The Songbird
is Singing

Scenes from a
Welsh Childhood in the 1920s

Alun Trevor had a Welsh country upbringing during the 1920s in Treuddyn, a coal-mining and farming village south of Mold, Flintshire. He was educated at the Coed Talon Elementary School and at the Alun Grammar School in Mold. After matriculation he began work with the Flintshire Education Department in 1938.

He volunteered for the RAF in 1940 and began five and half years of military service. Initially based at Jesus College, Cambridge, within the RAF education core, he was posted to Shaibah in Iraq. His service in the Middle East included spells in Baghdad and Tehran. He also used his leave to tour the Holy Land. He completed his RAF service with Bomber Command's Pathfinder Force and also completed his teacher training.

After World War II he developed a career in education including employment with Flintshire Schools before moving to Kent where he met his wife, Mary Addison. They married in 1952. At this time Alun Trevor also took part in an international exchange with Island Trees High School, Levittown, on Long Island in the United States. He travelled widely in the eastern United States and addressed the Utica New York Eisteddfod. On returning to the UK he moved to Malvern while continuing to study. He completed a BSc in Economics with the University of London which enabled him to broaden his teaching to economic history in adult education.

Since retiring in 1980 his main interests have been with the Clwyd Family History Society and the Chester Welsh Society. His bilingual publication *Cofio Cantorion: The Welsh Imperial Singers, the story of their tours of Britain and North America*, was published in 1991 at the time of the Mold National Eisteddfod. He has written widely on historical matters for magazines and journals including *Y Faner* and *Ninnau*.

His father, Jābez Trevor, was a miner who became a professional singer with the Welsh Imperial Singers.

The Songbird is Singing

Scenes from a
Welsh Childhood in the 1920s

Alun Trevor

Parthian
The Old Surgery
Napier Street
Cardigan
SA43 1ED
www.parthianbooks.co.uk

Published with the financial support of
the Welsh Books Council.

First published 2009
© Alun Trevor
All Rights Reserved

ISBN 978-1-906998-06-6

Editor: Penny Thomas

Cover design: www.theundercard.co.uk
Typeset by www.lucyllew.com

Printed and bound by Dinefwr Press, Llandybïe

The publisher acknowledges the financial support of the
Welsh Books Council.

British Library Cataloguing in Publication Data

A cataloguing record for this book is available from the
British Library

Er cof am
Arthur
a
fy nhad a mam

⁕

In memory of
Arthur
and
my father and mother

Contents

Preface

We were two small boys. Our home was a nine-acre hill farm in north-east Wales. It was hardly a living and Dad was a miner at the nearby colliery. The coal-mining area of Leeswood, Treuddyn and surroundings had achieved fame of a sort in the mid-nineteenth century when a block of coal weighing sixteen tons was brought to the surface. This 'black diamond' had been transported to London and displayed at the 1851 Great Exhibition at the Crystal Palace. But the Leeswood collieries had a more lasting fame as a source of cannel: a bituminous coal valued for its oil. This coal prompted the building of a railway branch line, winding its way up from the county town of Mold.

Our dad, Jäbez Trevor, was born in 1888 into a large, poor family. He was the seventh of nine children. His own father died when Jäbez was five years old. And like his father and brothers, Jäbez went to work below ground at the age of fourteen. From an early age his real interest was neither farming nor mining but singing, and his early musical education was in the hands of the headmaster of the Coedllai (Leeswood) Elementary School who also formed and conducted the Coedllai Male Voice Choir, the members being his former night school pupils. However, during these early years before his adult voice developed, the fourteen-year-old Jäbez joined the Silver Band in neighbouring Coed Talon, where playing the trombone gave fluency to his music reading. At eighteen he joined the Male Voice Choir, and very soon became their tenor soloist. He began competing at local eisteddfodau, and joined every choral group within reach, such as the Glee Singers in nearby Treuddyn, the Broughton (Wrexham) Choral Society and the Deeside Choir. In the 1914–18 war, when working at the coalface was essential war work, he gave much time to entertaining convalescing troops. After 1918 Jäbez Trevor became well known in North Wales and the north-west of England as a concert singer, winning at the Royal National Eisteddfod in 1923.

In 1926 the coal miners of Britain came out on strike for six months, meaning that Jäbez was available for many more concerts, and demands for him to sing came from ever farther afield. He 'swept the board', as the papers put it, with eisteddfodau successes, winning the prestigious challenge solo at the Anglesey and Pentrefoelas Eisteddfodau as well as the duet at Pentrefoelas, described as 'the largest one-day eisteddfod in Wales'. It was this last success probably more than any other which drew the attention of a certain visitor to Wales who was recruiting singers to form a professional group. With this group he planned to tour Britain and overseas.

He was an American. Visitors to our isolated hill farm were rare and besides, this one was different. He was short in stature, dapper in navy blue suit and red tie and had a theatrical air about him. He not only spoke English (our language was Welsh), but English with, to two small boys who rarely heard English anyway, a strange accent. We were barely old enough to understand the purpose of the visit, the first of a number. While conversing with the adults, he would, on each visit, delve into the four waistcoat pockets of his immaculate suit. Eventually out came a threepenny bit or a sixpence: once it was a quarter, which we managed to pass off as a shilling at the village store.

R. Festyn Davies was in fact Welsh born. He was a native of Trawsfynydd in Snowdonia. Snowdonia, he proudly told us, in American Welsh, was the home of the ancestors of the US Founding Father and third President, Thomas Jefferson. Also of Welsh descent were Charles Evans Hughes, who became Chief Justice of the US Supreme Court; Calvin Coolidge, the then US President; and David William Davis, who had recently been Governor of Idaho. And there were many, many more. In fact anybody who was anybody, past or present, was Welsh or of Welsh descent. Our American education started early.

But the nattily dressed Festyn Davies himself, so said the publicity material he gave us, was trained at the London Guildhall School of Music and also studied under the Italian tenor Enrico Duzensi. In 1908 he'd left England for America where his career began as soloist with the Filipino Constabulary Band. But with a 'dynamic personality' (his own words) he was destined to conduct some of the biggest musical festivals in the country, such as the Great Festival at Stanford University Stadium, where a chorus of 10,000 voices was accompanied by six full bands before a 50,000 audience. This same Festyn Davies was now back in Wales to recruit a professional male ensemble which would go on a world tour under his own direction, and he needed a tenor soloist. Thanks to the General Strike, the pumps had been out of action at

iii

the local mine; it flooded and was closed permanently, putting Jäbez (and 500 others) out of work. It was this that finally persuaded him to sing full time for a living.

And so the contract was signed.

The Welsh Imperial Singers were recruited from the whole of Wales. At first there were nineteen of them, but the group was reduced to twelve before they embarked for North America. They were noted for their well-trained, highly disciplined singing; voices blending in their sturdy songs. Press reports described them as Wales' 'finest combination' and 'a unique ensemble'. Their singing was 'spirited and expressive' with 'a delicate sense of feeling and harmony'. One critic said they sang as though the strings, woodwind and brass of a small orchestra had human hearts and voices built into them. And the *Toronto Telegram*, echoing this orchestral parallel, saw Festyn Davies doing what Stokowski did with the Philadelphia Orchestra: his singers were an instrument tempered and tuned to sing his interpretations, with delicate pianissimos and exquisite shades of tone, responding to every gesture of his baton. His name was bracketed with that of his contemporary, Sousa, the band conductor and composer of marches: they both had that electric leadership, apparently, which swayed audiences and inspired their musicians to perform their music from the heart. Whether the singers themselves viewed their egotistical director in this light is a different matter.

There is no doubt, however, that this male chorus, together with the soloists, captivated audiences. This was in the 1920s, when North American immigrant communities consisted of large numbers of recent arrivals from the Old World. People of all ethnic minorities, it seemed, fell under the spell of the Singers' beautifully controlled voices, as suggested by this verse from Illinois, written by one by the name of Marvil McCormick Schopp, not the most Welsh of names:

> Imperial Singers from grand old Wales
> Your voices echo o'er hill and dales.
> You live and love in a world of song –
> Ah, with such friendship one can't go wrong.
> Oh men of Wales, I so wish for you
> Much love – and prosper in all you do.
> And in our clasp may there ever be
> Hope, love and strength and sincerity.
> And far or near, over land or foam,
> Our land – 'tis yours! And our home your home.

The Welsh Imperial Singers existed from 1926 to 1939, but not continuously so. They came together for each tour, with change of personnel from time to time. They finally disbanded at the outbreak of war in 1939 whilst preparing for what would have been their sixth North American tour.

From the Canadian prairies came an englyn, that Welsh four-line alliterative stanza, the oldest metrical form in the language. It came from Enoch Davies of Bangor, Saskatchewan. To this settlement at the beginning of the century some hundreds of the Welsh of Patagonia had migrated. The englyn bade Festyn's ensemble farewell after their performances in Bangor. It wished them worldwide success. This 'worldwide' success never got beyond talk by Festyn of tours of South Africa, Australia and New Zealand. The Depression of the 1930s, and above all the talkies, put paid to such plans, but the British and North American tours continued, though reduced in extent. They disbanded for a time, and re-formed in 1938.

Yes, it was the Welsh of North America who naturally gave them the greatest welcome. Though of course among all the ethnic groups of the USA the Welsh were few in number, their influence was far in excess of their numbers and the tours of the Welsh Imperial Singers lingered in memories for many years.

The late Mr Owen C. Roberts, a former president of the St David's Society of Montreal, had childhood recollections of the visit of the Welsh Imperial Singers to that city to give two concerts at the Windsor Hall in 1928. During a later tour in 1930, the Ottawa St David's Society, with Mr G.F. Millward as its president, held a welcoming banquet. Mr Roland H. Jones remembers their frequent concerts in Chicago. In Kansas City MO, Mr Robert E. Jones recalls how his father, a Welsh immigrant, took his eight-year-old son to hear the Welsh Imperial Singers at the American Royal Building. The late Mr Gwynn Parri of Milwaukee distinctly remembered, fifty-eight years on, the group's disciplined singing and the costume worn on stage when they sang at the Immanuel Presbyterian Church.

On stage the Singers appeared in early nineteenth-century costume, supplied by Rayne, the London costumiers. They wore red swallow-tailed coats, brocaded waistcoats and puffed shirts, with tight trousers strapped under the foot. In contrast the conductor wore knee breeches, silk stockings and brown swallow-tailed coat. Immediately on his entrance, the Singers formed, with their conductor and accompanist, a small, close-knit group round the piano, making a visual impact in tune with their music-making. Their programme always opened with 'March of the Men of Harlech', followed by numbers from their printed programme ('Partial Repertoire: A Hundred Great Songs: Solos, Duets, Glees, Part-Songs and Choruses'), announced by the conductor from the stage. The Welsh Imperial Singers were widely acclaimed on both sides of the Atlantic, and were presented to the Duke of York (later King George VI) in 1928. The comment made by ex-Prime Minister Lloyd George was: 'This band of singers is different. Old melodies were new tonight.'

Before long Paramount were planning a movie: a travelogue about Wales, the land of song, mountains and princes. The Singers were to take the part of slate quarrymen singing at their work (one or two of them had been slate men in real life), and provide the soundtrack with the incidental music for the whole project. These were the very early days of talkies. But the film-making was bogged down from the start. Paramount had a tight budget. On location, rain caused delay. Then the good chapel-going people of Bethesda, the quarry town, objected to the making of a movie. In many parts of Wales at that time, movie houses, along with pubs and bars, were not allowed to open to the public on Sundays. And here was a film company making a movie, and wanting to do it on the Sabbath to make up for lost time! Snowdonia has one of the highest rainfalls in the British Isles and in the end rain washed the whole project away. So it was back into costume, with three days in seaside Llandudno and one-night stands along the North Wales coast. Then the signing of contracts for another American tour, the securing of visas and work permits, and the booking of passages for the voyage out of Liverpool.

The group was the feature musical attraction at the Rotary International Convention, Chicago, 1930. They made three '78' records, consisting of six songs, in Montreal for 'His Master's Voice' Victor. In 1938 they appeared at the Canadian Exhibition in Toronto. The later US tours need to be seen in the context of the times. In the mid 1930s neither Hitler nor Mussolini was seen as a threat to US security. Americans were protected by the Atlantic and there was disillusion because the First World War had not been followed by international cooperation. The USA was pre-eminently a country made by immigrants, and the early twentieth century had brought a large influx from eastern, southern and central Europe. The 1920 census recorded 106 million people, with the foreign element, including the first American generation, reaching twenty-four per cent of the white population. The outcome: isolationism and a neutral stance in the event of war. Even ex-President Hoover, while he condemned Nazism, thought that America could live in a world of victorious fascist nations, though it would be unpleasant. And supporting this stance were Charles Lindbergh and the influential Robert McCormick, publisher of the *Chicago Tribune*. But while Americans overwhelmingly rejected Hitlerism, the activities of the pro-Nazi German-American Bund were a blot on the land of democracy.

Yet the USA had a common language with Britain. The Welsh Imperial Singers, like other touring British entertainers and lecturers, were a constant reminder to their audiences that they shared a common heritage with Britain. The Singers sang in 465 US towns and cities. There were over fifty concerts in the Chicago area alone. Their influence was especially telling in the isolationist mid-West during their 1938–39 tour. It was the time when German troops entered Austria and Czechoslovakia. Highly praising the concert held in the People's Church in that city, the *St Paul (Minnesota) Pioneer Press* of December 18, 1938 concludes with the words: 'The engagement of the Welsh singers was a substitution for that of the Budapest University Choir, the American bookings of the latter having been cancelled by disturbed conditions in central Europe.' This says it all. So the Singers did their bit to strengthen President F.D. Roosevelt's hand: a policy of supporting Britain short of declaring war on the Axis Powers. They sang at the White House too.

At home and abroad, the group had sung in theatres, concert halls, schools, colleges, vaudeville, churches and conventions. They performed at chautauquas, that American institution that flourished until the early twentieth century, giving popular education with concerts and plays, often performed under canvas. In the Canadian Rockies, they sang in lumber camps. Numerous people heard them on North American local radio stations, and so did the passengers on ten transatlantic liners. They entertained women's clubs and sang at Kiwanis and Rotary functions. The total number of their performances ran into thousands.

For much of the time they were a group of twelve singers with their director and accompanist, but more than fifty singers appeared with them, some for only a short spell. They left to make their own careers as soloists. Their director, Festyn Davies, eventually retired to his native Trawsfynydd. Two emigrated to Canada. Jack Newbury, with his magnificent bass voice, formed his own male choir in his native Swansea, and was typical of the prominent part many of them played in the musical life of their own localities. Some pursued careers in opera, such as Ivor Evans who became principal bass with Sadler's Wells, and Wilfred O. Jones (tenor) who sang roles at Covent Garden. Only one singer, Watkin Edwards (tenor), sang with the group on each of the five North American tours. In the First World War he had been wounded, losing the use of his left arm, and on stage he wore a war medal pinned to his costume. He hailed from the coal-mining village of Rhos, Wrexham. A fuller account, in words and pictures, of these singers is contained in my bilingual book, *Cofio Cantorion: The Welsh Imperial Singers* (Gwasg Carreg Gwalch, 1991).

Jäbez Trevor sang with the Welsh Imperial Singers for nearly eight years. At the same time, despite repeated approaches from Festyn Davies to try to persuade him to rejoin his singers for yet another tour, he was building up his own, independent career as a concert singer.

A letter arrived at our farm, this time from Toronto. Festyn again, with an interesting line in persuasion. He had arrived late one night in Toronto from Montreal. His mission: making arrangements for a Canadian tour. He had disembarked at Halifax, Nova Scotia, early in the year. The St Lawrence was still frozen, preventing liners sailing upstream to Quebec and Montreal during the winter months. By his own account, he was met at the dockside by all sorts of reporters, had his picture in all the papers, with big write-ups on the arrival of this famous conductor. Then by train to Montreal and Toronto, where he put up at the best hotels, getting special rates of course. This, he pointed out, was something that carried great weight in North America. 'Big people' came to interview him about arrangements for the grand tour with his singers. But, unfortunately, the ground had been covered by poor choirs, including some from Wales, so it was hard to get support. However, his dynamic personality was getting results. The transcontinental Canadian National Railway was very much behind him, and with its radio stations along the line from coast to coast, his proposed tour had already been widely announced. It would be a great success. The railway officials were particularly pleased that he wanted to put things over big. R. Festyn Davies and his Welsh Imperial Singers would tour Canada yearly for the next ten years! All this in a letter in a flashy hand, written in Toronto's King Edward Hotel on the hotel's own quality notepaper, to 'My dear Jäbez Trevor'; to impress and persuade him to rejoin as soloist.

But the Memorandum of Agreement signified a tour of at least six months, with eight full concerts per week. An appearance in a movie theatre, which called for three or four performances daily, only counted as one full programme. This was too trying for a soloist who wished to pursue his own career as a concert singer. In the end a compromise allowed for Jäbez's own concert engagements as well as those of the tour.

Jäbez Trevor had a robust tenor voice, with dramatic

fervour, a virile style, and a charming lyricism which gave an intense, personal quality to his singing. His first radio broadcast came from the Dublin studio of the Dublin and Cork Broadcasting Station. The station broadcast a series of monthly programmes during 1927–28. They were directed by W.S. Gwynn Williams (1896–1978), the composer, author, conductor and editor, who took a leading part in establishing the Llangollen International Eisteddfod. These Dublin broadcasts, each ninety minutes long, were designed to compensate for the poor reception of transmissions from Cardiff in those early days of broadcasting. They were aimed specifically at the Welsh-speaking areas of north and mid Wales. Incidentally, other members of the Welsh Imperial Singers, such as the tenors Ernest Williams and J. Eifion Thomas, took their turn in this Dublin series after their time with R. Festyn Davies' professional group. Jäbez Trevor also broadcast in the 1930s from the newly opened Bangor (North Wales) studio of the BBC in a programme performed by 'Adar Alun' (The Birds of Alun), produced by Clydach-born Sam Jones.

Oratorio was Jäbez Trevor's favourite. His repertoire included operetta and operatic arias, ballads and of course Welsh songs, but in Chicago he also recorded a newly composed song, 'Dawn of Love'. Although of a somewhat later date, it was of the same genre as the Victorian and Edwardian songs and ballads which later singers have done so much to revive. *The Songbird is Singing* recalls the arrival of this gramophone recording by post at our hill farm. Recently this scene from the book was read, and the record played, on Chicago's Radio Station WFMT by the late Studs Terkel, in a bid to trace the composer, but without success.

With the outbreak of the Second World War in 1939, the British Government set up the Council for the Encouragement of Music and the Arts (CEMA), later known as the Arts Council. This organisation ensured that people in bombed cities were not entirely starved of music, by sponsoring concerts away from the bombed areas. Jäbez Trevor was involved with these concerts. He finished his singing career touring Britain extensively for ENSA, the organisation which entertained the Forces and people in war factories. In 1946 he retired. He died in 1972, nearly eighty-four years of age.

The Scenes from a Welsh Childhood that follow coincide with the early years of Jäbez Trevor's professional singing career. They are documentary, set in the late 1920s, the era of the Coolidge and Hoover administrations, of Prohibition and the gangster Al Capone, the 1920s Boom and the 1929 Crash, and the onset of the Depression all seen through the eyes of two small boys 3,000 miles away on a remote Welsh hill farm. For Dad, Jäbez, is in frequent contact through a stream of letters, picture postcards and parcels. The letters were usually on hotels' headed notepaper. And the printed address, in days long before zip codes, always ended with strange capital letters, which were puzzling: N.Y., PENN., S.D., N.D., ILL., WIS.... The last-named we thought to be the initials of the Welsh Imperial Singers themselves until the atlas solved the problem. Over a number of years, in five separate tours with brief periods between overseas tours back in the United Kingdom, the Singers sang, not only in Canada (coast-to-coast, twice), but also in thirty-four US states, and traversed another half-a-dozen, thus taking in forty of the then forty-eight states. The letters all describe for the boys a wonderful world only six days from Liverpool.

The Songbird is Singing has none of what the Welsh call 'y cythraul yn y canu' (the devil in the singing). If, in a touring group, there were disagreements over clauses in contracts, prolonged antagonisms between the members and the director, or disputes over pay and the length of a tour, then we eight and nine year olds were not to know of them. As the book gives a child's viewpoint, these disputes must necessarily be absent from it.

Running as a refrain through the narrative are the opening lines of the children's hymn by Alfa (1876–1931), 'Rwy'n Canu Fel Cana'r Aderyn'. Also, the English version, 'I Sing as the Songbird is Singing'. This was written by William J. Griffith (1882–1956). He was born in the village of Rhiwlas, near Bangor, North Wales, the son of a Wesleyan minister. After working at the slate quarry at Bethesda, he emigrated to America in 1907 and settled in Bangor, Pennsylvania. Later he became pastor of the Hebron Presbyterian Church in Chicago. His longing to pay a return visit to the land of his birth was never realised. Hebron Church was one of three churches in Chicago with Welsh-language services and was much frequented by some of the Welsh Imperial Singers during their many visits to that city.

These scenes are recalled, and clearly spring to life as memories do, after more than eighty years. And if after such a lapse of time these recollections are somewhat fragmented, they are far from fleeting impressions. The scenes and incidents converge on the book's central event to make the narrative a single whole. This event was the death of a child. It is, in fact, a child's-eye view of the death of a child.

The narrative is also a child's view of an age now gone: the close-knit Welsh upland village – church and chapel, village school and choir, the gamekeeper and the shoot, the Welsh language, the Band of Hope and magic lantern, the railway branch line, the coming of electricity... and always Dad, far away, but in close touch, giving them a vision of a New World.

Alun Trevor

The Songbird
is Singing

Scenes from a
Welsh Childhood in the 1920s

Alun Trevor

I
In the Beginning

The voice out of the gramophone was singing:

> I'm living o'er the mem'ries
> Of my childhood days now gone...

I adjusted the speed to put it exactly on 78, gave the winding handle another turn, and returned to the rocking chair by the fireside; picking up the atlas once more.

'Arthur, come and write to Dad,' called Mam from the back kitchen. Arthur was outside, in front of the house by the open window; he was a seven-year-old aspiring soccer star, forever playing with his football. Mam had been in the dairy, and now came into the living room. She carried a milk pail which she put down at the foot of the stairs near the front door, ready to go out milking. 'Arthur,' she called again.

'Mam,' I said, flicking over the page of the atlas, 'where's the town called Flint?'

But her mind was on Arthur. 'Wish I could get him to read,' she sighed. And turning to me: 'Mm? Fflint?' pronouncing it 'Fleent', the Welsh way. 'Oh, the other side of Mold.'

'Wrong. It's in Michigan.'

'Ah,' she said with a smile, peering through her thick lenses. She was very short-sighted.

My finger moved from the Midwest to the East Coast. 'Where's Bala Cynwyd?'

'Um, well...' she was playing the dunce now. 'Well, Alun, you go up the Tyrpeg...' (the Turnpike). The turnpike road was half a mile away at the end of our farm road. It climbed and wound its way upwards from the village railway station at Coed Talon on the eastern side and through the parish of Treuddyn. Three miles further on it crossed the county boundary to climb steeply through the heather of the Llandegla Moors. Up there on a clear day in spring or summer we could see the faraway Dee and Mersey Estuaries and a tiny smudge on the horizon, the port of Liverpool. The road continued south-west to Corwen. 'Bala Cynwyd's beyond Corwen,' said Mam.

'Wrong. It's in Pennsylvania.'

'Wrong again am I? Nought out of ten.'

'Where's...'

'Now it's time you put that atlas away. Go and get the cow in.'

It was milking time. It was always milking time. But when she opened the door, there was the cow staring over the farmyard gate, patiently waiting, so I was relieved of my twice-a-day task of fetching her from the lower fields. Mam picked up the pail, but paused in the doorway. She turned and said confidentially: 'Sometime, try and get Arthur to read. Can't read a word! And next birthday he'll be eight.' It was true he never picked up a book. 'You're a year older and you can help him...'

The rubber football bounced against a window pane with a crack.

'Arthur!' shouted Mam, sharply. And almost immediately the ball flew in through the open window, bouncing on the tiled floor.

'Arthur! Put that ball away in the spench.' This was the glory hole under the stairs.

He breezed in. 'I was only heading it into the goal,' he pleaded.

'Indeed, you'll damage...'

'No, no, it was only to make you jump,' he grinned.

'Well, practise reading instead while I do the milking. Alun will help you.'

As she went out of the front door the song on the gramophone record was coming to an end:

I want you ev'ry moment...

I put down the atlas and strode across, ready to pick up the sound box and swing the arm off the record. Mam's strong soprano voice, already out in the yard, joined in on the last line, making the most of the final note, a top G:

...Just because dear, I love you.

Vancouver... Edmonton... Winnipeg... back in the rocking chair and Western Canada. Arthur, clutching his rubber ball, was now sitting on the top step of the stairs, looking down on the living room, singing the song softly, the tune and words picked up from the gramophone:

I'm living o'er the mem'ries
Of my childhood days now gone...

Earlier, after feeding the hens, Arthur had joined me to sit in the spring sunshine on the low garden wall in front of the house. We were facing Hope Mountain with its irregular patchwork of green fields, unkempt with uncut, quick-set hedges, bright in the April sun. Below it was the wood, a fringe of treetops just coming into leaf, which ran the full length of the valley, curving round and marking the lower boundary of our smallholding. Rising steeply from the wood, our hayfields came right up to our garden with its lawn and lilac tree. The cat had joined us, sitting on the wall, blinking in the sun. She knew it was Arthur's job to give her a saucer of milk after milking. When I came in to read the atlas, Arthur had stayed out until he had successfully headed his ball in through the open window. The cat followed him in.

She now waited patiently at the foot of the stairs for him to come down to fill that saucer as soon as milking was done. But Arthur, at the top of the stairs, was in full song. Meanwhile, in the atlas I found for him towns called 'Arthur' and 'Port Arthur', but he took no notice. He sang: he did not want to read. I flicked the page back to the Middle West. 'Minneapolis... Milwaukee... Chicago... Chicago!' I said aloud, excitedly.

'Chicawgo!' called Arthur from the top of the stairs. 'You don't know how to say it.'

'Okay, bud,' I said. 'Chicawgo.' It was how they said it in Chicago. Dad had told us.

'Chicawgo,' said Arthur again. 'We're going there when we grow up.'

I shut the atlas. Yes. Dad was in Chicago. Touring the States singing. It was the 1920s.

Manhattan, New York City, nearly fifty years later. Strolling down Seventh Avenue. It was hearing a Midwest accent which reminded me of that little incident: Arthur's football coming in through the open window. Manhattan was at the height of the tourist season and the Middle West accents were tourists (from 'Chicawgo', maybe) – after all, most tourists in New York are Americans. And here was America celebrating its Bicentennial. I had had a prolonged and busy stay there in the 1950s, before returning home on the Queen Mary; and had walked, alone, down this same Seventh Avenue. Now I was a tourist myself, with time to listen and to linger: Carnegie Hall, Times Square, Broadway, the Empire State Building at 34th Street... time to remember the small Welsh farm: our childhood home. Yes, we had planned to visit all these places together when we grew up. But it was not to be. Within a year or two of that incident with the football, eight-year-old Arthur was dead.

But to begin at the beginning.

Dad's own childhood days were the 1890s. His father died in tragic circumstances when he was very young, leaving behind a large family. It was Mam who would tell us about Dad's childhood. He seldom spoke about himself. She would light the table lamp, sit at the sewing machine mending Arthur's shirt or patching trousers, and tell how his father and brothers were all colliers. Dad's whole life, from schooldays on, was singing. Arthur had the habit, from an early age, of sitting at the top of the stairs, looking down on us in our large living room. His voice would soar above the whirr of the sewing machine, singing our latest from the Coed Talon Elementary School or Band of Hope:

> Rwy'n canu fel cana'r aderyn,
> Yn hapus yn ymyl y lli...

It must have been a year or two later that I found an English version:

> I sing as the songbird is singing,
> So happy, unfettered and free...

It was in a book of Welsh melodies of the National Gymanfa Ganu Association of the United States and Canada (their hymn-singing festival), left behind by Dad when he was home.

At fourteen Dad had gone to work at Coedllai Colliery. In the same year he joined the Coed Talon Silver Band, playing the trombone. On the day of the Coronation of King Edward the Seventh, the band, in their new uniforms, had marched through the village playing 'Rule Britannia'.

On the bookshelf beside the rocking chair, tucked away at the bottom, were brass-band arrangements – most of them the full conductor's score – of 'Rule Britannia',

Rimsky-Korsakov's 'Scheherazade', Tchaikovsky's 'Marche Slave' and '1812 Overture', and Wagner's 'Lohengrin', 'Prelude to Act III' and the 'Overture to Tannhauser', all with neat pencil marks by the lines for the B-flat tenor trombone. These, and others, had all been unused for a long time (except that Arthur seemed to have some fascination for 'Rule Britannia'), for at eighteen Dad had joined the Coedllai Male Voice Choir, under the school-master T.G. Jones, known as T.G. They rehearsed in the Big Room of the council school, which the older people still called the Board School.

I well remember when I first heard them sing: my first memory. I must have been very young. It was that Welsh hymn, 'Llef' (Cry), with the words of David Charles:

O Iesu mawr! rho'th anian bur...

which, in the English version of Isaac Watts, becomes:

Come, gracious Lord, descend and dwell...

'And Jäbez,' T.G. had said, addressing the choir in the Big Room, 'I want you to sing the solo in this new piece.' And so began Dad's singing career: choir soloist, winning the tenor solo at local eisteddfodau and joining every choral group within reach, including the Glee Singers in the neighbouring parish of Treuddyn.

Mam sang in the church choir and with the Glee Singers. Her father was the blacksmith. At Whitsuntide 1918, Jane and Jäbez were married, and at the wedding reception in the parlour of our farmhouse, Pen-y-Wern, the bridegroom responded to the toast by singing Quilter's

7

setting of 'O Mistress Mine'. But it was Mam who was always singing it around the house, in the dairy and out in the fields:

> O mistress mine! where are you roaming?
> O! stay and hear; your true love's coming,
> That can sing both high and low...

Jäbez Trevor won at the National Eisteddfod held in Mold. A few years later I was reading our local quarterly magazine: '...in these days of rapid flights by air and news by wireless...' then a headline: 'A Brief History of Mr Jäbez Trevor'. I sat upright and nearly slid out of the rocking chair.

'Mam, Mam,' I called, 'it's about Dad.'

I read on. The article was about Dad's childhood, and how he used to amuse himself by singing and humming in his home the songs he heard sung by the famous singers of those far-off days.

'Mam,' I called more insistently, 'it's about Dad.'

Arthur was on the stairs again, singing – it was 'Rwy'n Canu' – at the top of his voice.

From an early age, said the article, Dad had mastered the modulator, and his voice had developed into 'a genuine tenor of power and range, which can express drama in music and spellbind with its lyricism... a quiet man (off-stage) who, when he sings, opens the depths and the heavens....' Many times the writer, when passing his home (2 Chapel Row, Coedllai), had heard Jäbez in full song. And now he has been engaged to sing professionally...

'Mam! Mam! Come and read it!'

The choir had presented him with a gentleman's

complete travelling outfit. 'We are extremely proud of his achievements, he who is one from amongst ourselves... a commanding figure, by his own efforts raised from the pit coalface to the concert platform...'

'Mam...!'

She had heard, and came hurrying in excitedly from the back of the house. 'What does it say?'

'"Jäbez sings with deep feeling; since marriage his voice moves you so much more. It comes from the heart..."'

'Ah...' she said. And, looking up at Arthur, 'Singing and sitting on top of the stairs again.'

His rubber football bounced down the stairs and came to rest against the front door. He came down rapidly after it. 'Mam,' he asked, 'can I have a football, a real one I mean, with a leather case?'

'Perhaps. When you've learnt to read. Go and feed the hens.' Then turning to me: 'Have you fetched water from the well?'

'No.' It was not the first time: immersing myself in books and the like usually led to neglect of the jobs I had to do.

'And don't let the fire go out,' called back Mam as she shut the door.

'Will you be giving us a solo at the evening service before you go?' It was the Reverend Cadwaladr Williams, BA, Vicar, Parish Church of St Mary, with his thin, piping voice, his slight build and poor eyesight. So, tomorrow, a mile and a half to the church with Dad, just for a run-through. It was to be 'Deeper and deeper still, Recitative and Aria', page 113 of Handel's *Jephtha*.

Jephtha was leather bound, on the bookshelf with *Hiawatha*, *Elijah*, *Messiah*, *Judas Maccabaeus*, *Acis and Galatia*, *The Creation* and *Welsh Songs*. There was, too, *Mozart Arias*, a bound volume of a size that stuck out of the shelf, and so always commanded the eye's attention before the others. There was a second copy of *Messiah*, Mam's copy, its leather worn with age and use. It had been Grandfather's, and had his copperplate signature inside the cover: 'John Roberts, his book, April 8, 1872'; and before that, Great-grandfather's, with his signature, 1868. Welsh words had been meticulously handwritten with Victorian thoroughness above the printed English for many of the choruses: 'Hallelujah! Yr Hollalluog Dduw a deyrnasa... for the Lord God omnipotent reigneth.' This *Messiah* was always next to *Jephtha*.

I took *Jephtha* down from the shelf and began reading page 113. '"Deeper and deeper still, thy goodness child pierceth a father's bleeding heart..."'

'Cor! Sounds good,' said Arthur.

'Mam, the page is torn.' It was fair wear and tear; this aria was popular.

'Well mend it with stamp-edging.' I searched but could find no stamp-edging.

Back to leather-bound *Jephtha*; '"My only daughter! – so dear a child... "'

'Daughter?' chipped in Arthur. 'Didn't know we had a sister?'

'"Doom'd by a father..."' I turned the page. '"Open thy marble jaws, O tomb! And hide me, earth, in thy dark womb!" Mam, what's womb?'

'Where you lived: before Pen-y-Wern.'

'Oh... don't remember...'

The Reverend Cadwaladr, gifted organist and, we thought, boring preacher, was at the organ console. He began the opening bars. Arthur and I were working the organ bellows, both hands on the long wooden arm which protruded four feet out of the slit in the organ's oak case. A sort of plumb line beside it inched its way up, showing more wind was needed in the bellows if the organ was not to go dead. Our combined strength was not enough. Exhausted, I fell to the floor; the long wooden arm, as it rose above my head, had slipped out of my hands. Arthur, much smaller and a mere four stone in weight, clung to the arm on tiptoes. It went irretrievably upward, Arthur dangling from it. The plumb line raced upwards too, and the organ stopped abruptly at the word 'pierceth'. Cadwaladr's legato gave way to his piping voice: 'Well, well, blowing the organ is hard work, isn't it.'

We tried again. But it was no use. Only a brief strangulated chord came out.

'We shouldn't expect two little boys to work the bellows. It's hard work.' He adjusted his thick specs. Turning to Dad, he raised his shrill voice: 'Jabez, shall I accompany you on the piano from the vestry?'

Dad had positioned himself at the top of the chancel steps, facing the nave. He was on stage.

'Won't take a minute to wheel it in.'

But he sang the first few bars of the recitative unaccompanied, to measure the size of the auditorium, just to know how much voice to give it.

'Are you sure?'

The vestry door opened. It was Mr Marshall the Post.

11

He was both postman and sexton. Ignoring us, he took hurried steps through the choir stalls to the bell rope behind the pulpit. The bell began to toll. Gwilym Gwern-y-Llyn had died, eighty-eight.

'Shall I pull the bell rope for you, Mr Marshall?' Arthur had scampered across, his hands already on the bell rope. Three pulls and the ring of the bell momentarily quickened. We hurried out. The Reverend Cadwaladr dashed to the vestry to put on his surplice for the funeral service which he had completely forgotten about; he was so forgetful. Arthur picked up his ball from under the vestry table.

Down the gravel path, past the sundial and the yew tree. The morning sun was warm and the birds were singing. The bell tolled with the measured regularity of an experienced ringer. Out in the open, in the clear morning air, it was a louder and more compelling summons.

But Arthur, with a life to live, was ahead, taking a short cut through the older part of the churchyard. He dribbled his ball speedily past Great-grandfather's grave. It had low ornamental iron railings, made and put there by his son, the dutiful, generous and good-natured John Roberts, better known as John y Go (John the Blacksmith), Mam's dad. The always full-of-fun John, who had served his apprenticeship with his blacksmith father, would give away his last penny. A church chorister, John had, like his father, sung *Messiah* many, many times. His own grave was alongside.

'Arthur, wait for us.' But he went on, weaving between the old, leaning headstones with their inscriptions facing east, the morning sun on them, until he reached the newer part of the churchyard with spaces for graves not yet dug.

He went headlong towards the open grave and stopped on top of the pile of earth beside it. Clutching his ball, he peered in.

'Arthur,' I called again, a little plaintively, 'don't go without us!' Oops! He fell over... backwards, picked himself up and leapt over the low churchyard wall into Glyn Ty'n Llan's field. Glyn's bullocks scattered.

Dad and I took our time along the path. It ran under the high churchyard wall with the overhanging yew and followed, over two stiles, the gurgling water of the brook. It then went down through a hollow where you would always see bumblebees with their underground nests in the springtime, collecting pollen from the flowers under the hedgerow – a warm, sheltered bee hollow, facing south and shielded from the north wind by the hedge and the dip of the land. Here the little brook joined the upper reach of a larger stream, Nant Byr, which, three miles downstream at Pontblyddyn, flowed into the Afon Alun, which joined the Dee at the English border; and the Dee flowed into the ocean.... The path crossed Nant Byr by a wooden footbridge.

I was some paces behind, carrying *Jephtha*. The sun, shining through the lower branches of the yew, made a flickering tracery on the open page:

Scenes of horror, scenes of woe...

I shuddered and turned the page:

... and I think the great Jehovah sleeps,
Like-Chemosh, and such fabled ditties.

Ditties? Comic songs? No. I had misread 'deities'.

> Therefore, tomorrow's dawn –
> I can no more.

I straightened out the torn page, shut the book and ran, vaulting over the stiles to catch up with Dad.

Arthur had reached the Tyrpeg, now a tarred motor road from Chester to Corwen. It was here that the great-grandfather with the iron railings round his grave had built a row of three houses, Britannia Terrace, red brick patterned with yellow, only a few paces above the Britannia Inn. Uncle Noah lived in one of them. Where the path reached the road, Great-grandfather's son, John the Blacksmith, had put an iron stile and gate in King Edward the Seventh's Coronation Year, the massive iron post topped with an iron crown. Arthur was sitting on this iron crown, still clutching his ball, legs dangling down. He was watching Satterthwaite's steam lorry, loaded with silica stone from the Bwlchgwyn quarries and destined for the Coed Talon Silica Works. It was passing Britannia Inn, with Wmphre'r Cipar (Wmphre the Game-keeper) coming out, unsteady in his gait. The steam lorry was chugg-chugging slowly, emitting steam and coming to a stop on its solid rubber tyres to fill its boiler at the well near the Beehive Stores.

The shop door bell tinkled. We had pennies to spend.

'Beehive,' said Arthur as he shambled in, dragging a foot through the sawdust on the floor, 'do we get stung? Buzz... zz...'

Mrs Williams Beehive smiled. She was behind the counter; a kind woman; her hair going slightly grey.

'Two bottles of pop please,' I said.

'Penny ha'penny each, ha'penny back on the bottle,' said Mrs Williams in her kind voice. We paid, and the bell tinkled on the cash register. We drank our pop and got our ha'pennies back. We pocketed the bottle tops. Then a bell rang in the house behind the shop.

'Listen!' I whispered to Arthur. 'That's a telephone bell.'

'Cor!' His eyes lit up.

'I read about it.'

Mrs Williams hurried away, shutting the door behind her.

We hastened out to catch up with Dad. We ran, passing Jesse Roberts' bakehouse, for Dad was well on his way down the Tyrpeg. It was a mile to our farm road, downhill all the way.

'Look, look, Dad, a motor car,' said Arthur, hopping dangerously into the roadway, and Dad immediately pulling him back on to the footpath. The approaching car stopped with its engine still running.

'"Sun... Sunbeam." It's a Sunbeam,' I told him.

Arthur spontaneously began singing the refrain of one of our Band of Hope tunes:

A sunbeam, a sunbeam,
Jesus wants me for a sunbeam...

'"Sunbeam Six Cylinder Tourer".' I peered at the car's radiator.

Arthur's singing was interrupted by the driver, calling to me above the purring engine: 'I say, young man...' It was a commanding voice with a pukka accent. An Englishman in tweeds, deerstalker and a moustache. 'I say, is this the road to Ll-lan... Ll-lan... something. Near Caw-wen.'

'Caw-wen?' I asked timidly.

'Yes, Caw-wen.'

'Please... where?'

'Caw-wen, my boy,' he repeated compellingly, but with a reassuring smile.

'Eh? Oh... you mean Corwen.' I rolled the R the Welsh way. And, spluttering, 'Y... yes, yes, straight on to Corwen.'

'Caw... rrr... when,' he imitated me.

His smile gave me confidence: 'Keep going up for seventeen miles.'

'Rightiho. Thank you my boy. Caw... rrr... when. Roll my Rs...' He revved the engine briefly; '...rrr... rev my engine, say what.'

On the back seat of the open tourer was a very small child. She stood up and leaned forward. 'Papa, will we be in time to say goodbye to you at Liverpool? Will we be vewy late?'

Mama sat in front. She turned round and said kindly, 'Sit down Molly dear, on the seat.'

The Englishman waved goodbye as he accelerated away. We noticed suitcases strapped on the back.

'Why don't they speak proper English?'

Arthur didn't hear; he was carried away in song.

A sunbeam, a sunbeam...

Dad had walked on. We sped once more to catch up, only to stop by a telegraph post. Pressing my ear against it, I heard the humming wind in the wires. 'Listen.'

16

Arthur did the same. 'I can hear people talking all the way to England.'

'That's nothing. You can send messages all the way to America.'

'Don't be daft.'

'You can. I read all about it. There's a cable all the way under the sea.'

'Oh you know everything,' he said, tossing back his head.

'It's true. Ask Mrs Williams Beehive, she's got a telephone.'

'Huh.' He clicked his tongue. And, relenting: 'Let me hear again.' We both pressed our ears for the second time.

The wind was now strumming the wires louder. 'No,' he said at last. 'It's lots of harps playing. Ooh! Angels!' And we ran on our way, bursting once more into song.

A sunbeam, a sunbeam...

Dad came into view as we rounded a corner. He was standing beside Hywel and his bicycle. Eleven-year-old Hywel delivered the papers. He was handing Dad the *Liverpool Post*, *Y Faner* (The Banner) and the *Chester Chronicle*. Straightening his bundle of papers, he remounted his bike and bade us 'Good morning'.

He had pedalled only a few paces when Arthur, imitating the Englishman's accent, called: 'Are you on the right road to Caw-wen?'

Hywel turned his head, puzzled; then pedalled on his way. A motorbike came into view: 'The Royal Mail'. It had a red mailbox alongside instead of a sidecar. Arthur yelled 'Hurray' until it disappeared downhill out of sight.

17

A horse neighed. The gypsies were back on the grass verge near the gate to our farm road. There was a clatter of utensils, a fire was burning out in the open and a dog barked as we approached.

'Hello Jäbez!' It was Jack, the manager of the Coed Talon Silica Works, approaching on foot and greeting us with the enthusiasm of a long-lost friend. And, after a few brief words he said, 'Well, Jäbez, off soon on your tour. All the best.' Chuckling (he was always chuckling), 'I remember you singing on your wedding day!'

'Any cigarette cards, Jack?' asked Arthur.

'Let me see...' he chuckled again and flicked open a packet. 'Here you are.'

'Who is it?' I asked.

Arthur peered at the soccer star's picture, unsure.

'You've got Dixie Dean.'

'You're Dixie Dean with that ball,' said Jack. 'Dixie' was hardly appropriate for Arthur. The real Dixie Dean was nicknamed 'Dixie' because he had dark curly hair. True, Arthur's was slightly curly, but he was fair with a pale complexion. 'Well Jäbez,' said Jack again, 'all the best.' As he walked away up the Tyrpeg, his non-musical, raucous voice broke into the popular song of the day, 'My Blue Heaven'.

We turned and opened the gate. Our farm road gave Dixie Dean half a mile of solo footwork all the way home.

'Mam, we saw a motor car! He was an English man!' This was our first excited greeting immediately we opened the door.

'Yes,' added Arthur. 'English people. In a Sunbeam motor car.'

'Where did you get that dirt on your best trousers?' Mam was quick to spot his churchyard tumble.

'And a motorbike,' – he ignored her rebuke – 'the Royal Mail going to Pontybodkin Post Office with letters.'

'Well,' said Mam, trying to be encouraging, 'you'll have to write letters to Dad when he's away, won't you.'

'Huh!' Arthur was not enthusiastic; he was reluctant to write as well as read. He turned to his collection of cigarette cards, shuffled them and began counting: 'Bastin...' he started defiantly. 'Alex James...' and raising his voice excitedly: 'Dixie Dean!' If he couldn't read the names, he recognised the faces.

I had settled into the rocking chair, idly scanning the newspaper, rocking gently in what had been Grandfather's rocking chair, and Great-grandfather's before that. Suddenly I stopped rocking: my eye spotted the football hints on the Junior Page: '"Our Soccer Series. Illustrated by Dixie Dean, the brilliant Everton centre forward."' And there was a picture of Dixie with the ball at his toe and another of him heading the ball. 'Listen to this,' I said to Arthur. '"Practise kicking a stationary ball hard and low... make sure you glue your eyes..."'

Glue your eyes, I thought, did he really mean that?

'Go on.' Arthur's attention was riveted.

'"... on the leather ball you are about to kick."'

He looked at Dixie Dean's photographs. 'It's a leather-case ball,' he said a little tearfully, 'like the one I want.'

'When you can read and write,' said Mam decisively.

'Then the handsome Pau-Puk-Keewis...'

I was reading aloud. *Jephtha* was back on the bookshelf.
It was *Hiawatha* now.

'Skilled was he... of quoits and ball-play...'

'Red Indians played football,' said Arthur.
　'Baseball.'
　'How d'you know, you know-all,' said Mam.
　Arthur wandered off. Eventually he reappeared at the
top of the stairs, singing. My head was buried in my book,
reading to myself:

　　'Then they said to Chibiabos...
　　To the sweetest of all singers,
　　"Sing to us, O Chibiabos!"'

I put the book back in its place.
　Mam said: 'Dad's singing *Hiawatha* in Corwen, then...
he'll be away.'
　Arthur came running down the stairs: 'Are we going to
Corwen to see him dressed up like a Red Indian?'
　'No. He'll be home late. Dad'll tell us about it in the
morning.' She took the table lamp to fill with paraffin in
the wash-house at the back of the house. Recently she'd
bought a new wick for the lamp, soaked it thoroughly for
an hour in vinegar and allowed it to dry – this was to
prevent the lamp smoking and to give a clear light. Her
soprano voice, through two closed doors, was now heard
taking up the strains of *Hiawatha's* tenor aria:

'Onaway! Awake, beloved...!'

Dad was poking the fire. Well, really tapping the poker gently on the grate to beat time to the music in his head. Arthur whispered: 'Dad's conducting.'

> 'Onaway! my heart sings to thee
> Sings with joy...'

The smouldering fire burst into flame. Dad returned to the rocking chair and opened *Hiawatha*. Coleridge-Taylor's music was coming through from the back of the house, loud and clear:

> 'When thou smilest, my beloved...'

But with Dad, the music flowed through him, seldom out loud in the house. Some fine mornings he would walk round the boundary hedges and fences of our nine acres.

> 'Smiles the earth, and smiles the waters
> Smile the cloudless skies above us...'

Our smallholding was no flat, vast, undulating prairie, but a collection of small fields on a steep slope. The house and farm buildings, built of nineteenth-century brick and Welsh slate by the same great-grandfather with the iron railings, were at the top. Below was the wood. Dad would supposedly be looking for gaps in the hedges and fences to repair, but really he wanted to be out alone to rehearse some new music in his mind.

As soon as he put down the *Hiawatha* music, I picked

it up again to read the Longfellow poem to its end:

> 'Spring had come with all its splendour...
> By the shore of Gitche Gumee.'

'Dad, where's Gitche Gumee?'
  'Lake Superior.'

> 'With the Famine and the Fever...
> She the dying Minnehaha.'

This provoked Arthur to some loud, mocking sobs. 'Minne...
haha,' he said, making play with the 'ha... ha...' This mock
laughter stopped when Mam brought in the table lamp.
  'You'll strain your eyes,' she said to me, 'all that
reading. Light the lamp. Always reading. Always learning.'
  But I was determined to reach the last page:

> 'He is dead, the sweet musician!
> He the sweetest of all singers.'

Arthur started a loud mock crying.
  'Oh Arthur, be quiet,' said Mam, quite put out. And
turning to me: 'Alun, light the lamp. I've got to help Dad
pack. I've so much to do.'

From Coed Talon Station take the LMS (London, Midland
and Scottish Railway) branch line to Brymbo; at Brymbo
change to the Great Western for Wrexham and main line
to London (Paddington) and the world. We were on the

station platform. There was a hiss of steam from the locomotive which drew the one coach. The white level-crossing gates were open, barring the Co-op horse-drawn cart delivering groceries. The horse waited patiently on the Tyrpeg. Dad, with his two suitcases and small music case, was already on board, leaning out of the window. Carriage doors shut, Mr Timms the Stationmaster hurried along the platform and the guard waved his flag.

We all quickly kissed goodbye.

The engine blew its whistle and drew its coach slowly away up the small incline where the single line ran parallel with the road leading up to Hope Mountain. We waved and waved and Dad waved back until the train disappeared round the curve.

The line to Brymbo ran on a mile through the marsh, with Hope Mountain rising steeply on one side, and the wood below our farm rising sharply from the edge of the marsh on the other. We walked home slowly along the Hope Mountain road as far as the Sion Chapel then took a footpath which crossed the railway track by the railway signal. The path followed the mineral railway line that went as far as Jack's Silica Works.

We approached our school with its empty playground. Leaning at an odd angle by the wall near the school gates was a newly erected black and white road sign: a torch of learning. It was like an ice cream cornet. 'Lick, all those who enter here,' said Arthur as we passed the school gates. He paused to peer into the empty playground with his nose pressed between the vertical iron bars of the tall gates.

Beyond the school the short side road petered out into a track along the lower edge of the wood. The ground now fell down to the marsh on one side, and the wood rose on the other. The path turned and climbed steeply upwards, making a tunnel through the trees. It emerged at the top by a gate and stile under a young sycamore tree. We had reached the lower fields of our little farm, Pen-y-Wern.

The cow saw us. She stopped grazing, raised her head and took a few paces in our direction. 'We'll take her up with us,' said Mam, out of breath. 'Milking time soon. Alun, you take her. She'll follow you.'

Arthur loitered, sitting on the stile. Then standing on the top bar of the stile, he was tempted, as he always was when we came home this way from school, to climb into the lower branches of the sycamore.

As I walked away the cow followed, and Mam called: 'Go easy with the cow-cake.'

We took the longer path round the hayfields and across the farmyard. The cow waited patiently as I opened the door; then made straight for her stall. She was always tethered by a loose, lightweight chain round her neck and she lowered her head for me to reach it off its hook. She understood. My arms were only just long enough to get the jangling chain round her big neck. She gave a brief, contented moo. 'There.' She snorted. 'Your cow-cake.' She stamped a hoof on the stone floor and munched away appreciatively. She'd had a calf, but it died. 'Want some extra?' I placed some more in the tub. 'Here you are then.'

Arthur was at the top of the stairs singing when Mam called: 'Come down and feed the hens.' But it was a sudden knock on the front door that brought Arthur hurrying down.

'Mr Marshall the Post,' he called excitedly. Mr Marshall

usually delivered early, on foot. To reach our farm he had already walked two miles from the post office. He had another seven miles to go; this was his daily round.

It was a letter from Dad, with a London postmark.

'Open it for me...' Mam wiped her hands on the hand towel. Arthur opened it, and she began reading: '"...all last week at the Brighton Royal Pavilion..."'

'Is it as big as our Pavilion?' This was a wooden structure with a corrugated iron roof, and wooden benches inside; it was built back to back with the Methodist Chapel. There we had our local Eisteddfod, where Dad in his younger days had once won the Challenge Solo.

'"This week at the Connaught Rooms..."' Her voice rose with excitement: '"... presented to His Royal Highness the Duke of York." Oh...!' She was overjoyed.

Some time later, when Dad was home, we saw the press cutting and heard how the noble Duke had said, 'You are a credit to Wales.'

'"Next week, Winter Gardens, Bournemouth – must make a good impression there. Then Birmingham Hippodrome. Shall be sending the boys a present. Parcel should arrive soon..."'

We cheered.

'"Keep it a secret – it'll be a surprise." Oh, I shouldn't have told you.'

'Bet it'll be a football...'

'Wait and see,' said Mam, trying to suppress Arthur's premature excitement.

'A leather-case ball!'

'Wait and see, wait and see.'

But Arthur began bouncing his rubber ball on the tiled floor, his excitement unsubdued.

'Go and feed the hens. And count them.'

Off he went with his ball. I followed, on the way to the coalhouse. The henhouse was at the back of the house, where we had our only flat field, Cae Cefn (Back Field), of about two acres. His voice almost drowned by the clucking hens, Arthur was counting. I returned, struggling with the full coal scuttle. He was still counting, with some difficulty, standing in the middle of the flock. Then: 'Only thirty-one. One missing.'

Back in the house: 'Mam, the Rhode Island Red's missing again.' The last time we saw her she was wandering off towards the hawthorn hedge, which was the boundary of our smallholding. She had her head on one side, not clucking, but making her funny, considering noise; to lay or not to lay...

'Oh, she'll turn up. Collect the eggs. Alun, go with him and make sure he doesn't break any.' And as we went out again: 'Take the egg basket.'

We were both in the henhouse. A hen was on her nest, clucking loudly. 'Put your hand under her... to get the egg out. Like this...'

'Brrr.' It was a pretence. 'She might peck me.'

'Go on. There is one.'

He extracted a white egg from under the Leghorn. 'It's warm... Not one brown egg from that Rhode Island Red.' He pined for his favourite: Little Rhody.

'Be careful...'

Before I could put the egg in the basket, he was performing. 'Can you balance an egg on your little finger... like this? See...'

'Don't!' The egg smashed to the floor. 'Oh! You'll have to tell Mam.'

His mock crying, with body shaking, lasted all the way back to the house.

We were back from school. As soon as we opened the front door Mam called from the back kitchen: 'Parcel's come.' There it was: a very large parcel, on the living-room table. We hurriedly unwrapped it, and Mam came in to see.

'Books!'

'Ugh...!' No sign of a leather-case ball. Arthur sank into a depth of disappointment.

'*Pictorial... Knowledge*': I read the gold lettering on the red binding, and counted the seven volumes.

'Well Arthur,' said Mam, trying to soothe, 'you'll have to read now, won't you, with all these.'

Sulking: 'I don't want any of them.'

I opened 'Volume One: Literature Through the Ages' and turned over a few pages, gazing at the illustrations on every page, until my eye caught King Arthur

'"King Arthur",' I read aloud. 'Look, Arthur. It's for you,' trying to placate. '"King Arthur and the Knights of the Round Table."'

But Arthur was not to be placated.

We were using the windowless gable-end of the wash-house as a goal, and of course Arthur's rubber ball. The wash-house jutted out at the back of the house, with a backyard open onto Cae Cefn. Mam was out too, throwing food scraps to the hens. The cat had just returned from her

27

prowls in the rabbit warren near the edge of the wood. She had been hunting. As she walked slowly and sedately across Cae Cefn towards us, she carried in her mouth a baby rabbit. She stopped and stood in front of me, proudly looking up to show me her victim, shaking it to draw my attention. Next she walked towards Mam; then to Arthur to show off again. And, as if to give him a gift, she deposited the mauled tiny rabbit at his feet. She knew Arthur would be giving her a saucer of milk at milking time.

We returned to our game. Arthur was about to shoot when we heard Jack's unmistakable raucous singing voice. He had come along our farm road, and was at the gate in the wall near the haystack. It led into Cae Cefn.

Arthur picked up his ball and ran to greet him. 'Any cigarette cards?'

'Hello Dixie Dean,' Jack grinned, and ruffled his hair as he called out to Mam: 'How's Jäbez? I hear he's going to be on the wireless.'

'Yes. Friday night. Well, come in.'

We showed Jack the programme that had come with Dad's last letter. It was headed 'The Dublin and Cork Broadcasting Station: A Programme of *Welsh Songs*'. He scanned through the items: 'Well...!' Then: 'At the Beehive, they've just had a wireless set...'

'Oh let's ask if we can listen in!' Mam had heard the wireless, once. Jack agreed to call at Beehive Stores and arrange it. We were thrilled.

I took the volume *Welsh Songs* off the bookshelf. Flicking over the pages, I said to Jack: 'Here's one Dad's going to sing: "Hob y Deri Dando",' thrusting the book before him.

'Mm? In Welsh. Can't read the Welsh.'

Meanwhile Mam was in the back kitchen, making him a cup of tea and, overhearing us, irresistibly took up the tune.

Jack turned to the English words on the opposite page. 'Jäbez singing this specially for you, Jane?' he called. His eye ran through the English verses and, chuckling, he raised his voice again for Mam to hear: the words were about Jane singing and in the wood, kissing. Laughing uproariously, he called out: 'In the wood, eh?'

Mam came in, embarrassed: 'Now, now, have this cup of tea.'

As he drank he said: 'You know, Beehive's wireless receiver has valves and a loudspeaker, instead of a crystal set with cat's whisker.' Mam protested she didn't understand these newfangled things. It was the only wireless in the village. We would be hearing Dad from across the Irish Sea; we marvelled. 'Yes,' confirmed Jack, 'and they have an aerial wire right across the Tyrpeg to the oak tree. That should pick up Jäbez singing, eh, Jane? Well,' he said as he rose, 'must be off.'

'Come and play football with us,' pleaded Arthur.

'No. On my way,' he said briskly. 'I'll tell them at the Beehive you'll be coming to listen in. Eight o'clock, Friday.'

There were static noises on the radio receiver, with whoops and shrieks, as Mr Williams Beehive turned the knob to get the dial firmly on Dublin 222.6 metres.

'Wonderful thing, the wireless,' said Mrs Williams.

The atmospheric crackles worsened. Mr Williams Beehive would have been happier behind the wheel of his new motor car. He now ran a village taxi service.

Arthur was in the chair nearest to the wireless loudspeaker, sitting upright with anticipation. Then, as it crackled on, unabated, he said in a subdued voice: 'Sounds like the frying pan.'

'Dad's frying eggs,' chuckled Mam quietly.

'Reception's bad today,' said Mrs Williams Beehive apologetically.

Suddenly we heard an orchestra briefly between the swelling and diminishing atmospherics. It was about to begin.

Many years later, Dad related this, his first broadcast in the early years of radio. It was on the first of June. He'd gone into a big room where a small orchestra was waiting. In the middle was the microphone; it looked like a meat safe on a big, wooden stand. He simply stood there and sang into it.

The crackle died away. The light orchestra was tuning up. Hushed, I leaned over to Arthur: 'There it is!'

'No. It's a band, not Dad.' Mam showed Mrs Williams Beehive the programme.

'Mm...' she said, with the orchestra still tuning, 'Jäbez singing "Fy Mlodwen" (My Blodwen).' This was the aria from the opera *Blodwen* by Joseph Parry (who wrote the hymn tune 'Aberystwyth – Jesu, Lover of my Soul'). In the aria Hywel, in the condemned cell, sings farewell to 'my Blodwen, my love, my all? ...the ribbon you gave me on the slope of the meadow... tie it, close to your heart.' On the programme too was 'Hen Groesffordd y Llan' (The Old Village Crossroad), where the singer sings the plaintive refrain 'P'le mae?' (Where art thou?); and the reply: 'buried 'neath the yew near the churchyard wall...' All this and more, on the wireless: Dad singing, and Dad not there!

Then the announcer's Irish accent emerged clearly above the crackle from the loudspeaker: 'This is the Dublin and Cork Broadcasting Station...'

'There it is!' burst out Arthur.

'Shush!' said Mam. We were all sitting up.

'For the next hour and a half...' (it was strange hearing a stranger's voice coming out of a box) '...we shall hear a programme of songs sung by the Welsh tenor, Jäbez Trevor, with the Station Orchestra.' He paused.

'Cor!'

Arthur was quelled again.

'We begin with...' Then suddenly the atmospheric crackle, dormant in the background behind the announcer, swelled up loudly, completely obliterating his voice.

There we sat for the whole hour and a half, listening to it, while Mr Williams Beehive, with apologies and frustration, occasionally twiddled the knob.

Then, sadly, we walked our mile and a half home.

Arthur was bouncing his ball on the tiled floor of the wash-house, where Mam had lit the boiler that morning. 'Arthur, keep away from the dolly tub. You'll have your ball into it!' But the ball-bouncing persisted. The mangle was turning. It was a beautiful morning: the sun shining and a slight breeze.

Off I went to do a daily task: water from the well. This was some three hundred yards away, across Cae Cefn and down the slope. It was a spring of clear water which never dried up even in the driest summer. The water bubbled out of the hillside near a clump of trees. Alongside was a trough where the cow could drink. This spring was the source of the smallest of streams, trickling down towards the wood, keeping the grass fresh and watering the wild flowers of wood and fields.

Back in the wash-house: 'Arthur, take your ball outside. Let me get on with the washing. It's a lovely day to get it on the line.' Mam was busy; only occasionally bursting into song.

I retreated to the living room and *Pictorial Knowledge*. I read how wireless telegraphy was the modern means of communication, and that it would supersede the cable under the sea. I was immersed in science.

We had originally decided to put all these new volumes in the parlour alongside the five books of *The Musical Educator*, 'a library of musical instruction'. These well-worn volumes in their faded green binding had come from the vicarage when the old vicar died. They told you about singing and voice production, and explained rhythm, melody and harmony; they told you about musical instruments like the organ and the harp, and about the great composers and singers of the past. In each volume the frontispiece (such as 'The Old Strad' from a painting), the plates (Mozart, Handel, Haydn...) and portraits (Melba, Madame Clara Butt...) were all protected by thin leaves of tissue paper, turning brown with age. These books were Sunday morning reading, with the fire lit in the parlour. But our new *Pictorial Knowledge* was eventually, with Dad's help when he was home for a few days, squeezed onto the bookshelf in the living room, where I could dip into it every day.

'Oh there you are,' said Mam, coming into the living room. And, slightly scoffing: 'Of course you've got your seven volumes. Come and help me carry the clothes basket. You should be out in the fresh air.'

In no time the clothes were flapping gently on the line out on Cae Cefn, the birds were singing and we were playing football. In the far corner of the field the cow was grazing, quietly swishing her tail. After milking that morning I had brought her round to Cae Cefn. The cat was prowling in the long grass by the garden wall.

'Play well away from the clothes line,' we were warned. The laden clothes line heaved as the clothes puffed out with the wind.

We decided to use the wash-house wall again, after Arthur had retrieved the ball from the nettles by the old pigsties. His rubber ball had narrowly missed getting in among the thorns of the hawthorn tree in the overgrown hedge. Our neighbouring farmer never cut his hedges, and this one was his. However it provided some shelter from the west wind; and in spring and summer the red evening sun shone low in the sky through its untidy gaps.

Arthur had taken only one shot at goal when I saw something peculiar in the sky. It was far away, over that same hedge on the western side. 'Look,' I said, leaving him to score into an open goal, 'what's that over there?'

He turned round and stared. 'A great big kite?' It was coming nearer, and we could now hear it faintly. 'A great big bird? No. Airship.'

'No. An aeroplane!' Then turning and shouting towards the wash-house door: 'Mam, Mam, come and look.' It was much nearer now, its engines roaring in the sky. And it was flying very low, only a few hundred feet above our fields. The frightened birds were twittering and darting from tree to bush. The hens began clucking loudly, flapping their wings. The cat sprang over the garden wall and bounded towards the front door but, finding it shut, crouched under the gooseberry bush. The cow looked up, turned and, with her tail in the air, ran along the boundary hedge towards the old pigsties, away from the approaching noise.

It had a silver-coloured fuselage with four big wings; our first sight of an aeroplane. It was near enough now to see the large letters 'IMPERIAL AIRWAYS' along its side.

'Goodness gracious,' said Mam, running up breathless, 'it's an aeroplane!'

'No, an airliner.' The letters G.A.A.G.X. were on its wings.

'Isn't it big.' Mam had to shout now to make herself heard above the roar. 'You'd think it would fall out of the sky.'

Arthur counted the windows along its side. 'Eight!' he shouted. 'Look, people inside.'

'Passengers,' I bellowed. 'It's a passenger airliner.' They were waving and looking down at us. One man was peering down as if trying to identify us. With the aero-engines at their most deafening, we three waved back and shouted 'Hurray!'

'Ooh! My washing. Ooh!' Mam ran towards the clothes line in panic. 'They'll see my washing on the line! I must take it in!' She furiously unpegged our sheets and shirts, calling: 'Come and help. Where's the clothes basket?'

Arthur and I stood and waved and waved until the plane's wings tilted slightly away from us as it turned. It was making for the gap in the hills, going round Hope Mountain.

'Going to London,' said Arthur.

'Yes. Looking for a place to land where it's flat. An aerodrome.'

34

Its wings were wobbling a little. It was moving away from us, now over our wood, with its wheels nearly touching the tops of the trees. Or so it seemed, from our angle of vision.

The engine noise was now distant; it had passed over our school at the bottom of the wood, over the railway station, skirting Dad's village, Coedllai, on the neighbouring hill. Between it and Hope Mountain was the narrow gap, The Nant, with Nant Byr flowing through it. Through this gap on this clear morning we could see the aeroplane heading slowly for the Cheshire Plain and England. It was receding gradually, now down to bird size. We watched until it was no more than a tiny speck.

'Did you see the pilot in the front window?'

'Yes,' said Arthur. 'I'm going to be a pilot. I'll bring Dad home from Dublin.'

'Can't. You'd have to cross the sea. It's got wheels, and wheels can't land on water. You could bring Dad home from London though.'

'I'd be the pilot and make it land on Cae Cefn.'

'No. Mam's clothes line's in the way. It's our only flat field. And it's only two acres. Not big enough.'

We walked indoors.

I made straight for *Pictorial Knowledge*. The aeroplane was the Handley Page 'Heracles'. I raised my voice to Arthur: 'Come and look!' It was a large fold-out illustration, inside the back cover, of this new Imperial Airways airliner.

'Cor!'

'It was the same aeroplane – the same letters on the wings: G.A.A.G.X. "X" means "unknown quantity" you know.'

'What's "quantity"?'

'Um... don't know really.' We opened the fold-out page to reveal the inside of the plane. It carried forty passengers and was the world's most luxurious airliner.

'Let me see.' He took a closer look. 'The pilot sits here.'

'Yes; and the man in the aeroplane can talk by wireless to the people on the ground.' The wireless aerial was let out of a tube under the nose of the plane to trail in the wind when the machine was in flight.

Mam approached, having heard our excitement. 'Let me see.' She looked at the passenger cabin revealed under the fold-out: 'Mm! Lovely upholstered seats inside, with arms. Nicer even than our parlour chairs.' These, our crimson plush chairs and sofa, had come, at the same time as the volumes of *The Musical Educator*, from the vicarage, and were her pride and joy.

I identified the luggage compartment with the help of the number on the picture and the key which named each part. And also the mail compartments. 'It carries letters!'

'Arthur,' said Mam, 'if you write to Dad it might go by airmail.' But it brought no response. I found a refreshment room. There were sixty-seven different things to identify, from engine exhaust pipes to escape door. Where would they escape to? In the picture, the aeroplane was crossing the coast, heading out over the sea.

'Curtains on the windows.' Mam was still in the passenger cabin.

'And landing wheels with pneumatic tyres.'

Mam turned to Arthur: 'The kind you blow up with a bicycle pump; like pumping up a real football. If you write to Dad...'

'Yes. Yes...' interrupted Arthur so as not to hear. 'Bet

if I was pilot I'd land on Cae Cefn.'

The top wings had a span of a hundred and thirty feet
and its cruising speed was one hundred miles per hour!

Mam concluded: 'Dad could be home from London in
two hours.'

That morning we had seen one of the world's latest and
largest airliners; perhaps on its proving flight.

We were in the school playground early. 'Did you see the
aeroplane...?' 'Imperial Airways... the world's largest
passenger airliner...' There was only one topic in the boys'
playground.

'Going to England,' said Arthur, when the school bell
rang. The chatter subsided. We lined up, an arm's length
apart from each other, and marched in through the porch.

Today it was singing with Mr Hayes in the Big Room.
It started with the usual first five minutes practising tonic
sol-fa, Mr Hayes giving the key note, sometimes from the
piano, sometimes with a tuning fork.

The singing began indifferently enough.

'Rwy'n canu fel cana'r...'

This was not singing as the songbird is singing. (Our
minds were too much on that aeroplane.)

'No, no, no,' said Mr Hayes in his teacher's voice. He
was at the piano. 'Stand up.'

We stood, raising the squeaking seats of our desks.

'And sing up.'

We began again, but at the second line up went Mr

Hayes' groan of despair: 'Oh!... stop! You're supposed to sing as the songbird sings, happy and free....' He looked towards Arthur who, because he was short, was in the front row. And after glaring at the rest of us with an eye which made us wither with inadequacy, he turned to him again and said, 'Arthur. Sing the first two lines.'

Arthur quietly cleared his throat, and sang them in full voice.

'Right. Now we'll all sing it like that.'

And so the lesson continued with more robust singing until it was time for Handwriting.

'Pens down.' Mr Hayes was poised to make an announcement to the class.

We had carefully copied from the blackboard, in copperplate:

> Oh to be in England
> Now that April's there...

(Airliner there too; our minds were still not entirely on our work.)

> While the chaffinch sings on the orchard bough
> In England – now!

(And Dad sings in England now; back from Dublin. Manchester Free Trade Hall I think.) Arthur had taken a long time to reach 'England' in the first line. He had dipped the steel nib of his pen deep into the inkwell, with the black ink reaching the tips of his finger and thumb. But so far he had avoided the worst crime, a blot. We had all written painstakingly with the right hand whether right-handed or not, with elbow well tucked in to the side, sitting up straight with the palm of the left hand keeping the copybook steady on the sloping desk. A quiet lesson, except for the occasional stifled cough and the scratching pens of those of us who didn't hold the pen at the right angle to the paper, just so.

We stopped writing, placing our pens in the groove along the top of the desk with the wet pen nib over the inkwell. Not a spot of ink was allowed on the desk.

'Pay attention everyone.'

We sat with arms folded, ready to listen.

'The school trip to Rhyl by charabanc,' announced Mr Hayes, 'will be… on Friday, the twenty-second of July.'

Murmurs of excitement from the class.

'Your mothers can come. Half a crown each.'

'Mr Hayes…' it was Arthur bubbling over.

'Put your hand up.'

His hand shot up. 'Mr Hayes, please sir, can I bring my football to play on the sands?'

'No, the tide will be in.'

He persisted: 'Can we play polo on the donkeys?'

With the ink of our copybooks now dry, we shut them; they were collected methodically. We stood to march out to play.

But Arthur had to stay in playtime to finish his handwriting.

At midday we rushed home, up through the tunnel in the wood and over the stile by the sycamore tree. We did not dare take the short cut up through our hayfields – it was summertime, the grass was long and it would be haytime soon. Haymaking was one of the jobs that needed outside help. Dad had arranged for Uncle George, Uncle Tom, and always Uncle Noah, to come regularly to do the seasonal jobs. They were all glad to have the work; times were hard, and coal miners were often working only three or four shifts a week. And so the hedge-cutting, muck-spreading, and of course the haymaking with many hands, were done. Haytime was the event of the year. Price Tir-Paenau, whose farm we could see across the valley on the upper slopes of Hope Mountain, would be bringing his two horses and mowing machine one of these fine summer days. Then with the mown hay turned and thoroughly dried and the fields dotted with haycocks, his haycart would come; a new haystack would rise in the yard and the hayloft would be full.

But now it was Rhyl. Despite taking the longer path to avoid the hayfields, we reached home before Mam had time to prepare our midday meal.

'Mam, Mam...' Arthur rushed into the house first, breathless and excited. 'We're going to Rhyl on the school trip!'

'On Friday,' I said, trying to get my breath back, 'the twenty-second of July.'

'Well...' began Mam. 'I don't know... we'll go if Arthur will try to read, and write to Dad.'

Our faces dropped.

Then, after a pause: 'When...? Twenty-second?' She walked over to the Co-op calendar on the wall. 'I think that's the week Dad's in concert at the Rhyl Pavilion.' She lifted the pages of the calendar, reading what Dad had written the last time he was home: 'Manchester Free Trade Hall… Argyle Theatre, Birkenhead…' and then flicking over another page: 'Yes. That's right. Rhyl Pavilion. All week.'

'Hurray! We'll see Dad…! We'll see Dad…!' We were too excited to eat.

⚬⚬⚬

By charabanc! This was something new. We had been on the train before of course. We were up early that morning. While Arthur fed the hens, I fetched the cow. Rabbits were nibbling at the grass a full field away from their burrows, hardly noticing me. Daisies in the dew and the sun hardly above the rim of Hope Mountain: a summer morning. The milking was over and the cow back in the field by seven o'clock. At least, I had not heard the seven o'clock train. We relied on the train to tell us the time, for there was no reliable clock in the house. Not that Mam would have taken much notice of it had there been one. She had little regard for time by the clock; each day was timeless, except when the LMS train whistle intruded. We knew when it was Sunday: there were no trains, and I had taken on the task of crossing off each day on the calendar, day by day. We changed into our best suits and walked down through the wood to the charabanc parked near the station, ready to leave at eight.

It was already nearly full of excited children. We were in good time, more by luck than design. Mam sat behind us. When every one of the bench seats was full, the driver climbed into the driver's seat. As he started the engine, a cheer went up. A small group had come to wave us off, and we waved and cheered as the charabanc moved away down the Tyrpeg. With its hood folded down, our heads were open to the sky.

Down through The Nant, the road twisting and turning as it followed Nant Byr through the trees in the narrow gap in the hills. Then at a crossroad came the bab-bab of the charabanc's horn. We turned into what for us was new territory with strangers flashing by: a postman on foot, a man going to work on a bike, a boy bringing a cow from a meadow. We overtook farmers in horse-drawn traps, cart horses not yet harnessed, a district nurse on her bicycle. A car flashed by in the other direction: our new doctor, said someone. An Englishman. We went on for miles and miles.

'Rwy'n canu fel cana'r aderyn...'

Arthur in full voice again, singing like the songbird. And we all joined in. The driver, as we went over the brow of a hill, gave repeated bab-babs on his horn, turning round and pointing to draw our attention towards the horizon.

'Look, the sea, the sea...!' someone shouted above the singing, which immediately changed to a loud 'Hurray!'

Arthur took up the singing again until the charabanc drew to a halt alongside the Promenade with the parading holiday crowd, the seagulls and the waves on the beach.

Dad was there.

'Dad, shall we go on the sands and ride the donkeys?' We did. It was a ride with a baby donkey trotting beside its mother. Arthur answered the braying donkey: 'You sound like an broken-down old harp.' The donkey brayed again, more appealingly. 'But you try your best. Let me stroke you.'

'Dad, shall we walk along the Promenade?' We did. We watched Punch and Judy, rode tricycles, walked on the pier, and saw the Rhyl Pavilion with Dad's name in big letters outside.

'Dad, shall we ride on the little train round the Marine Lake?' We did. And rolled coins in the fairground's 'roll-a-penny'.

'Dad, shall we listen to the Pierrots?' We did. There was an open air audience on folding chairs, some with rugs over their knees. On the small stage was a tinny piano accompanying a man singing Jack's song, 'My Blue Heaven'. The small ensemble followed with 'It Ain't Goin' to Rain No Mo', No Mo''.

'Dad, does the sun always shine in Rhyl?'

'The sun shines in Rhyl for ever,' said Mam. 'Look at the sunset over the Great Orme. Dad's in Llandudno all next week, aren't you Dad.'

'Let's all go.'

We wandered back to the beach, strolled along the water's edge, and back to the Promenade and the waiting charabanc. Not far away were the Pierrots, the male soloist now pounding out 'Yes We Have No Bananas'. We kissed goodbye to Dad, and climbed aboard.

We were home very late.

⸎

Arthur yawned: 'I'm not getting up today.'

Mam's voice came up from the bottom of the stairs: 'Get up. Breakfast time.'

'Come on. I'm hungry. I'll get dressed before you.' He

jumped out of bed with a thud on the bedroom floor. As he dressed he began singing his own Welsh version of the Pierrot:

'Oes mae genni banana...'

I climbed out of bed and took up the second line:

'Mae genni banana today.'

'Hey,' I said, 'you've put on my trousers.'

There was a loud knock on the front door at the foot of the stairs. 'Mr Marshall the Post,' said Arthur, racing down.

I came down to find Mam reading a letter. 'Dad's been offered a six-month contract to tour Canada and the USA.'

'Ooh! Will he see Red Indians? Real ones?'

Mam was clearly a little worried. 'Dad will be away a long time I'm afraid. You'll have to write to him. Regularly. Both of you. Arthur, you must practise.'

'He'll go by Imperial Airways...!' Arthur was bubbling over.

'No, by ocean steam liner.'

'See,' said Mam to him, 'your letter would go on a steamship. Come on and practise reading: now.'

II
SS *Laurentic*

After Dad's spell at home, the first letter to arrive had 'White Star Line: on board *SS Laurentic*' printed on the envelope. The notepaper had a picture of the ship at the top. Dad had written it soon after she left Liverpool, posting it on board before she called at Belfast, where mail was taken off. We got the letter two days later.

Mam sat in the rocking chair, reading the letter, while Arthur and I looked over her shoulder, absorbing the details of the ship in the picture. '"Dear Jane and the boys... a pleasant voyage so far..."'

We noticed the wireless aerial strung from mast to mast, like the one at the Beehive. Perhaps we would hear Dad on the wireless from the ship!

'Let me read it: "This liner is like a big floating city..."' She was 18,000 tons, with shops, a hairdresser, a library and a swimming pool.

'Is there somewhere to play football?' Arthur decided you could dribble on deck round the two funnels, using the masts for goalposts.

'"...these jabbering Germans, enough to moider one..."'
The transatlantic flow of emigrants from Europe to the
New World had restarted, tentatively, after the Great War.
They could make a leisurely six-day crossing of the
Herring Pond with Liverpool the premier port of
departure; ports of call at Belfast, Glasgow, St Johns
(Newfoundland) and Quebec to Montreal; or calling at
Halifax (Nova Scotia) and Boston if sailing to New York.

Mam was now reading more to herself: '"...Enclosing
cheque..."' And concluding aloud for us: '"With love from
Dad. PS. Had press photo taken before I embarked."' Later
we found it on the front page of the *Liverpool Courier*.

I rushed to the bookshelf, to bring out the volume with
a chapter on Modern Ships. The *SS Laurentic* had
telescopic masts, and they were lowered to go under
Quebec Bridge.

'Now get Arthur to read that.'

But Arthur was bouncing his ball. I tried tempting him
with the many pictures of modern liners. But the ball
bounced more persistently.

The *Laurentic* was a fairly new ship, and one of the last
North Atlantic liners to be built as a coal burner. She was
the first of many that took Dad to North America. He
sailed on the *Newfoundland*, *Nova Scotia*, *Baltic*, *Adriatic*,
Britannic – all out of Liverpool either from Gladstone Dock
or the Princes Landing Stage. And once on the *Majestic*
from Southampton. He came home on one occasion to
Plymouth on the American ship *President Harding*.

Mam made one more attempt that morning: 'And
Arthur, if you learn to read, we could go to Liverpool to
meet Dad when he comes home.'

Quickly taking notice: 'Would we see the ship?'

'And you must write to Dad too.'

'Would we go on board and meet the captain?'

'Perhaps,' she said, turning to me with a wink, feeling she was making progress at last. 'If you will really try...'

Besides the regular letters to Mam came a stream of coloured picture postcards. They usually came in twos. Sometimes the letter had with it a snapshot or two and the occasional newspaper cutting.

'Dear Alun....' This was the message on the back of a picture of the Canadian Parliament Building. The card had a two cent King George the Fifth stamp. The tour had already taken in St John's (Newfoundland), Halifax (Nova Scotia), Quebec and Montreal. 'I suppose you know Ottawa is the capital of Canada. Love from Dad.' The message was always brief, often educational.

Arthur hesitated at the small print under his picture of toboggans on Mount Royal, Montreal. And so the postcards came: Canadian Mounties, Lumber Raft on the Ottawa River, the Canadian Lynx...

A Canadian National Railway card arrived: 'In Canada they have goods trains two miles long.' From Coed Talon... halfway to Brymbo! A train the length of our wood, beyond the Pant-y-Stên level crossing and beyond Llanfynydd, the next station up the line!

Arthur's card showed the Canadian Prairie. A team of eight horses were cutting the grain 'at great speed'. The small print explained: 'Prairie means "meadow".'

'What a big meadow,' said Arthur, 'as big as from here to Pontybodkin.' Pontybodkin, half a mile below the station, was our nearest post office, where we posted our letters and sometimes a rolled-up local paper.

Manitoba was 'God's own Country of the Prairie'.

'Does God live there?'

And Winnipeg was the Queen of the Prairies. *Winnipeg*! The name amused us. Saskatoon, Saskatchewan; Moose Jaw... Medicine Hat was where a Cree Indian medicine man lost his war bonnet in the river during a war with Blackfoot Indians.

Banff, Alberta. Banff, with two Fs, like Welsh. A beautiful calendar arrived. The Rocky Mountains now – it was the 'vacation land' of Canadians.

Kicking Horse Pass with the spiralling tunnels of the Canadian Pacific Railroad under Cathedral Mountain.

'Cor!' Arthur looked at this spectacular postcard. 'Better than our Brymbo Express.'

Snapshots came of Dad standing beside a huge steam locomotive, and on the rear platform of the train. On the back he had written: 'Canadian National Railway: Continental Limited.'

'Canadian National Railway's much better than Canadian Pacific.'

'Oh yes,' nodded Arthur with worldly wisdom, 'much better.' Mam smiled to herself.

Dad's route took in Calgary, Edmonton, Kamloops, Penticton... and postcards came from them all.

Mam, with all these cards coming in one direction, thought we should find postcards with local views to send to him. It would be a subtle way of getting Arthur to write. At Beehive Stores we found two: one was of the walk by the brook with the bee hollow, near the church and the overhanging yew, where I had read *Jephtha*. We failed to get Arthur to write it. The other was taken by Georgie Jones who lived by the station. He had taken his camera, big wooden tripod and black cloth up to the top of Pen-y-Boncyn. The result: a dull, underexposed picture postcard of Coed Talon complete with the colliery's smoking chimney stack and the railway cutting. I addressed it to Dad, care of his Canadian agent in Montreal, Mr Desautels (Mam never could spell that name), and stuck on a penny stamp. Then I wrote 'Pontybodkin in the far distance' and hurried down the fields and wood to catch the evening post at Pontybodkin Post Office.

'Dear Jābez. The boys are now in bed...' (Mam's letter came to light many years later.) 'They love the picture postcards. Keep sending them. Hope your cold is better. Can you get Nostrolene over there? It's done Alun's catarrh a world of good...'

Vancouver: the latest card, showing totem poles in Stanley Park.

'Red Indians!' Arthur raised his voice with excitement.

With a letter was a newspaper cutting. The headline ran: 'Welsh Singers to Tour the States'.

We were frantically opening a parcel.

'Presents!' Arthur tore open the brown paper after Mam had cut the string. It had United States stamps.

It was not Dad's first US tour. In those early years it became the pattern – first Canada, then the States, but never once going to the US West Coast. He had previously entered the United States at Port Huron on the overnight train from Montreal to Chicago. Later he was to sail to New York direct.

After another spell at home he was back once more in Canada, and now the USA again, this time to take in the Middle West.

We had begun an interest in stamp collecting. The stamps showed a picture of a US president, but it was hard to tell which because of the franking mark. 'Thought you knew everything,' said Arthur.

He lifted the lid off the box. It was a book. 'Ugh...' – his face fell. It was an atlas. *Atlas of North America*: page after page of coloured maps.

Arthur discovered in the box another wrapped parcel and soon had it unwrapped. It was a flashlight. 'For me! For me!' His mounting excitement had the wrapping paper all over the floor. He switched on his new electric torch. It had a gadget to produce coloured light. 'Look, a red light; and green as well!'

There was another small item, a necklace for Mam, with a letter. Dad had just worked his way through the Dakotas, and now had a week in Minneapolis. This was the land of Minnehaha – the state of Minnesota, Mother of the Mississippi, the Father of Waters. Then on to Milwaukee which was in Wisconsin, the state south of Lake Superior – the Gitche Gumee in Longfellow's poem. The letter said: '"Tour going fine..."'

'Oh look,' interrupted Arthur. He had found a picture postcard at the bottom of the box. It showed a tornado which destroyed hundreds of houses in Minnesota. This worried Mam for a moment – it was not very safe for Dad there.

Then back to the letter. He was planning a long stay in

Chicago. '"Will you send letters care of my US agent, Redpath Bureau..."'

'Redpath!' Arthur lowered his normally high-pitched voice an octave to sound menacing. 'There'll be Redskins there, on the warpath!'

And Dad gave the agent's address; Kimball Building, Chicago. '"Is Arthur beginning to read?"'

But Arthur was still rummaging in the box and had found the other postcard for me. It was a huge steam locomotive: Great Northern Railway's Empire Builder, standing at Union Station in St Paul, Minneapolis' twin city.

'Let Arthur try reading it.' But almost immediately the letter recaptured Mam: '"Shall be taking the overnight train..."'

'All aboard!' called Arthur loudly, imitating the train conductor. Dad had told us about North American trains. In fact, he and the other singers travelled in the USA mainly by their own bus, in contrast to Canada, where they travelled for the most part by train. And it was American trains that captivated us now. There was a chapter in one of our books about observation cars and cowcatchers; about crack trains like Twentieth Century Limited ('The Greatest Train in the World': Chicago to New York – for every minute it is late, the railroad company pays you back a dollar); Broadway Limited (also to New York); the Detroiter and the Wolverine (New York via Lower Ontario and Buffalo). And railroads like the Illinois Central, New York Central, the Pennsylvania and the Baltimore and Ohio; and even the New York, New Haven and Hartford.

'Listen,' commanded Mam. '"The boys would love to see one of these trains – red plush seats in the coach, electric lights..."'

'The electric light on the train. Gee.'

'"...and when it's hot, an electric fan..."'

'Gee whiz.' (We now knew American words, picked up from Dad when he was home.)

The Negro porter wore a white jacket with brass buttons, and came walking down the aisle, delivering a telegram and things. '"I had dinner on the train..."'

But how do you do the cooking, on a train? Books left a lot unexplained. And, asked Arthur, how could you pour the tea going over the Rocky Mountains?

'Chicago's a long way from the Rocky Mountains silly. Fifty miles! Further than Rhyl.'

Did they stop the train to get water from a well, we wondered?

'Let me finish,' said Mam, moving to get more light from the window. '"There's a Pullman sleeping car where I go to bed..."'

'How can you go to bed on a train?'

'"...and the porter shines your shoes for you and gets you a pillow."'

'How can you sleep on a train?'

'Well, Arthur,' she said, smiling and looking at him through her thick glasses, 'you slept on the train once, in my arms, all the way from Brymbo.'

'Yes,' persisted Arthur again, 'but how can you go upstairs to bed? On a train?'

Suddenly we heard the whistle of the half-past four Brymbo Express. We could not see it. It was hidden by the trees. But we saw the billowing white smoke rising in the sunlight from below the wood and heard the faint clattering of the train wheels telling us the time. 'That's our train,' said Mam, looking out of the window. 'It's late.

Come on. Feed the hens. Fetch the cow.' And as the cat meowed, 'Give the cat some milk.' And, hurrying towards the back kitchen: 'Alun, fetch water from the well.'

That evening, just before our bedtime, Mam was writing a letter. It was her habit to write standing up. The writing pad and inkstand (with its two pen holders and two ink bottles, blue-black and red) were on the dresser. Her pen moved furiously. When her hand moved over to dip the pen in the ink, she would miss her aim and almost knock the ink bottle over, her eyes never moving from the lines she had written: 'They are growing fast. Alun's going to be tall like you. We are going to have photos to send you. Georgie Jones is coming with his camera...'

'Georgie, why does the camera have to have three legs?' Arthur was examining all his apparatus.

'To keep it steady,' said Georgie Jones in his unruffled voice. 'Now if you'll all come and sit under the lilac tree.' He was almost the professional. 'Camera's ready.'

He had carried his camera with its large and clumsy wooden folding tripod up through the wood. We had gone down as far as the stile by the sycamore tree to meet him, supposedly to help him carry his awkward load, but really because we were curious to see this strange apparatus.

The camera was on its tripod. The cat came and rubbed her back against his legs. 'Shall we have the cat? Alun, you hold her,' he said, picking her up and handing her to me. 'There.' He now had us seated on the wooden seat on the lawn at the bottom of the garden near the lilac tree. Beyond, the ground fell away sharply down to our nearest hayfield and, perhaps not consciously, he had chosen as backcloth a panorama – the irregular patchwork of green fields which was Hope Mountain. He stooped to peer into the viewfinder, pulling his black cloth first over the top of the camera and then over his head.

'Georgie, why are you putting that black cloth over your head?'

'Arthur, you... you're going to hold your ball are you?' Arthur held his ball close to his chest. We were ready.

'Right. Watch the dickie bird.' The shutter clicked. 'There we are.' We dispersed.

'Where's Jäbez now?' he asked as he packed his camera.

'Chicawgo,' said Arthur, pronouncing it the way Dad did when he was last home.

Then Georgie reminisced about Dad, when young, competing with more ambition than experience – he was not yet twenty-one – at a National Eisteddfod, singing a very difficult test piece, 'O Loveliness Beyond Compare' from Mozart's *The Magic Flute*. The adjudicator had said, 'This young singer will go far.'

'Well yes,' chipped in Arthur, 'he's already been as far as Vancouver.'

Georgie chuckled. 'Now Vancouver, is that near New York?'

'Well... er... it's a long way by train. A hundred miles.'

'He has travelled far.' And, after a pause: 'I remember how we went in horse wagonettes to Caerwys Eisteddfod. In nineteen hundred and nine.'

'Before I was born,' said Arthur.

'The whole choir. And we walked over Hope Mountain there,' said Georgie with a sweep of his arm, 'to Cymau to compete, had tea and a final rehearsal in a field...'

The mountain road to Cymau started near the station. By Sion Chapel it turned, rising steeply for half a mile up the mountain. Then it turned again by Tri-Thy (Three Houses) to follow the contour line for much of the mountain's length. Across the valley, this was roughly at our level. It was on this road in threshing time that we would watch a steam traction engine drawing the thresher, puffing slowly along, visiting the farms in turn – Tir-Paenau, Tri-Thy, Cae-Glas, Y Fron.... Silently, for it was a mile across the valley, the tiny puffs of white smoke would rise against the steeply sloping green fields. Then the road defied gravity again, to rise to the moorland at the crest. At eleven hundred feet above sea level, and five hundred above us at Pen-y-Wern, it was the roof of the world that touched the sky. Somewhere up there was Hope Mountain's other chapel, the tiny Horeb, standing all alone in splendid isolation, out of sight. Horeb: Mount Sinai? Then there it was, up in the sky. The road disappeared over the top, passing Horeb down to the hamlet of Cymau.

'We were young then. Aye.'

Before he left we showed him our new photo of Dad, wearing evening dress. It was a large photograph in a gilt frame, and it hung on the wall in the parlour, above the plush sofa. He paused on his way out through the gate: 'Your dad, now, he's got stage presence.'

And turning to Mam as he walked away across the yard: 'Remember me to Jäbez.'

More parcels, postcards and letters for Mam: Mr Marshall the Post brought them regularly. This time it was a parcel.

'What is it?' Arthur was impetuous as usual. 'Handle with care' and 'Fragile' were stamped on the sides in large letters, and the postmark was 'Chicago, Illinois'.

Mam came in from the barn, having heard Mr Marshall crossing the yard. We were up late that Saturday morning; no one heard the train. 'Let's open it,' she said, coming into the living room and wiping her hands.

'Bet it's a leather-case football for me!' Arthur was prancing with excitement.

'Hand me the scissors.' She was trying to calm him. 'We'll cut the string... carefully.' The scissors snipped the neatly knotted string stuck down with sealing wax. Removing the outer wrapping revealed a box.

'Take the lid off,' said Arthur impatiently.

'Have patience, have patience...' Mam removed his hand from the lid, and then carefully lifted it. The box was packed with straw and newspaper: obviously something breakable. Crockery; a watch or something? Or an alarm clock? Instead of depending on the train... without a reliable clock... not that it would have made any difference having the most accurate clock in the world.

My eye caught the newspaper title: 'Chicago Daily Tribune: The World's Greatest Newspaper.' And in small print: 'Two Cents: Pay No More!' Removing this news-paper packing revealed something round. A plate, possibly, to hang on the wall?

'No, it's a wheel, with a hole in the middle,' decided Arthur. It was a flat object, and its cardboard cover cut away at the centre to reveal a printed label. At the head of the label was a picture of a dog with its head on one side, his ear close to what looked like a trumpet.

'"Victor Talking Machine Company".'

'Talking Machine?'

And Mam, with a sudden revelation: 'It's a gramophone record!'

'A what?'

The small print curved round the label's edge: '"Electrically... recorded." They've got the electric in Chicago then.'

'Talking machine?' Arthur still disbelieving.

'We'll have to buy a gramophone to play it.'

'What, to make a man talk on it?' Arthur had picked up the breakable record, now out of its plain cardboard sleeve.

'Arthur, handle it carefully!'

'Look, I can roll it along the edge of the table.'

'Oh... give it to me!' Mam lunged forward to rescue it. 'We'd better put it back in its sleeve.'

There was a copy of sheet music at the bottom of the box: '*Dawn of Love*. Song.' It must be something Dad found in a music shop in Chicago, thought Mam. The price was 50c.

'That's about... two bob,' Arthur calculated quickly.

Rummaging in the box, he found a letter. Mam adjusted her thick glasses: '"Just a note... with a record of a new song. Made... at the Recording Studios."'

'What, on the talking machine?' Then Mam, suddenly excited: 'Look at the record. What does it say? Your eyesight's better than mine.' I peered again at the gold lettering on the round black label: '"His... Master's... Voice".'

'No, here. Below the dog. The small print.'

'"Dawn of Love". Same as the music copy.'

'Yes, go on... go on... read the rest.'

'"Sung by Jäbez Trevor, tenor!"'

'Oh!' Her joy was complete.

'"Accompanied by the composer."'

'We're going to buy a gramophone. Today. We're going to Cranes Music Shop, Wrexham. Hurry. Get your boots on.' We scurried. Arthur broke his boot lace and quickly knotted it together again. 'And coats. Quick. No time to change into your best suits.' Mam quickly looked out of the window up at the sky. 'What time is it? The sun is high. If we hurry... we'll catch the eleven o'clock train to Brymbo... change to the Great Western...'

We were both ready, but Mam was still upstairs getting dressed. I couldn't resist a glance at the words of the new song:

...And then came life's awakening...

'Alun! Put that music copy down!' She came hurrying down the stairs. 'Hurry!'

But I took another brief glance:

my childhood days... now gone...

She opened the front door. 'If we run we'll catch that train.'

We shut the door with a bang, without locking it – but that was quite usual – no one came our way. The cat, sitting on the low red-brick wall in front of the house, darted out of our way. The few hens scratching in the yard clucked and flapped their wings as we hurried across to the footpath down the fields. And the cow stopped grazing to look up at us as we ran, Arthur first, down to the stile and the tunnel through the wood.

So this was a gramophone. It was just like the picture on the record label. The meaning of 'His Master's Voice' dawned on me. Mam quickly put the kettle on the fire before joining us. I had the book of instructions: *How to Operate the Gramophone*. '"First place the horn in position and swivel in desired direction. Place record on turntable."' After consulting the drawing in the instructions, the record was in place with the spindle at the centre fitting neatly into the tiny round hole in the record.

'"Attach needle to sound box."' The man in Cranes Music Shop had shown me how. He had given me a tiny tin box full of short and very sharp steel needles. To play a record a new needle had to be inserted and screwed into its socket. '"Wind the motor."'

'Let me.' Arthur turned the handle at the side.

'"Set speed of turntable at seventy-eight revolutions per minute."' A silver-coloured lever jutted out from under the turntable. The pointer was set on 78.

'"Lower sound box gently with needle in the spiralling groove at edge of disc." Disc? Must be the gramophone record.'

'We're going to hear a talking machine with a talking man': Arthur was hushed and excited.

'Singing,' said Mam, no less excited. 'And a very special man.'

The kettle was boiling. 'Oh, wait.' She strode over to

take it off the fire and returned to watch me swing the arm over gingerly so that the needle rested in the groove at the record's edge.

But nothing happened.

'Silence,' said Arthur solemnly. Then, after a pause and perplexed glances at one another and again at the record, Arthur said in his normal voice: 'You haven't switched it on!'

The cockerel crowed. It had come over the stone wall from Cae Cefn into the garden. 'Arthur, go and shoo it out.' When he opened the front door, the cat came in. She leapt on to the chair beside the table to watch the gramophone.

'Wait for me, wait for me...' Arthur was back in a moment, with: 'He's gone. Gone to lay an egg.' Now back at the table, one hand stroking the cat, the other propping up his chin close to the turntable, he had an intent look; he sniffled.

'Wipe your nose. You can't listen to Dad with a dirty nose.'

All was set to switch on.

'Wait. Let me...' Mam moved over to the mantelpiece for a comb '...let me tidy my hair...'

Arthur whispered behind his hand: 'The talking man might see!'

I switched it on. The turntable turned with a hum. I swung the arm once again, letting the needle down, the record spinning round this time. The cat was watching every move.

There was a piano introduction. Then:

> I'm living o'er the mem'ries
> Of my childhood days now gone...

60

'Cor! It's Dad!'

'Shush!'

Dad's voice was unmistakable. We played the record to its end. We played it again, and this time I had the music copy in my hand, following the notes and sometimes glancing at the words.

And then came life's awakening...

The voice soared out of the gramophone:

> I want you in the morning
> When the dawn comes stealing in...

And pianissimo:

> I want you in the night time
> When the whole world is at rest...

It finished fortissimo on a high note:

> Just because dear, I love you.

We played it again. 'Open the door... open it wide...' said Mam, elated. 'Turn the horn towards the door so that Dad can be heard right across to Hope Mountain. Let them hear in Tir-Paenau and Tri-Thy!'

'Top G,' said Arthur at the final note.

'You're right. "Do not slur. Optional ending."' I had the music copy again. I turned back to the beginning, this time concentrating on the words (by Helen Hindson and Margaret Ringgold), reading them all the way through:

Dawn of Love
(Dedicated to the HY-EECH-KA Club of Tulsa)

I'm living o'er the mem'ries
Of my childhood days now gone...
The mem'ries ever dear to me,
While the years go rolling on.
They passed me by as swiftly
As the grey clouds drift above.
And then came life's awakening,
'Twas the Dawn, the Dawn of Love.

I want you in the morning
When the dawn comes stealing in;
I want you at the noontide,
'Mid the bustle and the din.
I want you in the evening
When the sun sinks in the west,
I want you in the night time
When the whole world is at rest.

I want you when I'm happy
And when I'm lonely too,
I want you ev'ry moment
Just because dear, I love you.

Before long Arthur had picked up words and music from
the record, and was singing it sitting at the top of the
stairs, an addition to his repertoire, alongside *I Sing as the
Songbird is Singing*.

'Let's have it again and again,' said Mam ecstatically.
And soon we heard her, sometimes in duet with the

gramophone, sometimes in snatches heard coming from the back kitchen or the dairy:

And then came life's awakening...

We listened to her voice caressing the words as it came through from the back of the house.

'Dad's song for Mam,' said Arthur as he turned to me. And pausing a moment to listen, with a hushed 'Yes...!' he smiled and nodded his pleasure and delight.

In the evening when milking and meal were over, the table lamp was refilled with paraffin and its wick trimmed. Lit and placed on the table, it flooded the living room with a warm light. I settled into the rocking chair with the newspaper used for packing the record, the *Chicago Daily Tribune*.

But the record was on constantly when we were in the house. When Mam was busy out of doors and the sun was shining, her powerful soprano voice rang out. I'll warrant they really heard her a mile away on Hope Mountain in Tir-Paenau and Tri-Thy. Especially on that final ('Do not slur') top G.

I took the somewhat crumpled *Chicago Daily Tribune* and laid it out flat, page one uppermost, on the living room table. With the palm of my hand I tried to iron out the creases to make it more presentable. 'The World's Greatest Newspaper' had suffered the indignity of being mere packing. It was the forerunner of something else Mr Marshall the Post delivered: a rolled-up American newspaper. From time to time came the *St Louis Post-Dispatch*, the *Baltimore Sun*, the *New York Times*, the *Boston Globe*, the *Philadelphia Record*, the *Ladies Home Journal* (for Mam), the *Ohio State Journal* (from Columbus, Ohio), the Welsh-American monthly *Y Drych* (The Mirror)... Sometimes there was a funny paper, that separate supplement in American newspapers containing comic strips. And sometimes the funny paper came on its own, addressed to Arthur, all part of a concerted effort to get him to read, if only captions on cartoons. He wouldn't so much as look at the printed word. Mam had got Hywel to deliver the *Children's Newspaper*. I had tried tempting him with jokes from the back page. We had the Welsh monthly for children, *Cymru'r Plant*, with a series of articles about flying – the Wright Brothers, Lindbergh, airships and Imperial Airways. But all to no avail. All he would do was glance at the pictures, gazing for some time at the airships.

'*Chicago Daily Tribune*: this newspaper's great,' I announced after scanning the front page. I had returned to the rocking chair.

'Well get Arthur to try reading it. Give him the funny paper.' But Arthur even avoided that, going out instead to feed the hens, and returning to sit with me on the low garden wall in the spring sunshine, clutching his ball and stroking the cat.

'Arthur, look. Pictures.' We were back in the house. I read to him the front page of the Chicago paper. Seven members of the Moran Gang had been lined up against a wall and killed by Al Capone's gang. It was a massacre in a garage, the rubbing out of one gang by another. The gangster Al Capone wore an eleven-and-a-half-carat diamond ring; rode in his steel-plated, custom-built, bulletproof limousine, a Cadillac; and he had a mansion in Chicago's Grand Crossing district. He was now the underworld supremo. His picture showed him wearing a straw hat.

'Al Capone. Al! That's you! Al,' chuckled Arthur to me, 'you're wearing a straw hat.'

Capone, said the paper, was now in Florida.

'Hold 'em up! I'm Public Enemy Number One!'

'Arthur! Put that bread knife down!' said Mam, startled by his realistic play.

'Oh shucks' – I joined in – 'I'll give you a dime if you'll put your gun away.'

'Okay. Money talks.' The bread knife returned to the table.

Mam however was stern. 'Look, Arthur. You are going to try reading. Alun, get the atlas. Let him read places where Dad's been. Show him Chicago.' She retreated to the back kitchen.

I opened the atlas, but my attention wandered to finding familiar Welsh place names in the USA – Flint, Bala Cynwyd, Berwyn (by Chicago)... and Bryn Mawr. (And from Bryn Mawr Station, Dad said, there was an Illinois Central suburban electric train into Chicago. Electric!)

The gramophone was playing. Arthur, meantime, went out again in front of the house, this time to play with his football. That was when he scored his goal by heading the ball through the open window. When the ball flew in on to the living-room floor, Mam was really sharp with him, and her worry about his unwillingness to read broke out afresh. But it was milking time, and out she went with milk pail, singing the closing bars of the song with the gramophone. Arthur, now in the house, stealthily climbed to the top of the stairs, still cradling his ball, to sing softly to himself, while I traversed Western Canada, mouthing the places to myself: 'Vancouver... Edmonton... Winnipeg...' I turned the page back to the Middle West.

'Arthur,' I called up to him, 'there's a town called Arthur in Nebraska.' I paused. 'And one in North Dakota. And in Illinois.' No response. He was still singing softly, not to be lured. 'And there's Port Arthur down in Texas... and Port Arthur in Ontario. There's a picture in *Pictorial Knowledge*. With grain elevators. Want to see it?' He made no move. 'By Lake Superior. Very superior.' I looked up hopefully. But the flattery didn't work.

Then picking up Dad's trail, mouthing to myself again: 'Minneapolis... Milwaukee... Chicago...' And aloud, excitedly: 'Chicago!'

'Chicawgo!' called down Arthur from the top of the stairs. 'You don't know how to say it.' That was how Chicago people said it.

'Okay bud, Chicawgo.'

Milking over, Mam came in. Arthur promptly gave the cat her saucer of milk. And, seeing me quietly sitting in the rocking chair, Mam said: 'Still with your head in your atlas. Why aren't you helping Arthur read it?'

'Chicawgo! Al Capone!' Arthur fired with the thrills of the spoken, if not the printed, word.

'I don't think it's safe for Dad to be in Chicago with gangsters.'

'Oh yes it is,' I reassured her, 'all the policemen have guns to protect you.' But the truth was different. Later, when Dad was home again, we overheard him tell Jack,

Georgie Jones and others of an incident he saw in the street. It was a hold-up. He heard bullets firing and a man fell down dead on the pavement. Police with revolvers gave chase in their cars and so captured the gang. Then back they came to recover the body. And that was that: all over. This was normal. 'No need to worry. Al Capone's in Florida anyway.'

'But Dad'll be going there before long.'

I returned to the newspaper. There was a new US President, Herbert Hoover. Mr Hoover had spent part of his childhood in Indian Territory (now Oklahoma) and his father, like Mam's, had been a blacksmith. Having the son of a blacksmith for President seemed to relieve Mam's anxiety. Mr Hoover spoke of the urgency of law enforcement, of the streets of Chicago, New York and Detroit smeared with blood; of killings by gangsters. Public Enemy Number One had an income from bootlegging running into millions of dollars. Government agents were taking bribes from speakeasy owners. The fight against the breaking of Prohibition laws was being lost. The 'noble experiment' to compel America to be sober wasn't going too well.

'Mam, can we go to the Band of Hope?'

She hesitated. The Band of Hope temperance meeting was at night, in the Sion Chapel under Hope Mountain.

'It's not far,' we pleaded.

'But it'll be dark when you come home.'

'It's only just on the other side of the railway.'

First this meant going down through the wood. Away from the path, the wood, like the railway, was forbidden territory. Somewhere deep in the trees there were old mine workings we had never seen, disused shafts not worked since Grandad was a young man. (At one time he had been the blacksmith at this colliery in the wood.) There was a seam of coal not far below the surface under the steep-sloping woodland and fields. We at Pen-y-Wern were sitting on top of a huge lump of coal. These old shafts were dangerous. But it was the danger of the railway that preoccupied Mam at the moment, triggered off by reading in the paper of a young child wandering on to the LMS main line somewhere in England and being killed by an express. 'Yes, and you might go playing on the railway track. And that in the dark.'

'Oh no we won't.'

'Well, perhaps.' She was almost relenting. 'It'll be a full moon.' Then worried about our safety again: 'But you have to come home through the wood. And that path up the tunnel is very dark.'

'We'll stick to the path.'

'We'll be able to sign the pledge, and get a certificate. Shall we?'

'And we'll see the magic lantern.' This from Arthur nearly brought victory.

But she hesitated; and our hopes were all but dashed: 'I don't want you meeting Wmphre'r Cipar.' Wmphre the Gamekeeper lived in his keeper's cottage a mile away at the other end of the wood near the Pant-y-Stên level crossing. He was employed by the Plas Teg estate, the Jacobean mansion by the River Alun on the other side of Hope Mountain. Our Pen-y-Wern, house and farm buildings, had been built by our great-grandfather on land leased from this estate, but with the expiry of the lease, we now paid rent. The Plas Teg posh people came to 'our' wood for their annual shoot, and Wmphre'r Cipar was seen occasionally, chasing us out once when we went to gather bluebells. He had been seen at night, not quite sober, returning home along the path up our fields, from the Railway or Britannia Inns. 'He's after poachers and he'll frighten the life out of you.'

'Please.'

'Well, all right.' But she was still concerned: 'You must hurry straight home. And take the paraffin hurricane lamp.'

'Won't need to,' said Arthur triumphantly. 'I'll take my flashlight.'

⌁

> A sunbeam, a sunbeam,
> Jesus wants me for a sunbeam...

We sang the last hymn before signing the certificate and seeing the magic lantern.

Sion Chapel was lit with four paraffin oil lamps, a fifth hanging in the centre above the pulpit, y sêt fawr (the deacons' seat) and the harmonium. We had sung, with harmonium, a mixture of Welsh and English children's hymns: Arthur's favourite, 'Rwy'n Canu'; Stainer's 'There's a Friend for Little Children'; 'Calon Lan' (A Pure Heart); 'In the Sweet By and By'; and many more. Arthur's voice had been prominent in each, the words of one of the English songs swelling to the rafters:

> A song which even angels,
> Can never, never sing...

During that hymn the lamp in front of us, suspended at the end of its long chain, had flickered menacingly, the flame licking the glass funnel. The wick needs turning down, I thought. But before the last verse the enlarged flame flickered again, then died.

We finished the Moody and Sankey, and sat down.

Our preceptor was a stranger to his young congregation; and that, together with his bold voice, compelled attention: 'Boys and girls: one drop of the demon drink...'

'Lemonade,' whispered Arthur. We were in the front row, and the preceptor's voice and gaze carried over our heads to the rows behind.

'...one drop, and you have bought a first-class railway ticket...'

'To Brymbo,' I nudged.

'No, Chicawgo.'

'...I tell you boys and girls... I tell you...'

'Yep,' I said almost aloud, nodding my head like old Gwilym Gwern-y-Llyn (now dead) and all the other old men in the Sunday congregation.

'...a ticket to take you... to the gutter.'

'To the midden,' Arthur whispered quickly in my ear.

'Ych,' I said aloud, which brought a reproving cough from the harmonium accompanist sitting in the deacon seat in front of us.

'Bet you can buy a drink on the Chicawgo express.'

'No. It would spill.'

We lost track of the oratory until he mentioned what we had really come to see, the magic lantern. He now moved closer to his audience so that we in the front row had to lean back and look up, stretching our necks, to see his face almost immediately above us.

'And all of you who are about to sign the pledge will see, on the magic lantern...'

'Oh...!' The murmurings of expectation and excitement made him pause.

'"The Good Samaritan", "The Prodigal Son" and "The Wine at the Wedding Feast". But first, the Pledge...'

Under the pulpit was a little table with pen and ink and a sheaf of certificates. There was a hubbub of children approaching this table in a semblance of single file; he raised his voice above the chatter and pen-scratching: 'Note what you promise.' He picked up a certificate and began: '"By divine assistance I will abstain from..."' But his voice was all but drowned out. 'Now, now, come along boys and girls...' He had lost our attention.

Arthur had signed first, and was looking at his certificate adorned with roses and lilies: 'Mam will like the flowers all round it. What...' He hesitated, unsure whether to ask me: 'What... does it say?'

I began: '"I will abstain from all..."' only to become stuck on a word, '"...al... al... alco..."'

Arthur laughed. 'Ha, you can't read it.'

'Yes I can.' Annoyed and challenged I tried again: '"Alco... Horlick..." No. "Al... al... Al Capone... ic liquor." No. I've got it: "Alco... holy... liquor."'

The hubbub died down and though we were still standing about in a motley crowd, the preceptor regained our attention:

'"...I will abstain from all alcoholic liquor and discountenance all the causes and practices of intemperance." Now read the mottoes on your certificate: "Look not upon the wine for at the last it biteth like a serpent and stingeth like an adder."'

'Ooh!' said Arthur aloud, then dropping to a whisper: 'must be tasty.'

'"Prevention is better than cure."'

'Cure what?'

'"Wine is a mocker, strong drink is raging and whosoever is deceived thereby is not wise. Abhor that which is evil; cleave to that which is good. Lead us not... into temptation."'

'...into the station.' Arthur was audible enough for the children standing near to giggle.

'And now: the Magic Lantern.'

Our excitement swelled up out of control while the white screen, which looked like a bed sheet stretched within a wooden frame, was put in position before the pulpit. After some commotion and delay because those near the harmonium couldn't see, the show was on.

At the end, the preceptor apologised for keeping us late, having also shown us 'Scenes from Missionary Lands' for good measure. 'We will end with a short prayer, with our hands together.' Then, raising his voice for God to hear: 'Our Father...' (In the pause, his face shook with passion and was turned up towards the rafters; his eyes firmly shut: perhaps he could see God that way.) '...guide our feet towards thee.' (We looked through our hands together down at our feet; well, they were muddy boots; must remember to wipe feet going into heaven.) We joined with him saying 'Amen'. Then a moment's silence before opening our eyes and stealing another glance up at him, but his hands were still reverently together with upward turned face, and his eyes were still firmly shut in deep reverie. Arthur conspicuously cleared his throat and added another 'Amen', loud, deep-throated with a long A and an American accent, bringing the reverie to an abrupt end.

⟝⟞

'Get your flashlight out.'

The moon lit our path along the lower edge of the wood. It reflected in the calm water of the marsh on our left and made Hope Mountain a silvery ghost. We had reached the lower end of the tunnel, where the path turned up through the wood.

Arthur switched on the light. 'We'll have it red,' he said, sliding the red glass over. 'No: green.' The beam of light, changing colour and direction erratically, produced a weird effect on the trees over our heads.

'Don't shine it up in the trees!' Our pace slowed down on the steep path; we breathed heavily, speaking in subdued voices.

Suddenly a flapping of wings, fairly close. 'Pheasant!' Arthur directed the light upwards again, searching the trees.

I half-stumbled where the path was particularly steep. 'Shine it on the path.' Another pause for breath. We stood still a moment, the light now red again on the broken ground immediately ahead. An owl screeched. The beam searched the trees once more. Arthur had scratched his knees; he had walked too close to the undergrowth along the edge of the path. 'Shine it on the path!'

'Let's go.' He swung the now green light round haphazardly. For a fleeting moment it lit up his face, making it cold and unrecognisable. We kept going.

'Stop,' I whispered, grabbing his arm.

We heard the incoherent slobbering mumblings of a human voice.

'What's that?'

'Shine your light to the side of the path... over there.' Someone was sprawled on the ground alongside the path. We inched our way up, keeping our distance on the far side.

'It's a man.' The maudlin mutterings seemed more menacing in Arthur's light.

'He's drunk!' And, with fright: 'It's Wmphre the Gamekeeper...' We ran for dear life; Arthur's shorter legs were first over the stile by the sycamore tree, up the shorter path through the hayfields, across the yard, bursting in at the front door, exhausted.

Another American newspaper. The hypocrites in the Senate, said the paper, were the men who voted dry and drank wet. What could that possibly mean...?

'Perhaps it doesn't rain much in Chicago,' was Mam's offered explanation.

'Oh?' I turned to the weather column. But it forecast rain for Chicago and its vicinity. Puzzling.

The news item – and it was front page news – spoke of a man who sneaked a drink for himself and then voted to send his fellow men to jail for drinking whiskey (spelt with an 'e'). Another column was about Prohibitionists at a great convention.

'Like Band of Hope,' explained Arthur.

And on the table at this convention was a quart of whiskey. We could send it to Wmphre. And tell him it was from Britannia Inn. Houston, Texas, reported the newspaper, was the driest city in the driest state in the world...

'Sahara Desert.' Arthur was taking an interest; perhaps he would try reading it. A pint of liquor was eight dollars, which he calculated to be two pounds.

'Ha!' said Mam, 'a pint of our old grey cow's liquor is only tuppence ha-penny.'

Prohibition, concluded the article, was the breeding place of crime; it was the liquor business in the dark. In the wood! With Wmphre!

'Yes,' said Arthur with an exaggerated shiver. 'Wmphre's just a hobo.'

'Yes. Rears pheasant chicks... so that they can be shot when Plas Teg posh people come for their shoot.'

'Bet he's got a hip flask. Full of moonshine.'

Mam chuckled: 'On a moonlit night.'

'We'll go sell moonshine,' said Arthur. 'Make it in the wood. Gallons of it. Sell it by the pint.'

'Well, come on,' said Mam. 'Let's get on with our liquor business: it's churning today.' She walked out through the back kitchen to the dairy: 'With our old grey cow's liquor...'

With only one cow since Dad had been away, we did not churn very often, so it was an event. We were in the dairy. Mam, using a small mirror with a tarnished frame which was on the windowsill, tied a scarf round her head. She was preparing for butter-making, singing away:

> '...I want you in the morning
> When the dawn comes stealing in...'

Turning the oak barrel of the churn required strength, so all we could do was watch. Watching soon turned into playing:

'I'm the best bootlegger in Chicago.'

'Yes, Chicago: Indian word. Means "a place of strong smells".'

'Ych...'

And so this play and make-believe went on until the churn stopped. Its lid was unscrewed and then removed, and the butter skimmed off.

'I own all the speakeasies and drink parlours.'

'Okay Scarface, I'm going to take you for a ride.'

Mam tilted the churn to pour out the buttermilk.

'Where do you get all this stuff from?' The buttermilk poured into the big earthenware pot on the floor.

'Montreal,' said Scarface. 'No: straight off the boat.' We had heard how bootleggers brought the illegal liquor either from Canada or straight off the boat. They would buy expensive yachts, deck them with girls in bathing costumes to disguise their real mission: to pick up booze off ships just outside territorial waters.

'Okay, show me real money. I want twenty-five per cent.'

Arthur paid over, and gulped down his mug of buttermilk.

'I'm the Prohibition Agent. What's that you drinking?' A state attorney had ordered Prohibition into effect. (This was about ten years late, for it was soon after the Great War that the manufacture, sale, importation and exportation of intoxicating liquors for beverage purposes were prohibited by an Amendment to the US Constitution.) The dry lid had to be clamped down immediately, he had said, to destroy the power of the gangsters by shutting off the flood of money coming into their coffers. Booze sales in speakeasies, saloons and drink parlours must end; the law was being openly flouted. Fifty police captains, the police commissioner and his deputies had moved into action. 'I'm the Prohibition Agent,' I repeated with the voice of the law. 'What's that you drinking?'

'Buttermilk,' said Arthur, laughing.

'Gi'me that milk ladle.' I filled the ladle and sniffed. 'Smells good. I'll confiscate it...' Gulping it down and nearly choking I added, '...in the name of the law.'

Mam by this time was a little harassed; we were underfoot and she sent us to play in the wash-house instead.

I opened the wash-house outside door, wide enough to put my fist round to give a heavy door-knock: 'I'm the Revenue Officer.'

'Come on in.'

'What's that you brewing in that dolly tub?'

'Soap suds...' he laughed. 'Try some. Let me fill your hip flask.'

'What in holy hell are you up to?'

'It's Monday, washing day.'

'It ain't Monday today. Okay okay. Hand over a five dollar bill.'

Mam in the dairy, singing in full voice:

'And then came life's awakening...'

And pausing, probably to pat the butter:

''Twas the Dawn... the Dawn of Love...'

That evening she was writing, standing at her usual place by the dresser: 'Dear Jäbez.... Since you were last home, they are for ever using those American words. Do all Americans talk like that...?'

━◦━⟨▷✕◁⟩━◦━

'We've got plenty of time.' We were on our way back to school. 'The one o'clock train hasn't gone up to Brymbo yet.'

'Yes. Let's explore!'

We were almost halfway down the tunnel through the wood, near the spot where we had seen Wmphre sprawled on the ground. There was a gap in the trees to the right, tempting. We had seen it many times, wondering where it led. But there was never time to stray from the path.

The gap led to what seemed like an overgrown footpath leading deeper into the wood. We pushed through the undergrowth. The sun shone and there was a gentle breeze in the trees. Arthur was ahead.

Suddenly a bird sang close by. I stopped to listen to it, a cheerful, sweet, warbling song. 'Oh, what bird is that?' It was out of sight. I spoke mostly to myself for Arthur had forged ahead deeper into the trees. Then it was gone. That evening, back in the rocking chair, thumbing through the pages of my books, I found a bird's description that seemed to fit that of the bird call: 'The bluebird of eastern North America sings with a cheerful, sweet warble. The young, when only two months old, help feed the nestlings of the second brood and clean out the nest. It is the herald of spring and symbol of happiness.'

'Mam,' I called, 'do we have the bluebird in this country?' But she was busy at the back of the house and did not hear. I tried to get Arthur to read it. But no luck. I never did find out for certain what that bird was. But on that bright, sunny midday on the way back to school it took a moment to recover from the joy of its beautiful song.

I caught up with Arthur. 'Look,' he said, 'a footpath we've never seen before.' At one time the trodden ground had obviously been a well-used path.

Brushing aside the undergrowth I said, 'Bet it's a short cut down to the railway.'

'A secret path!' Arthur's eyes lit up. 'Let's call it our secret path!'

'Yes. Indian trail.' We pushed ahead; the path turning downhill.

'Nuts!' There was an abundance of hazelnuts – a neglected, overgrown copse in a small clearing, untouched; a whole harvest, and all for us! The clusters were hard, brown and ripe. 'I'm going to fill my pockets.' We crammed them full and, taking a suitably sized stone to crack the shells, climbed a nearby oak and sat astride a crooked, wide-spreading lower branch. Then holding a nut between finger and thumb on the grey, thick bark of the branch, we used the stone as a hammer to crack the shells one by one. It was a feast. The unusually warm October sun shone through the few dull-brown autumn leaves still on the oak, making a pattern on the ground below. The light wind blew through the leaves on to our faces.

There was a distant barking of dogs. We thought no more of it until it was accompanied by men's voices.

'Listen!' They were coming nearer.

It was the shoot. Men and dogs now closer; the men were beating the undergrowth. There were two or three rapid gunshots. A startled pheasant on the ground close by clucked its hoarse call and flapped its wings vigorously, rocketing upwards on to a low branch. It was near enough for us to notice the purple markings in its feathers, the scarlet round the eyes and tufts behind the ears. It made a loud, far-carrying, explosive cry, with a thumping of rapid wing beats. We looked at each other, frightened.

'I'm climbing down,' said Arthur, one leg already dangling down.

'No!' – I subdued my voice – 'Don't climb down! If you're on the ground, they'll think you're a rabbit and set the dogs on you. Stay still, perfectly still. If you shake the branch they'll think you're a pheasant and shoot this way.' He carefully and quietly straightened himself back on his seat. We sat clinging with both hands. We peered through the leaves down to the ground expecting to see but hoping not to see the shoot. Wmphre would be one of them. We hoped they wouldn't see us.

A gunshot whistled overhead. 'Ooh. That was near!'

'Phew!' said Arthur aloud.

'Ssh... Don't move.'

We sat motionless.

At last men and dogs moved away into the distance. We heaved a sigh of relief.

'They nearly shooted us,' said Arthur at last.

'Shot us, silly. You're a hick.'

'Go on you... you're a hillbilly.'

'I'm going to pick more nuts.'

'Me too.' We climbed down.

Our pockets almost full again, Arthur paused in his harvesting and looked at me: 'What are we going to tell Mam?'

'Mm... Nothing.' There was a short, sharp whistle of the train and the rumble of train wheels, louder than usual. We were nearer the railway than we thought.

'Come on. We'll be late for school.'

'Oh, there's plenty of time, plenty of time to pick a few more.'

'I'm going. Come on. We'll have to run.'

As I quickly brushed my way back along our secret path, he called after me: 'Plenty of time...'

'One seven is seven, two sevens are fourteen...' The class was chanting tables; an extra afternoon dose because of the poor performance in that morning's arithmetic.

But Arthur and I knew them. Mam had taught us at an early age in the way she had been taught by her father: she sang them. The first four lines of the seven-times table made the first verse, the whole table made three verses: the second line a repeat, the third a run up the scale...

So we learnt tables, along with sung Welsh nursery rhymes, before our first day at school. And in this way we learnt English names for numbers before speaking English.

'...three sevens are twenty-one, four sevens are twenty-eight...': the class chanted, eyes shut, arms folded. The multiplication table had been written on the blackboard, which stood on its easel between the fireplace and the door. Mr Hayes had retired to his desk to do his paperwork. The master's large sloping desk was on a dais and, seated there, he could keep one eye on us, his roving gaze surveying the whole class. '...five sevens are thirty-five...'

We suddenly stopped and opened our eyes. Mr Hayes looked up, then towards the door; the whole class was watching the brass doorknob turning slowly with a squeak. The door opened a few inches. In squeezed

Arthur, shutting the door gently. We sat in silence, watching him walk across to Mr Hayes' desk, his boots making a resounding noise on the wooden floor.

Mr Hayes, more annoyed than stern: 'Where've you been?'

'Lost in the wood, sir. Watching pheasants.'

'Don't be late again.'

He walked to his place, and the class resumed: '...six sevens are forty-two, seven sevens are forty-nine...'

'"Hotel Sherman, Chicago.... Only another week in this Windy City..." I hope it's safe for Dad in Chicago. He's still there. All those gangsters...'

'Sure he's safe. Al Capone kills other gangsters, not the people...'

'I'm not so sure.' Mam was worried.

'Well,' said Arthur in support, 'it's like the shoot. They shoot pheasants, not the...'

'Ahem... not the... not the gamekeepers.'

'Yes, that's right,' said Arthur cheerfully. 'Not the other people watching.'

'Nobody watches pheasant-shooting,' she said rather crossly, lowering her voice. 'It's too dangerous.'

'Yes,' I added quickly.

'Er... yes... yes...' echoed Arthur, not very convincingly.

'And keep away from the wood when they come shooting.'

'Yes Mam.'

'Yes Mam.'

She looked at us, her glance quickly moving from one

to the other. 'And on your way to school stay right on that path down through the wood.'

'Yes Mam.'

'Yes Mam.'

'We'll go hunt pheasants in Dakota instead.'

'Okay. Come on.' And out we went through the back door on to the Cae Cefn prairie.

Later, that evening, I glanced through Dad's letter: '...hope the boys are not getting out of hand.... Still a few more engagements in the Middle West before I move on...'

Dad always spent some time in the Middle West. In the granite of Mount Rushmore, in the Black Hills of South Dakota, he saw the beginnings of the massive sculptured head of George Washington, seventy feet high. From Columbus, Ohio, came a photograph with the caption: 'Welsh Singers with Governor at Capitol'. A St Louis paper spelt Dad's name 'Trevoire'. 'Will you be taking a trip on the river, Mr Trevoire?' The hotels there had magnificent dining rooms, and coloured waiters who wore evening clothes.

Occasionally came newspaper cuttings (which Dad called clippings) about his concerts: 'a mature artist'; 'a thrilling, vibrant tone'; 'climaxes of operatic fire and intensity' ; 'he travels because he loves his native music...'

The reverse side of one of these clippings had the headline, 'Hobo on Rape Charge'.

'Mam, what's rape?'

'Oh... something American.'

But my books said: 'Rape: European plant grown as food for sheep.'

The 1920s were a busy time for Dad with as many as eleven concerts in a week. He went 'out in the sticks', visited a 'corn, hog and cattle' farm and gave an afternoon recital in the high school of a small town. He saw a one-teacher schoolhouse, built of wood and painted white. The children were doing their handwriting from the blackboard. Dad copied the verse to send to us:

     _____ ____ is my name;
America's my nation.
   _____ my dwelling place
And Heaven's my destination.

You wrote in your name and where you lived. Dad's idea was to get Arthur writing. But still to no avail. In this one-room schoolhouse were eight rows of kids; first grade (seven year olds) sat in front. And the eighth grade (fourteen year olds) sat in the back row. 'Like our Standard Seven,' said Arthur. Behind them was a heating stove. Each row took turns to recite the verse while the rest wrote. Their playtime was called 'recess time'. The school had a water pump in the yard. There had been a time when the older boys came to school on horseback, hitching their horses to a hitching post. Out in the yard too there was a cave where the children could be safe during a cyclone. Dad passed a farm with the barn blown away and the orchard reduced to scarred, twisted trees.

A birthday card with a verse inside:

Engine, engine, number nine
Ring the bell when it is time...

The Brymbo Express was now the yowl of the Illinois Central: it ran all over the Middle West:

Engine, engine, number nine
Running on Chicago line.
When she's polished, she will shine,
Engine, engine, number nine.

Indianapolis, Cincinnati, Nashville, Memphis, Jackson... then cards with a New Orleans postmark. 'NOO Orlins,' corrected Arthur. We heard about jazz – clarinets and saxophones. But we had no idea what jazz sounded like. And from Atlanta, for Arthur: 'In Georgia, they grow cotton and peanuts, what you call monkey nuts.'

'Penn'orth of monkey nuts please.'
Mrs Williams Beehive weighed the unshelled monkey nuts on the scales.
'Thanks.'
'Thank you,' said Mrs Williams, taking Arthur's penny. Then turning to me: 'And you?'
'Penn'orth Mint Imperials please.' They were tipped out of their glass jar and weighed. 'Thank you, Mrs Williams.'
Out on the road, as he broke the peanut shells, Arthur asked: 'Why did you get Mint Imperials?'
'Well, Imperial Airways, Mint Imperials, see?'

'Oh yes. Mint Imperial Airways.' Then, with his mouth full: 'And Jack Dempsey... he owns an Imperial... a Chrysler Imperial motor car.'

'Better than Model T. Any darn fool can drive that.'

'Or a Chevrolet. Yes...' said Arthur emphatically, 'and he's been world heavyweight champion.'

We had forgotten the Welsh Imperial Singers.

'D'you want a fight?' Arthur, short in stature, had taken a prizefighter's stance in front of a big boy nearly twice his size. It was outside the school gate. 'Hey,' said the big boy, his voice in a lower register. 'Hey. Listen to this rum little 'un.'

'Come on Jack Dempsey,' said another, running up.

'You couldn't knock the skin off a rice pudding,' said the big boy, giving Arthur a one-handed slight push on the shoulder which nearly made him topple over.

But Arthur advanced again: 'D'you want a fight?' He pretended to spit rapidly into his palms, rubbed his palms together, then resumed his stance. A small crowd of boys had gathered round. 'D'you want a fight,' repeated Arthur, his fists now safely in his trousers pockets. And looking up and grinning at the big boy: 'I'll hold your coat.'

The talk turned to football. The bigger boys had long been planning a football match, and were trying to persuade Arthur to play and be Dixie Dean; and bring his new leather-case ball which he was forever telling them Dad was going to send. But where to play? There was only the Tyrpeg road, where Arthur and I were forbidden to play. Arthur was not allowed even to take his rubber ball with him on our frequent walks half a mile down the Tyrpeg to Pontybodkin Post Office. But many of the boys lived near a short stretch of the road, straight and reasonably level, immediately above the railway station. There, after school, they would kick around an old and worn leather case, its stitching at the seams coming apart. It was stuffed with old rags. But the Tyrpeg was now dangerous with motor cars. A little boy, Reggie, about Arthur's age, had been killed. He ran straight into a vehicle, the first motor car accident in the parish. So the Tyrpeg was out of the question for their football match. Arthur had hinted Cae Cefn would be grand, if Mam would allow. Cae Cefn could be Wembley Stadium! (Not many years previously the papers had been full of pictures of this newly built stadium, a Mecca for 100,000 soccer spectators.) But the thought of a horde of boys trampling all over our fields had brought a point-blank refusal. So plans for a great Wembley Cup Final Match, revived and discussed in the school playground from time to time, had so far come to nothing.

The group of boys entered the school gate and trailed across the girls' yard towards their own on the railway side of the school. The very young children used the girls' playground. They were being shown by one or two of the older girls, determinedly cheerful on a damp morning, how to play a singing game, and were formed into a ring with clasped hands and raised arms. As a young one entered the ring, they all called 'Bluebird', 'Yellowbird'... according to the colour worn, and sang:

Here comes a bluebird through the window,
High diddle dum day...

The bell rang. We dashed through the small gate dividing the two playgrounds, hurried into line, and marched into school.

Mr Hayes was addressing the whole school in the Big Room: 'Today... is the eleventh of November. We are gathered to remember the Fallen. At the eleventh hour, on this day, the world will stand still...'

'What are we going to do?' whispered Arthur.

We had been positioned with our backs to the glass-fronted bookcase with the black bibles. Fifty English bibles had pride of place on the top shelves. (On the lower shelves were the forty-three Welsh bibles, *Y Beibi Cysegr Lân*, like two rows of third-class passengers on the Brymbo train from Mold on market day.) After each morning's prayers and hymn, Mr Hayes would allocate New Testament verses for learning by heart, such as John, Chapter One, Verse One: 'Yn y dechreuad yr oedd y Gair...' or, if top shelf: 'In the beginning was the Word...' He would then mark the attendance register and deal with miscreants and latecomers while we the class would quietly read our bibles. These bibles and their glass case were a gift in the 1890s to our newly opened non-denominational board school, from the churches and chapels of all denominations in the locality. The verses learnt, you then quietly held the bible on its end with spine resting on the desk, letting the hard black covers fall outwards; and lo, the holy book fell open at a preordained, well-thumbed page with a 'bad word'. These bibles, trained every school morning since the bequest of thirty years ago, had developed a conditioned response. It was impossible not to open at a naughty page. Silence reigned over the studious class working at the vocabulary of naughty words for nine year olds.

But this morning was different: we had had our playtime early, and had assembled for the second time, at a few minutes before eleven o'clock. We were glad to be in from the damp fog that hung over the yard and enveloped the railway semaphore signal close by.

'What are we going to do?' insisted Arthur.

'They made the supreme sacrifice...' continued Mr Hayes' unusually long address, '...they gave their lives...' (They didn't give their lives, I thought, they were taken from them. We knew one was the Beehive son, killed 1918, aged 19.) I watched the flames flickering in the fireplace.

Above the fireplace was a heavy plaster-of-Paris model map of North Wales, with its wooden frame screwed to the wall. The model's exaggerated vertical scale made the peaks of Snowdonia stand out like the peaks of the Canadian Rockies, where snow-capped Mount Robson was nearly four times the height of Snowdon. Trawsfynydd was Kicking Horse Pass, and Llyn Padarn Lake Louise. Snowdon itself, with peak chipped off to reveal the white plaster under the paint, was topped with 'snow' for ever. Across the sea, to the left of the wooden frame, somewhere on the grimy wall, would be Dublin. And far, far to the left, out of the window and the space beyond, Chicago and the clear air of the Rocky Mountains. But in the Big Room that morning it was crowded and stuffy, the whole school assembled.

'...the motor cars will all stop on the Tyrpeg, the eleven

o'clock Brymbo train will stop at the signal... for two minutes' silence...' Mr Hayes glanced at the clock on the wall, '...in remembrance of those killed in the Great War.'

'Why did they die?' whispered Arthur.

As Mr Hayes spoke, his back to the coal fire in the grate, puffs of black smoke occasionally escaped the chimney to rise and blacken the southern slopes of all the high ground on the model map, from the Berwyns to the sea. Even Hope Mountain, eleven hundred feet above sea level, a mere hiccup in the south-east corner of the scale model, was blackened at the Cymau end. And our fields and wood, all on a south-and-east-facing slope, were no more than a tiny black smudge above a curving black line that signified 'Branch Railway'. Outside, on that November morning, Hope Mountain was lost in low cloud, the mist hung over the marsh and the smoke from the train was a pall over the wood.

'We will all stand.' We all stood. 'We shall remember them.' Mr Hayes raised his voice:

> 'They shall grow not old, as we that are left grow old...'

'I'm not old.'

'Ssh.' I gave Arthur a sideways kick on the boot.

> 'At the going down of the sun and in the morning
> We will remember them.'

'Amen,' said Arthur, aloud.

'That's not a prayer...' I spoke too loudly; Mr Hayes was looking at us, '...it's a poem.'

90

'We will place our hands together, close our eyes, and for two minutes...' he took his watch out of his waistcoat pocket. 'Stand in silence.'

We obeyed. We all stood perfectly still, eyes shut, hands together, heads bowed. The heavy tick of the clock on the wall timed the silence, broken only by a few intermittent stifled coughs. It was a long two minutes...

'Attishoo!'

'Your poppy's fallen on the floor.' Then, with my hands hiding my whispers, 'Shut your eyes.'

'How d'you know, if your eyes are shut?'

'You're squinting through your fingers.'

Arthur was screwing up his face, opening and shutting one eye, then the other. His 'Attishoo' had been an excuse not only to get out a handkerchief, but a monkey nut too. He crushed the shell between the palms held close to his face, and tried to thrust a monkey nut into my hand.

'Ssh... give me one later.'

He munched. The empty shell fell on the floor. He put out his foot to squash it and kept his foot there to hide the shell. The commotion brought a loud, rebuking cough from Mr Hayes.... A short, sharp train whistle outside, the eleven o'clock train moving off. Our two minutes were over. The tension relaxed. We sang 'O God Our Help in Ages Past':

> Time, like an ever-rolling stream,
> Bears all its sons away...

and then returned to our lessons.

'Mam, why in America do they put a belt round the bible?'

'A belt?'

'Yes.'

'Well, they don't.'

'Yes they do.' I flicked back the page and read aloud to her: '"The Bible Belt stretches from Georgia through Tennessee to Texas."' I looked up, but she had gone, busy at the back of the house. I was puzzled: must be a long belt.

Postcards from Florida now: Miami orange groves ('Look, trees with oranges on them'); the Everglades, with alligators and flamingoes; and Daytona Beach, the scene of attempts to break the land-speed record.

'For you Arthur: a Sunbeam racing motor car.'

'Like the Sunbeam motor car we saw on the Tyrpeg.'

'No. No. This is one thousand horsepower, and it does two hundred and three miles an hour. World record!'

'Ooh! Faster than Imperial Airways!'

'Twice as fast. Driven by Seagrave.'

'Seagrave?' said Mam. 'What a sad name.'

'I'm going to drive a Sunbeam,' said Arthur, revving his car round the room.

'Mam, letter for you. Postmark "Tennessee".'

It was breakfast time. She put down the bread knife and opened the envelope. '"...met for the first time my cousin Thomas, who emigrated when he was twenty-one to Tennessee..."'

Tennessee: nicknamed the Monkey State. Every state had its nickname. Tennessee was traditionally 'The

Volunteer State': it raised volunteers for the Mexican War of 1847. But 'The Monkey State' was a reference to the recent Scopes 'Monkey Trial' which banned the teaching of the theory of human evolution in the state schools.

'Yes,' said Arthur without a shred of evidence, 'Monkey State, because there they have monkeys and they eat monkey nuts.'

'"He's sixty-two now, and coming to visit the Old Country. He's the Reverend Thomas Trevor..."'

'Wow! The Reverend. A Bible-punching cousin.'

'Well, hurry with your breakfast,' said Mam, a little impatiently, 'What will you have to drink? Cocoa?'

'A Tennessee inch of whiskey please. How about splitting a quart with me, Al?'

'Hurry and be off to school; I want to finish Dad's letter.' But before we went we heard: '"... and would love to preach in his childhood chapel, the Sion Chapel under Hope Mountain..."'

The text of his sermon was Psalm 137: 'By the waters of Babylon...' which in his Southern drawl became: 'By the waters of Tennessee, I sat down and wept... when we remembered thee, O Sion.' Capel Sion had a hushed congregation that Sunday: '...As for our harps, we hanged them up... How shall we sing the Lord's song in a strange land?'

We heard how, as a twelve year old in the 1880s, he had moved with his family to a coal-mining area in County Durham in England. Then, aged twenty-one, he had emigrated to the New World. It was the age of steamers, though a few sailing ships still plied the trade routes out of

93

Liverpool. He disembarked in New York and headed for Tennessee. There was still the spirit of 'Go West, young man, and grow up with the country' – the land of opportunity. And so, still in his youth, he had left Tennessee to set off on a quest for what he called 'The American Dream': a paradise on earth. It was 'Hail, Columbia! Happy land!' with all the individualism that had won the West. It had been the 'manifest destiny' of Americans to spread and multiply over a whole continent. And, quite literally for him, it was 'Oh my America! My new-found-land...' Success meant moving on; you had to move on. But his life thus far had been without meaning; there was no pattern... Old travel-stained Original Sin had crossed over too from the Old World to the New. (Land of opportunity for Original Sin? We didn't quite follow all this. Did poor old beggar Original Sin come over steerage or super-cabin?) And besides, life was hard, mighty hard, out West. After enduring many dangers and temptations, he had returned to Tennessee. But still a young man, and inspired by Moody and Sankey revivalist meetings, he gave up devotion to the almighty dollar and discovered the Lord Almighty. And so we heard how he became a pastor. He attended night school. Then he worked his way through college.... His descriptions gave vivid glimpses of life out West and in the Monkey State – freedom for the slaves, the Tennessee floods, cotton plantations, Nashville and Memphis, the Mississippi. We had history, geography and religion all in an hour-long sermon.

The service had begun with a hymn, in English especially for the visitor. Appropriately it began:

> Glorious things of thee are spoken,
> Sion, city of our God...

In mid-hymn he had climbed the pulpit steps, ready for his sermon, singing lustily all the way. And at the last two lines:

> Solid joys and lasting treasure
> None but Sion's children know

he had looked down at us the children (sitting together on this special occasion in the front seats), with a twinkle in his eye, a happy man, back home in his native land. He was lodging in the village, and on successive Sundays had attended in turn the other three chapels, Jerusalem, Ebenezer and Berea; each time putting three pounds (three pounds!) in the collection. ('Millionaire,' said Arthur.) As he climbed those pulpit steps we had noticed that his dark suit was slightly shabby. (A bachelor, Mam explained later, without a wife to make him buy a new suit.) He looked elderly: Dad's cousin, but much, much older than Dad.

The sermon drew to a climax. His Southern drawl sounded strange: '...and evil men tell us we are descended from monkeys...'

'Give him a monkey nut,' Arthur murmured, munching.

'...and from the apes. I tell you...'

'Where's his tail?' Stern taps on the shoulder from adults behind us.

'...we are God's own children... we are God's own creatures....' Every word in the bible was true; God had made the world in six days. The novelty for us was hearing a sermon in English in chapel (we heard English in church); and the novelty too of a sermon in American English. Dad telling us American words when he was home was one thing; but a sermon! I whispered: 'He doesn't know Welsh!'

'...we are immortal...'

'What's "immortal"?' Arthur was attentive.

Our fascinated attention was captured by the oratory: '...In Tennessee, we cleave to God, we cling to the Rock of Ages; we do not reckon, we do not calculate, the ages of the rocks... and here in the chapel of my childhood, let me repeat, let me restate: that Hope Mountain...' with a sweep of his right arm he pointed towards the windows where the mountain's slope came down to the chapel's side '...that Mountain of Hope shines like a beacon confirming God is the Maker...; those fields, those hedgerows...' there was a break in his voice '...they speak to me...'

'Ghosts...! Holy ghosts... brrr...' Arthur shivered.

'We were created by Him. And He alone offers us everlasting life. Amen.'

'Amen... Amen...' responded solo male voices in the congregation, a succession of two-note 'Amen' chimes rising from the bass in the second row to a high tenor at the back, their ringing voices floating upward to the rafters.

The deacon rose to his feet. 'Our American guest will call on the children to recite a verse from the bible after our next hymn.' As we sang 'Bydd Canu yn y Nefoedd' (There'll be singing up in heaven), I said to Arthur: 'Shall I say a verse in Welsh or English?'

He chuckled: 'Say it in American.' We spoke freely; the singing hid our voices from those near.

'I know: I'll say "In the beginning was the Word..." Short and sweet.'

'No. Say that one in Welsh, so he won't understand!'

The hymn ended; we sat down. The Reverend in the

dark suit had descended near the deacon's seat, to be more informal: 'My apologies for addressing you in English. I have been away from the land of my birth for fifty years.'

Murmurs of pleasant surprise, amazement and wonder rose from the congregation. Then looking at us, and in a more intimate Tennessee drawl: 'Now which boy or girl is going to be first?'

There was a pause, with undercurrents of whisperings from the congregation. Children looked at one another, full of indecision.

Arthur, in my ear: 'Go on. You be first.'

I stood, cleared my throat, and began reciting aloud, in Welsh, John, Chapter One, Verse One: 'Yn y dechreuad yr oedd y Gair...' (In the beginning was the Word...) but the preacher interrupted, taking up the verse, in Welsh and with an immaculate Welsh accent: '...a'r Gair...' (I was perplexed: he was speaking Welsh! And he changed the words!) '...yn y dechreuad, oedd y gair Cymraeg...': the word, in the beginning, was Welsh; the word when I was a child... it was a torrent of Welsh without a trace of American twang.

'You'll have to sit down,' whispered Arthur to me. 'Hard luck.' I sat down, crumpled. And Arthur, munching more monkey nuts, whispered: 'Here, have one.' We gaped at the minister. Arthur nudged me: 'Say kiddo, you'll never make a preacher like this one.'

We heard how, as a child, he ran down the wood half a century ago. He remembered the building of the branch line to Brymbo during his early childhood; and the coal trains in the siding near the marsh to take the coal from the colliery in the wood – all this long before our Coed Talon Council School was built. He revelled in his native tongue, back in his own parish, back in the days when he knew only Welsh. And he had heard no word of Welsh – there was a lump in his throat – 'tan y rŵan...' till now. His handkerchief was out. He broke down in tears: 'Yn y dechreuad...' In the beginning was the Word.... He sat down. Immediately there was a swelling up of the congregation's embarrassment and shufflings. The deacon rose to his feet, flustered: 'We will sing... we will repeat... the last verse... of our last hymn.' He had mixed his Welsh and his English in total confusion. The singing began with a ragged entry, the harmonium coming in late.

'Fancy – away for fifty years!'

And Arthur, boasting: 'I'm going to be away... a hundred years!'

'Which state of the USA has the same name as Tennessee River?'

Arthur's hand shot up.

It was the geography lesson: The Rivers of North America. Last week it was Rivers of North Wales: Dee, Clwyd, Conway.... Now it was St Lawrence, Hudson, Potomac; Pee-Dee ('Pee in the Dee,' whispered someone amid titters from the class, which Mr Hayes ignored); Savannah, Suwannee.... A huge map of North America draped the blackboard and the teacher pointed with a long pointer.

'Which state has the same name as Tennessee River?'

Arthur's hand was still up, stretched out to the utmost; he was half off his seat, and his sotto voce 'Sir, Sir...' breathless and frantic.

Mr Hayes ignored him with a wave of his hand, while

trying to elicit the answer from someone else. There was no response. 'Which state...?' In despair, he turned to Arthur for the answer:

'Please may I be excused?'

With a sigh and a gesture Mr Hayes gave permission, his map pointer drooping to the floor. Arthur went out to the lavatories across the yard.

When he returned, the schoolmaster was still trying to extract an answer, studiously avoiding my half-raised hand. On this particular day, the class was abnormally dull and docile. Quite lifeless.

Mr Hayes, pointing once more to the river and the state's name on the map, repeated his question yet again, emphasising each word: 'Which state has the same name as Tennessee River?'

'The Monkey State,' blurted out Arthur, shooting his hand up like a flash and bringing the class to life with convulsions of laughter.

III
The Leaving of Liverpool

Dad was home again, but not for long. A few weeks with
us, a spell touring Britain, then abroad once more.

We were in the school playground. A small group of
children were chanting a nonsense verse:

> Ar y ffordd wrth fynd i Lerpwl
> Gwelais ddyn yn bwyta siwgr...

(On the road to Liverpool I saw a man eating sugar...)
Others were jumping around, laughing and scrapping.
Arthur and I, excited, were surrounded by another group.

'We're going to Liverpool! Yes! We're going to see the
ship!'

The first group approached us, chanting with
exuberance, relishing and emphasising the rhyme:

> Gof'nais iddo beth o'n wneud,
> Bwyta siwgr, paid a deud.

(I asked him what he was doing, eating sugar, don't tell.)

'We're going on board! The world's largest steamship!'

'The *Majestic*. Fifty-six thousand tons!'

The chanting group, with even more exuberance, were step-hopping together; away they went, chanting their rhyme over again in chorus, to the limit of their voices, and then tumbling in a heap on the ground.

Everyone was infected by Arthur's excitement: 'The largest steamer in the world?'

'Yes!'

'We're going on board. To see Dad's cabin.'

The other children were on their feet again; this time their nonsense was in English:

> ''Twas in the month of Liverpool
> In the city of July
> The snow was raining heavily,
> The streets were very dry...'

'We'll see the ship's wireless,' continued Arthur. 'And the engines, and meet the captain! We're going to take Dad to Liverpool in Mr Williams Beehive's taxi motor car. Dad inside and luggage on the back.' It was a Vauxhall 'Cadet', seventeen horsepower, costing two hundred and eighty pounds. Dad had told us.

A boy ran up: 'Tip... you're it.' He rapidly sped away while watching us over his shoulder. We were too immersed to bother.

'Big ship, *Majestic*. Three funnels.'

'Built in Germany.'

'We won her as first prize because we won the Great War.' She was seized by Britain as part of war reparations,

101

and renamed.

The boy who would play tip approached again: 'What does a ship do when she comes into port?'

'Er... don't know,' said Arthur.

'Ties up!' said the boy, pulling out Arthur's tie from under his jersey and running away.

We were in the Big Room; Mr Hayes at the piano. We were singing the refrain of a sea song, about a sailing ship in the olden days:

'So fare thee well, my own true love,
And when I return, united we will be...'

'Good. Now the third line.'

'It's not the leaving of Liverpool that grieves me...'

'No!' The words were difficult to fit to the crotchets. He demonstrated by speaking the line to the rhythm and note values of the music. Then after another try unaccompanied, still finding it difficult, he said: 'Arthur. You sing it.'

'Okay. Okey-doke.' Arthur grinning; more cheerful than impertinent. Subdued giggles broke out from the class.

'Where did you learn that sort of language?'

'Don't know sir.'

Then after a short pause Mr Hayes said: 'Right. On your own.'

As he sang, the sun shone through the window, lighting up his face. The rays darted through the chalk dust slowly settling on the piano. He sang to perfection, right to the end of the refrain:

'...But, my darling, when I think of thee.'

'Arthur, you must sing at the Urdd Eisteddfod.' This was the children's competitive festival. 'When you are old enough. How old are you?'

'Eight sir.'

'Right.' He spoke to the whole class: 'Now, from the beginning. Sing the words clearly...' He spoke the first two lines of the first verse to demonstrate. Then we sang, inspired:

'Fare thee well, the Princes Landing Stage,
River Mersey, fare thee well...'

The car was riding jerkily in low gear over the rough track which was our farm road. Jolts made the car springs squeak. It slowed down as it approached the first farm gate. I got out and opened it; Arthur opened the next one. Our old grey cow raised her head to watch us go. 'She's going to be on her own all day,' said Mam. 'We'll be back in time for milking though, won't we, Mr Williams?'

'Oh yes.'

We now moved a little faster, still riding jerkily.

'Grand things these pneumatic tyres,' said Mr Williams Beehive. The car gave a sudden, violent jolt into the rut made by the Co-op cart which delivered our groceries. Then another jolt out again.

Dad sat in front. We were on the back seat getting the full force of the jolts. 'These tyres,' I said to Arthur, 'they're tyres you blow up.'

'Yes. Like the leather-case football I'm going to get from Dad...'

'Wait and see.'

'Then we'll have our football match!'

'Wait and see.'

The grown-ups weren't listening; they were too busy talking. 'This is better than the horse and trap,' said Mam. We had come to the Tyrpeg. 'It'll be nice to ride in a motor car on a real tarred road.' The gypsies were still there on the grass verge; their dog barked. Satterthwaite's steam lorry came chugg-chugging up the hill.

'Old Satterthwaite...' chuckled Mr Williams, 'and his solid rubber tyres!' It passed; and we turned into the road, the car travelling smoothly downhill.

'Not cheap to run,' said Mr Williams Beehive at last, raising his voice above the engine noise. 'Petrol one and nine a gallon.' We came to a crossroads, with a beep-beep on the horn.

It was downhill all the way until, many miles later, Mam said: 'Isn't it flat.'

'We're in England now, Cheshire.' I had looked up the route: Pontybodkin, Pontblyddyn, Pen-y-ffordd, Penymynydd; down the Dingle to Hawarden, over the Dee at Queensferry... and into England. 'A lot of English people live here.'

'Got your passport, Jäbez?' said Mam belatedly.

'Dad's got his photo in his passport,' said Arthur.

'Handsome too,' said Mam, half to herself.

'Dad's got a safety razor. Mr Williams...' said Arthur, leaning forward to tap him on the shoulder, 'Mr Williams, bet you haven't got a safety razor.' And it was ten cents for a shave; and shaving cream came out of a tube you squeeze. We noticed new things every time he was home.

Some miles later Mr Williams said: 'Soon be in Birkenhead. We pass the Cammell Laird Shipyard. Then tuppence to cross on the Mersey Ferry.'

'Look at all the motors,' said Mam as we entered the built-up area. There were trams, buses, petrol lorries and an occasional horse and dray on a big wide road with shops all the way along it.

We left the car near Woodside Station; Mr Williams helping to carry the suitcases to the ferry. We put our coins in the slot and went briskly through the turnstile with the crowds talking in their strange Lancashire accents.

'What a lot of people.'

'Don't they speak funny? Where are they all going?'

Seagulls squawking; ferry boats coming and going with their paddle-wheels churning. We boarded our ferry.

Cargo vessels were at anchor in mid-estuary. 'What a lot of ships!' Arthur gave an elongated slurred whistle, descending the scale. 'Fantastic!' We gazed in wonder. 'Look at that one. Its flag's got a lion on it, front paws holding a football.' Was it American Football? Or baseball? A ship's siren in the distance diverted our gaze for a moment. Then looking again at the flag now we were nearer, the lion was holding a globe – a model of the world. So it was the Cunard flag.

'She's not one of ours. We want White Star Line.'

'Yes, white star on a red flag. RMS Majestic. Cor! We're going on board!'

We had wandered round to the rail on the other side of the ferry to see the Liverpool shore approaching, with the

Royal Liver Building, each of its cupolas surmounted by a figure of the mythical liver bird with wings outstretched. To Arthur it was a bird perched on a big football.

The churning paddle-wheels slowed down as we drew alongside; and the gangway was lowered. We stepped ashore.

The Princes Landing Stage, downriver from the Pier Head, was a low, floating raft, half a mile long, linked to the shore by covered ramps. It was wide, about eighty feet, and with crowds of people on it like a promenade – like Rhyl, except this one was floating alongside the estuary. Farther downstream was the new Gladstone Dock from which Dad had sailed on the *Laurentic* and other liners. And *Majestic* was three times the size of *Laurentic*! And took only five days to cross the Herring Pond.

There was a cold wind blowing off the river; Mam hitched up her fox fur round her neck. Seagulls screeched and swooped to pick up scraps out of the murky water. The landing stage heaved gently and a pilot boat rocked alongside. Our ferry and its threshing paddle-wheels had left on its return to Birkenhead. Shorehands were coiling up ropes ready to tie up the next ferry. They came and went, with clanging bells and cheeky hoots.

From out in midstream came the long, deep hoots of the cargo ships, raising their anchors to head down to the open sea. The northern half of the landing stage was for the big ocean liners, so we walked along, to wait for Royal Mail Ship *Majestic* to come alongside to take passengers aboard.

'Yes,' said Arthur with mounting excitement. 'The biggest. The world's biggest!' And skipping and prancing on the wooden deck: 'We're going on board.'

'She'll be in soon.' We scanned all the ships in mid-river, identifying them not only by their flags: Cunard, red funnel with black top; 'our' White Star Line, yellow funnel with black top. *Majestic* would have too the flag of the Commodore of the White Star fleet – a White Star Line flag edged with white, flying from the mainmast (I had read all this in *Pictorial Knowledge*.)

'There she is!'

I looked for her name on the bow, but it was difficult to see, for she was out in mid-river.

'She'll come alongside soon,' added Arthur, beside himself with excitement. 'It's great!'

Many more people, burdened with luggage, now arrived from the Riverside Station behind the landing stage. Porters were busy, to and fro. And many more people like us, there to say goodbye. But our unhappiness at Dad's leaving was half-forgotten as we looked forward to going aboard the liner: it was a mixture of dread and exhilaration, sadness and excitement. The voices of officials, porters and stewards behind us were getting louder.

'Attention all!' A loudspeaker. 'Passengers for the *Adriatic* please board the tender now approaching the landing stage.' So she was not the *Majestic*. What disappointment! We were not going to see the world's largest liner. We had to make do with the *Adriatic*, an old liner and one of the 'Big Four' built about 1904. There had been a change in Dad's plans, and it had not come through to us boys. The *Majestic* sailed from Southampton: I should have known. (He was to sail on her later.) But now it was the *Adriatic*.

There was a hoot from the tender as it tied alongside. 'We regret,' added the loudspeaker, 'it will not be possible for others to go on board.'

'Oh!' We looked at each other: disappointment upon utter disappointment!

So we had to say goodbye to Dad on the landing stage. The tender was named *Magnetic*. Dad went on board. It was crowded with passengers, this inelegant, rusty little boat, not worthy of a name. Huh! *Magnetic*: what a silly name. It had cruelly snatched Dad away from us and denied us our tour on board the transatlantic liner. Then without ceremony it hooted fussily and left the landing stage to race to midstream and deposit its packed human cargo on the *Adriatic*. It quickly disappeared behind the liner's stern, to enable the passengers to board on the port side.

The *SS Adriatic*'s deep-throated siren boomed out three times.

'Two octaves below middle A,' muttered Arthur. She moved slowly to begin her voyage. A thrill to watch... until we realised she had left behind a huge emptiness in the middle of the river...

The cock crowed. Arthur yawned.

'Get up!' I shook him.

He yawned again.

'Alun! Arthur!' Mam at the bottom of the stairs. 'Postcards!'

That did it. We were up out of bed like a flash, racing down the stairs not dressed, our bare feet on the cold linoleum. Arthur's card showed icebergs off Newfoundland; mine the *SS Adriatic*. And it was not far from Newfoundland, I reminded Arthur, that the Titanic went down. He looked at my picture postcard: all the

108

white ventilators on the open deck, he insisted, were giant saxophones.

Mam was immersed in her letter: '"Just a word before we land in New York in a few hours..."'

But Arthur couldn't resist interrupting to show her the icebergs. They were bigger than the ship! Mam was afraid that Dad's ship would strike one of them and sink. But we reassured her that SS *Adriatic* had already been to New York, and had sailed back to Liverpool with these postcards. 'She carries mail you know.'

Mam went back to her letter: '"The ship has an orchestra..."'

'That's why there's all those saxophones,' explained Arthur.

'"There are nearly a thousand passengers..." gracious me! "...and many famous people travelling..."'

'And Dad. Yes?'

'Yes, and Dad.'

There was a palm court. But how could palm trees grow on a ship? And a swimming pool with 'mixed bathing'. There were twenty-five cats on board. The *Adriatic* was like a floating city: drawing rooms, like a mansion, with a big grand piano; a wireless room; hairdresser; a library: '"and one old lady reads one book every day, and has crossed the Atlantic forty-seven times..."' There was the White Star magazine with a scarlet front cover which Dad promised to send.

'"...the Captain's Dinner last night. Had a nice voyage. Will write again when ashore... PS. A small parcel is on the way."' We hoped it would come soon.

The menu for the Captain's Dinner was printed inside the letter. It included grapefruit, boiled salmon...

'Did they fish for it in the sea?'

And roast turkey, baked American ham... peach jelly, ice cream, apples, oranges, bananas, pineapple...

We groaned.

'Poor Dad,' said Mam, 'eating all that and then singing in an after-dinner concert.'

But Dad was already in New York, and the next postcards confirmed it: '"Yankee Stadium, the home of Babe Ruth." Mam, who's Babe Ruth?'

She played the willing pupil: 'Um... your Auntie Ruth when she was a baby.'

'Wrong. He's a baseball player...'

'A man?'

'... and the world's greatest. Like Dixie Dean in football.'

Arthur's card showed Broadway: '"...once the Indian Trail, now the Great White Way."'

'Because the white man is there.'

'No, because it's lit up at night.'

'Like when the full moon shines on Hope Mountain?'

'Yes.'

Then came a New York newspaper. '"Stock market going mad. Dow Jones climbs to new peak."'

'He's climbing mountains in the Rockies,' explained Arthur.

'No. No. This is in New York.' Then, turning to Mam: 'But who is Mr Dow Jones?'

'Must be the New York auctioneer, if it's the stock market,' she said. 'Lots of auctioneers are called Jones.'

Mm... Dow Jones, Dow the Cow. Then the next

headline: '"The Bull Market at Full Rampage".'

'Oh!' exclaimed Mam. 'Can't be shorthorns like our quiet old grey cow.'

Another headline spoke of a stampede of bulls on Wall Street. 'Bulls out in the street!' said Arthur, looking over my shoulder hoping to see a picture. 'With all those motor cars' – his picture of Broadway showed cars galore – 'I'd like to be there!'

Arthur's next card, 'New York City', showed cars and more cars. Wheels, wheels... America was a nation on wheels, a nation on the move... 'There are many times more cars in New York City than in the whole of Wales. Ford Model T is still all the go here, but there's a new Model A, forty horsepower, sixty miles per hour. Love from Dad.'

'Give me a Chevy,' said Arthur. 'No. I'll have a Chrysler Imperial. Like Jack Dempsey.'

'I'll have a Model T.'

'Model T in high gear; that's you singing...' sniggered Arthur to me, imitating the high-pitched engine.

The latest was a car fitted out with a wireless set. It had a loudspeaker under the floorboards. Dad could listen to *Grand Ole Opry* and *Amos and Andy*. Perhaps it worked better than Beehive's wireless set.

After some thought, Arthur turned to Mam: 'Why can't we have a motor car? It could be a Model T. Tin Lizzie. And only sixty pounds.'

'Only?' said Mam. 'We could buy two cows for that!'

Dad had said in his letter from the *Adriatic* that a small parcel was on its way. Impatiently, every morning, we looked up the 'Overseas Mails' column on the back page of the daily paper, until we saw 'Mails expected tomorrow from USA, Canada and Bermuda.' When it came it consisted of two tiny presentation boxes parcelled together.

'Pocketknife!' Arthur was first to open his box. Mine was identical: a two-bladed knife with a picture of *SS Adriatic* on its ivory holder, bought in a shop on board. We wanted to try them out right away, but it was milking time.

'Five o'clock': Mam was prompted by the train whistle. 'Who's going to fetch the cow? It's late. You can play with your pocketknives later.'

'They're not for playing with. They're real.'

Arthur clutched his new knife while he gazed yet again at the cars on his New York picture postcards. 'Mam,' he pleaded, 'shall we have a motor car? A real one I mean?' President Hoover was supposed to have said something about a chicken in every pot and two cars in every garage. We could make the old stable into a garage. And of course we had the chickens. So why not a car?

'Who would drive it?' said Mam.

'You could.'

'Oh, ladies don't drive motor cars!'

'Well, I could help by putting my hand on the steering wheel.' Arthur 'revved up' his car.

'Now if you both go and drive the old cow in for milking you'll be doing your job.'

'Okay Mom,' said Arthur, not quite hiding his disappointment. 'While we're out, you order a car by mail from Sears Roebuck.' And as we went out of the house: 'Only ten bucks.'

If we were late milking, the cow usually made her way up to the farmyard gate. But today, late though it was, for some reason she was as far away as it was possible to be: right down by the sycamore tree, at our boundary by the stile on the edge of the wood. As we approached, she mooed disconsolately, clearly upset by something. 'Ty'd o'na...' (Come on...) But my words wouldn't comfort her.

I patted her on the neck which helped to pacify her. It was well past her milking time.

Arthur was looking up into the sycamore tree. 'I'm going to try out my pocketknife...'

'We haven't time.'

'...up on that branch.'

He leapt on to the top rung of the stile and then up on to the lowest branch. 'Carve my initials.' He began chipping away. 'Easy on sycamore bark.'

'What if Wmphre the Gamekeeper comes?'

'I can take on any man in this section.' Though strictly speaking, we were not in the wood, only on its boundary.

'Okay, Babe Trevor. Five minutes.' I climbed up. A breeze blew through the branches. Then the wind dropped and the sky became overcast. We chipped away at the greyish-brown smooth bark. 'Yes! It's good. I'm doing my initials too.'

But we had the same initials, A.T. So why not do one letter each? We could do Mam and Dad's as well. And they both had the same – J.T. – J. for Jäbez and J. for Jane. After giving the matter a brief talking over, and marking out on the trunk where the letters should be, the decision was made. The chips of bark flew in all directions.

The cow, standing close by, suddenly looked up towards the house. 'Alun...! Arthur...!' It was Mam at the top of her voice, in the far distance; more singing than calling.

'Come on, we've got to go.'

'Alun...! Arthur...!' Her voice rang out, nearly a quarter of a mile away, with a sustained high note on the second syllables, and loud enough to be heard across to Hope Mountain. 'Where are you...?'

'Okay,' said Arthur. 'We'll finish it sometime on the way to school. Big job.' We hurriedly climbed down.

'I'll bring the cow.'

She was swishing her tail and stamping a hoof on the stone floor of her stall. I had put the chain round her neck and fed her. She gave a discontented moo. Mam was sitting on the stool with milk pail, the milk pinging into the pail. I sat on the spare stool with a newspaper, moving it nearer the door to get more light. Arthur was the other side of the cow, in and out of the spare stall, bouncing his rubber ball. The cat came and sat beside me, her tail curled round her front paws, watching and waiting for milk to be poured into her saucer.

'We've never been so late milking!' Mam was angry. Her head against the cow's side, she turned her face round towards the open door: 'And it looks like rain.'

'Yes,' I said, turning to the weather forecast at the head of the front page: '"Rain today and probably tomorrow."'

'There you are, see. We must get the milking done quickly or you'll get wet taking her back to the field.' After a pause: 'But is that today's paper?'

'Tuesday, 29th.'

'Oh that paper's old!'

'Yes... oh! It's a New York paper: "Two Cents."'

'Oh!' Mam's milking stopped briefly as she jerked her

head round towards me. The cow stamped the floor and moved her rear. 'Steady there...'

The front page headlines were unusually numerous and large, stretching right across the page: '"Unexpected torrent of liquid... liquidation...'"

'Must be heavy rain in New York. Floods.' Arthur's ball bounced on the hard floor, disturbing the cow.

'Arthur,' said Mam. 'That ball!'

'Okay.' He retreated into the spare stall, crouching with his back against the whitewashed wall, holding the ball close to his chest, pondering. Then: 'When my new football comes, can we have a football match?' But Mam was concentrating on milking. 'Cow'll be dry soon. Then we'll have to buy milk...'

'Oh no we won't,' interrupted Arthur, jumping up to his feet and taking a stride towards the cow's rear; and with a hand outstretched: 'I'll pump her tail.'

'Keep away!' said Mam sharply as the cow stamped a hoof. 'She's ever so fidgety.' Then, after a while, turning to me: 'Any other American news – stale news in that old paper?'

The paper had 'Wall St Crash – Special Edition' printed at the head. I read for her the biggest headline: '"Great Crash on Wall Street."'

'That's where the stock market is.'

'Yes. Livestock.'

'Must be all those fast American motor cars. Crashing.'

'"Stampede in Stock Market..."'

'Good gracious!'

'"Collapse of market..." The roof fell in!' I laughed.

'It's not funny,' said Mam seriously. 'All those American cows rushing into the street. No wonder there was a crash.'

'Model T,' said Arthur, 'crashing into a Chevrolet.'

'People must have been trapped and killed inside the building...'

'"Bear market takes over..."'

'Bears?' Mam looked up, puzzled. 'Who would want to buy bears? Bears are dangerous. America sounds a strange country.'

'"Investors fearful of being caught in a bear trap..."'

'Hm. Exciting! Go on.' Arthur was now on his feet again, giving his ball a hard bounce on the floor.

'Arthur!' said Mam angrily. 'Not here while I'm milking.' But the bouncing and Mam's anger had completely unsettled the cow. She gave a loud moo, tossed her head and half turned round. Then her rear pushed against Mam on her stool, causing her to spill some milk out of the pail. The cat darted forward, but retreated before getting too near the swish of the cow's tail.

'Don't disturb her...' And turning to me, with rising anger: 'And you reading the paper while I try to hurry...'

The cow gave another sudden movement of her rear. The milk poured on to the floor, with pail crashing after it. 'Now look what you've made me do!'

The pail rattled and rolled. I got up, rushed forward to pick it up, but hesitated...

'Well don't just stand there holding the newspaper... pick up the pail!'

'The milk... it's... running all over the floor...'

The cow's tail was up. 'Wants to wee-wee,' said Arthur.

'Watch out!' called Mam.

I retreated away from the splash.

'Stand back: Niagara Falls,' said Arthur.

And then there was muck all over the floor.

'Ych!'

'Pick it up!'

'It's... it's in the muck.'

'Oh I'll have to pick it up...' she picked up the pail and put it on one side; went out; and came back with a clean one.

'Start over again,' she said with a heavy sigh as she placed the overturned stool upright, back in position. As the milk pinged again into the pail: 'We'd better get rid of this cow.'

'Oh no,' I protested, a little tearfully.

'She's getting old.'

'She's quiet usually. Far better than the red one we used to have.' This young red cow had been sold when Dad went away singing, to reduce the work. It was in the Mold Stock Market, and because school was closed for the half-term holiday ('Teachers' Rest'), we had gone too. When she was taken from her pen and prodded violently into the ring, the auctioneer rapidly reeled off prices, firing away... (we couldn't understand a word of it) then down came his hammer, and the red cow was driven heartlessly into a cattle lorry with 'Smith Abattoir' on its cab door. ('Slaughterhouse,' explained Mam.) So selling our old grey cow would mean taking her to the Mold Stock Market. My tears were welling up. 'She's only a bit excited since she lost her calf...'

'Dad could buy one in New York Stock Market,' said Arthur. 'See what the paper says.'

Reluctantly I turned to the inside pages and found 'Stocks Quoted'. Glancing down the list: 'I don't want any of these: "Santa Fe... Wells Fargo..." Funny names for cows. They're cheap. Can't be much good. All these cows are cheap. "Canadian Pacific..."'

'Dad's train in Canada,' said Arthur.

'"Lucky Stores..."'

'Like Beehive Stores.'

'"Singer..." Singer!' I chuckled. 'Name of a cow!'

This set off Arthur singing softly: 'Moo moo... moo...' to the tune of the opening line on our record.

'"Bell Telephone... Hudson Bay... J.P. Morgan... "'

'He's a man, not a cow. He's the money man. You pay him dollars for the cow,' said Arthur. Then: 'I know. He's Captain Morgan, the Welsh pirate.'

'No. That was long ago. "Woolworth... Bethlehem Steel..."'

Arthur instantly broke into song again, this time a Negro spiritual.

> 'Steal away, steal away home...
> I ain't got long to stay here.'

He sang softly, but the cow stamped her hoof. Mam stopped milking momentarily: 'Arthur,' she said, subduing her voice, 'I'm trying to milk.'

'Here's one.' Looking down the list, my eye caught one that took my fancy: '"National Dairy."' If we really had to have a new one, we'd need a dairy cow. 'American breed. Only forty-nine cents.'

'Can't be,' said Mam. 'We sold the red cow for thirty pounds. It's a misprint.'

'No. All these cows are cheap because it says "Collapse of prices. National Dairy Inc." Yes: Inc. "The bottom dropped out of the stock market." The bottom dropped out?' I laughed, nearly falling off my stool. '"Disastrous decline rocked Wall Street..."'

118

'Earthquake!' Arthur was back to the spiritual:

'He calls me by the thunder...'

'"Prices swept downward." No, it's a flood. "Millionaires slaughtered! Bears stampede to sell..." Funny livestock market.'

'Dad had better not go there even if he is in New York.' Mam had finished milking. And as she got up: 'And how would he bring her home?' She carefully put down the pail. Then slapped the cow's haunch: 'Move over.'

I scanned the news columns. President Hoover was reassuring everyone and saying that the business of the country was fundamentally sound. And the US President himself must have thought that buying National Dairy was a good idea because his opinion was that stocks were excellent buys at their present levels.

'Now you just look after this one.' Mam had released the cow, prodding her out of the stall. 'And keep her out of the hayfields.'

Arthur thought we could have two cows.

'Yes,' I said enthusiastically. 'Yes. One Welsh and one American.'

But Mam brushed the idea aside: 'Get your mackintosh. It's going to rain. And your wellingtons.' The day had become cold and dank. And turning to Arthur: 'Get the saucer. Let me pour the cat some milk.'

It was a heavy shower. The cow waited for me in the yard. Out in the field, the grass was sodden underfoot. She veered to the hedge, looking for shelter and I patted her wet back. 'You can shelter under the sycamore tree by the stile.' And a few paces later: 'When it stops raining, you can go in the hayfield; I'll leave the gate open for you.' She gave a quiet moo and shook the rain off her head and neck. I patted her again. 'We won't get rid of you. Honest.' Always I walked alongside, near her shoulder. She would move along with you, even when you changed direction. So unlike the young red one: she would race on ahead, going the wrong way; then stop, and bolt in another direction. But our old grey cow was different. When Uncle Noah occasionally came to milk and help out, she would give less milk, for it upset her regular routine. She was old and set in her ways. And when I now put my hand in my jacket pocket under my raincoat, she knew it was to bring out a piece of cow-cake. 'There you are.' Contentedly she munched. Then quietly and slowly she walked away down the field.

By the time I had returned to the house, the rain had eased off. Mam was telling Arthur: 'Go easy with the Indian corn.' He was about to feed the hens, and Mam said I had better go with him.

At the back of the house, Arthur soon had the clucking hens round him, coming out of the henhouse to be fed. 'Here you are. Here you are.' He scattered the corn on the wet ground. 'Plenty more in the Prairies.'

He paused to look round at the pecking flock. 'Rhode Island Red? Little Rhody, where are you?' And to me: 'Missing again.'

And as we returned to the house he added: 'She'll turn up.'

◄◆►

'"Just a note with parcel..."' Mam had opened something for us with a New York NY postmark. It was a metal replica, about nine inches high, of the new Empire State Building going up in Manhattan. 'It's to be the highest building in the world,' wrote Dad.

I had read about the construction of this new skyscraper in *Pictorial Knowledge*, and the last newspaper from New York was full of it. The financier J.J. Raskob had made a speech in which he said that it would symbolise the America he believed in: a country which reached for the sky yet with its feet firmly on the ground. The architect of this wonderful new building had said it was to be like a pencil pointing to the sky. I rested the base firmly on my palm, and pointed with the forefinger of the other hand to the topmost point, which really was like a pencil point.

'It's going to be a quarter of a mile high,' said Arthur, recalling what I had read to him. 'Think about it...' He was now looking at the pictures of the building site in the newspaper: road trucks unloading, cranes lifting girders, a crowd assembled, press cameras clicking, and speeches being made. J.J. Raskob had also said that it was faith in the stock market which had enabled financiers to raise the sixty million dollars needed.

'Sixty *million* dollars!' said Arthur, picking up the model, caressing it and stroking the copper-coloured metal with the tips of his fingers. It was a scale model too: with one hundred and two floors.

A few days previously, late one afternoon after milking, I had counted its windows in the picture in *Pictorial Knowledge*. The book was on the rag rug in front of the hearth. The grate of our living-room kitchen range was looking spick and span, black-leaded that morning. The heavy iron kettle on the fire was coming up to the boil. It was just before teatime. The volume was propped against the fender with its oval-shaped pattern and the words 'Home Sweet Home'. I counted the skyscraper's windows and at the same time held the long-handled toasting fork in front of the fire – burning the toast of course.

Arthur now started counting the tiny windows on the replica, starting from the base, but soon gave up. He then held it close to his eye, as if trying to peep in. 'Will it have the electric light?'

I scanned the news columns again to try to enlighten him, but all I could find was J.J. Raskob saying that the building was to be a symbol of hope and proof of prosperity ahead.

We were so absorbed in the Empire State Building that we had not realised there was a second item in the parcel: a pencil set for Arthur. 'Just the thing for writing to Dad,' ventured Mam. 'With your letter you could send him a drawing of this new skyscraper...'

He was distinctly unmoved.

'Or you'll never get that leather-case ball...'

But he dismissed the idea with a shrug.

The replica of what was to be the world's highest building had a pencil sharpener in its base. 'You could sharpen all those pencils.'

'Oh yes,' he said, more cheerfully.

'Where are we going to put it?' asked Mam.

'On the mantelpiece.'

The mantel shelf was rearranged so that the copper-coloured Empire State Building became the centrepiece, with our two metal, silver-coloured money boxes on either side. These money boxes had slots for the different coin sizes, with separate compartments for the pennies, shillings and half-crowns. The last time Dad was home he had given Arthur a quarter, with George Washington on it. This quarter (nicknamed 'two bits' said Dad) was worth about a shilling, and was the same size. It now rattled along with the shillings in Arthur's shillings compartment as we rearranged the shelf. The money boxes, and now the skyscraper, were reflected in the big mirror behind them.

'Why don't we have that little mirror as well?' Arthur dashed off to the dairy. This mirror was the one Mam used when tying a scarf round her head before butter-making. Arthur returned and propped it on the mantel shelf so that it mirrored the Empire State Building beside it. This little looking glass in its turn was reflected in the big mirror behind.

'See,' said Arthur, up on top of a chair to get a better view of the double reflection, 'lots of skyscrapers.' It was our vista of Manhattan. 'Look... it goes on and on... into the far distance... and I'm going to go on... and on...'

'Up Fifth Avenue,' I said, pushing him aside to look.

'No.'

'Up Broadway.'

'No. I...'

'It's only the two mirrors reflecting each other,' said Mam, trying to calm him down.

'I can see Carnegie Hall. In the distance.' Arthur immediately broke into song. It was Puccini's 'Your Tiny Hand is Frozen'. 'I'll sing from the top of the Empire State Building.'

For months we had progress reports on the building of this skyscraper: from Dad's letters and postcards; from New York daily papers, tabloids with lots of pictures; and a booklet that Dad sent, giving all the details. And there was always *Pictorial Knowledge* with its descriptions. The miniature replica held pride of place. This building was to be higher than the Eiffel Tower and two hundred feet higher than that other new skyscraper, the Chrysler Building. At 34th Street and Fifth Avenue, the old Waldorf-Astoria Hotel had been pulled down to make way. After twenty-three weeks, and ahead of schedule, the 57,000 tons of the steel skeleton had been topped out, towering 1,250 feet above the sidewalk.

'Higher than Hope Mountain. Much higher.'

'Holy *Moses!*'

'It covers one acre. On a two-acre site.'

'Big enough for a football pitch. Just like Cae Cefn.'

'If they built it on Cae Cefn we could climb to the top, look over Hope Mountain and see Plas Teg. And because from the top you can see fifty miles, we'd see England. *England!*'

'We'd see America.'

'Don't be silly, America's far, far away, over the horizon. To the west, over the Cae Cefn boundary hedge. Up the Tyrpeg. Beyond Corwen.'

'Well, I'd climb to the top anyway.'

'In an elevator.' It was going to have seventy-three elevators with speeds up to 1,200 feet per minute, with seven miles of elevator shafts. 'What's elevator?' asked Mam.

'It lifts you up when you want to go upstairs to bed.'

'Oh I wouldn't trust it. I'd climb the stairs.'

There would be 1,860 steps! And the building would have 6,500 windows. Who would clean them all? 'And on the top, right up there...' I pointed to the pencil-point tip of the replica: '...there will be a mooring mast for airships.'

'No!' said Arthur, incredulously.

'Yes. I'll show you in *Pictorial Knowledge*.' The volume was propped on the seat of the rocking chair, while I sat on the rag rug on the hearth, turning over the pages of sepia-coloured pictures of other skyscrapers until I found the page.

Arthur was bubbling over. 'We could go by airship to hear Dad. And shout "Encore". What does it say?' He stooped over me and slowly turned a page, then turned it back and forth, saying again with agitation: 'What... what does it say?'

Mam whispered to me: 'Let *him* read it.'

'Er...' His finger pointed to the words. We were both now on the hearth rug.

'There aren't many long words. I'll help you.'

'Try,' said Mam. Then: 'Come on, Cariad.'

But Arthur, instead, picked up the booklet Dad had sent, and slowly turned over its pages. Then perking up, he ostentatiously cleared his throat, and read its title: '"The Empire State Boo... boo... booilding..."'

'Building,' I said.

'Boo-ilding. And boo to you too.' He picked a page at random: '"It will be the ninnth..."'

'Ninth.'

'I know, I know. "...ninth wonder of the world. It will have a steel frame, with enough steel to build a railway from Noo York..."'

'New York.'

'Noo York: that's how you say it, you Limey. "...railway from *Noo* York to Miami." Holy Moses! "There are 3,000 workmen building this Mam's... hat... on skyscraper."'

'Manhattan,' I said, laughing.

'Finished.' He shut the booklet.

'Just a little more': Mam, trying to be persuasive, but to no effect. He sulked. Then she said, 'We'll be able to tell Dad you can read.'

He slowly reopened the booklet and found the page. 'Er... where were we?' His finger more or less found the place: '"... on Manhattan Iss-land... is land..."'

'Manhattan Island.'

'Manhattan is land,' he repeated emphatically. 'It's land if it's an island. "Many records have been broken. Building site stories have now become leg end..."'

'Legend,' I said, looking at the word.

'T'isn't. It's leg end. Broken legs. Builders falling off the ladder, see?' He violently turned a page. 'Oh, gee whiz, this is the bit about the airship!' And reading rapidly: '"It-has-one-hundred-and-two-floors-and..."'

'There's a comma there.'

'Don't,' said Mam. 'Let him.'

'"...and comma there at the top is the mast for airships which..."'

'Full stop.'

'"...which they full stop in New York when they comma with passengers. Passengers please..."' – and rapidly flicking over a page – '"Passengers please turn over... on this two acre site. Will be the world's tallest building."'

From there on he read half to himself in a continuous monotone, barely audible. He was now in the rocking chair with the booklet on his lap. Embarked on a lifetime's reading and the pleasure from it, said Mam to me, softly. Yes, he'd finally caught on.

Mam walked over to the dresser, picked up the pen and wrote on the writing pad: 'Dear Jäbez. Arthur can now read. It's wonderful…'

I walked over to Arthur and, bending over him, said quietly: 'I reckon you knew how to read all along.'

'Maybe, maybe,' he said, not taking his eyes off the printed word and shrugging me off.

Mam was writing, unable to restrain her joy: 'He's suddenly taken to it. It was this skyscraper building from Woolworth's that did it. And the booklet you sent…'

Arthur's reading was an indistinct mumbling. He was concentrating, never taking his eyes off the page. It continued for some time. Then suddenly, out loud: 'Finished.' He shut the booklet with a flourish. 'I've read five pages. I'm thirsty. How about a highball?'

'Or a Manhattan.'

'Yes,' said Arthur, going through the motions of raising his glass and simulating drinking by drawing saliva through his teeth. 'Ah. That's better. I'm going to read some more.'

A knock on the door.

'Mr Marshall,' said Arthur. 'Another parcel. My football!'

But it couldn't be Mr Marshall the Post at that time of day. When the knock was repeated, it was obviously not the familiar knock of the postman.

'Alun,' said Mam, a little worried, 'look through the window.'

I raised the curtain slightly. It was a lady. And with the side of my head pressing against the pane, I could see she carried a large basket.

127

'What's she like?' asked Mam in a whisper, approaching the window.

She had a long dress; it was gaudy and bulky. Her hair was very dark, and she wore earrings.

Mam looked, adjusting her thick, rimless spectacles. 'Gypsy woman!' Moving towards the door but clearly disturbed by the intruder she said: 'We'll send her away.'

We followed.

'Lavender bags? Lace?' said the swarthy gypsy, displaying her wares.

'Not today thank you.'

Then dipping into her basket: 'Clothes pegs?'

'Have you any Winnipegs?' asked Arthur.

'No thank you,' repeated Mam, more sharply.

'...Clothes pegs only a penny each.' And, with a mixture of persuasion and menace, 'If you don't buy, you may get bad luck.'

'No thank you,' said Mam again, brusquely.

'You never know,' said the slightly hoarse, rasping voice. 'You may be sorry...'

'Not today, I haven't time.' Mam pulled Arthur out of the doorway as she half-shut the door.

Then with persistent persuasion: 'May I tell your fortune? Only a shilling.'

'Well...'

I whispered: 'No. Waste of money.'

'No,' said Mam, biting her lip, 'I'm busy.' Then, not without threat, the gypsy woman said: 'You'll regret it. A serious ill will befall you...'

The door was slammed shut. And bolted.

'Perhaps I should...' Mam was upset. 'Look out of the window. See if she pinches things from the barn.' I looked, and saw her go out through the gate, carefully shutting it. 'Perhaps I should have bought...' There was distress in Mam's voice. 'She put a curse on me. Bring bad luck.'

'No.'

'Perhaps I should have had my fortune told.'

'No.'

'You never can tell. Best to know how you are... it's like... it's like going to the doctor when you're not well... it's best to know. It gives you peace of mind.' She was in this state of agitation for some time, unable to settle down to chores around the house.

Then, still not her happy self, she approached the gramophone. 'Alun. Come and show me again how to put it on.'

'Easy,' I said, putting my newspaper down and walking over. 'Switch it on.' The turntable began its rumble, spinning round. 'And put the needle in the groove.'

Mam cheered up, humming with the piano introduction and then began a duet with the gramophone. But at the words 'The mem'ries ever dear...' the turntable slowed down and gradually came to a stop.

'Oh, it's broken. Oh no!'

It only needed winding up. A few turns of the winding handle and the speed was back to normal:

'...the years go rolling on...'

'Oh, thank goodness we've still got Dad,' she said with a sigh of relief. When the song came to the words:

'And then came life's awakening...'

129

she was back to her duet, fondly and tenderly embracing the top note on the word 'awakening'.

    ''Twas the Dawn, the Dawn of Love....'

And she sang it to the end.

I rewound and replayed the gramophone, changing the needle two or three times as she sang and went about the house, back now to her normal self. While the gramophone played I sat in the rocking chair with *Old Moore's Almanac*. It was about the Big Slump: the world was heading for depression. 'Mam, what's depression?'

'It's when you have a headache and a bellyache at the same time,' she called from the back kitchen, breaking off momentarily from her duet. She was now singing robustly and rapturously, in and out of the living room.

I picked up the daily paper, and spotted an item of American news: factories were shutting down, stocks were skidding, breadlines stretched down the streets, and three thousand US banks had gone bust in three years.

The cheque that came out of the envelope with Dad's letter was not the usual one. Normally Mam would cash it at the bank in Mold, usually on market day when we were at school. But this cheque, 'To the order of: Jäbez Trevor, Redpath Bureau, Kimball Bld, Chicago, Ill.', was headed with the bank's name, and 'In Receivership'. The bank had gone bankrupt, explained Mam. She was very upset. Dad had lost money. Typewritten on the cheque were the words 'Pay creditor the sum of 49 cents.'

'Is that all?' she said, nervously picking it up, peering at it, then holding it up to get more light from the window.

'It would buy that American cow, National Dairy,' said Arthur.

Fortunately the amount we lost was not large. Dad described the way things were going. He had seen a shanty town in Central Park, New York – the out-of-work down-and-outs living in ramshackle huts, contrasting with the wealthy Park Avenue close by. We had already heard of similar places in Chicago: they were called 'Hoovervilles', after President Hoover. In them the homeless unemployed lived in cardboard hovels. In a small town in the Midwest he had seen a hunger march to the City Hall on a bitterly cold day. Prosperity was just round the corner, insisted President Hoover. And now the Depression was doubly brought home to us with: '"I've heard from my cousin in Tennessee... he's now unemployed. In the States right now millions are out of work. Sending you money..."' There between the sheets of notepaper was his regular cheque. '"Sorry it's less than usual, but box office bookings are down, and I bought these new shirts with collars attached, very handy..."'

'Oh, let's send something to Dad,' said Arthur.

'Yes!' It would cheer him up. Yes, a present. But what?

'A tie,' said Mam. 'A tie to go with his new shirt.'

'Co-op cart's been,' were Mam's first words when we got home from school. 'Help me put away the groceries. Alun, count the Co-op checks.' Another flimsy pink slip to stick on the gummed sheet. 'Tea... sugar... butter.' She checked off the order list: the tea and sugar weighed and measured out into bags; the butter weighed and wrapped – all done at the shop; nothing was pre-packed. 'Now the cow's dry we have to buy milk and butter.'

Arthur picked up a tin of condensed milk and placed it the right way up on the table. I looked at its label: '"Product... of..."'

'Let me, let me,' he said, pushing me away and getting his eyes down to the small print, anxious to show he could read: '"Product of... USA." From National Dairy Inc, you bet. Why don't *our* cows put their milk in tins?'

As we put the groceries away, Mam said: 'And I've ordered the tie to send to Dad. You must write and tell him: parcel with tie on the way soon... and ask for your football.' We both looked at him. No response.

Then I added: 'Put "Tie from the Co-op."'

'No, we don't say it's from the Co-op,' said Mam as she began humming the opening bars of 'Dawn of Love'. 'Alun, let's have the record.'

She began, with the gramophone, singing it moderato espressivo, just as the music said.

Dad was touring the East now: Boston, Philadelphia, Syracuse, NY.... The postcards came regularly: 'New England in the Fall', 'On the Boardwalk, Atlantic City', and two written on board the New York Central: 'Niagara Falls' and 'Buffalo'.

Buffalo was an inland port on Lake Erie, with half a million people, and where a US President, William McKinley, was assassinated in 1901. It had a big Polish population, with Polish newspapers.

'Buffalo,' said Arthur, now keen to read his own cards. 'Full of Poles. Sure is a mighty great pleasure to meet you, Mr Trevorski.'

'I'm not pulling them in like the last tour. My agent says try less Handel and more Lehár, but I don't know. Anyhow, I've bought a copy of "Oh Maiden, My Maiden", from his latest...'

Of course Mam knew this number from Lehár's *Frederica*. She had heard Dad sing it only the last time he was home. It captivated her and became her song of the moment around the house and out of doors. With Mam's voice ringing in the background, Arthur said to me: 'Well old Alunski, let's go some place.'

After a moment's thought: 'Carve initials?'

'Yes. Sycamore tree.'

It was something we hadn't done for some time. So we stealthily hurried off with our pocketknives, running down the fields, leaving Mam happy and singing to her heart's content.

In no time we were down at the stile, climbing up to sit on the branches, chipping away at the bark of the trunk. Arthur seemed none too secure on his branch, furiously working at it.

I paused for a rest. And to think about Dad's latest letter: 'Mam always sings Dad's operetta. Never oratorio. Never opera.'

'I do,' said Arthur, his eyes lighting up. He jerked the branch dangerously as he burst into opera. It was the same Puccini aria. Suddenly he stopped.

The branch creaked. 'Oh...! Oh...!' It was breaking with Arthur clinging on to it. He was laughing. 'This branch

133

has me all balled up. Oh...! I'm falling. I...' He hit the ground with a thud, on his behind. Then picking himself up, brushing the dirt off his jacket and noting a rip in his trousers, he straightened himself. 'Gi'me the big hand,' he shouted up to me.

I jumped down, and gave an exaggerated clap: 'You wow 'em off their seats, and how. Take three bows and an encore.'

He complied.

Then suddenly, breaking off his encore: 'I cleaned up a thousand bucks last month. I'm hungry. Let's go eat.'

We trudged up the fields back home, spurred on by the thought of food. Mam had recently been sent an American cookbook. It told you how to make Philadelphia sticky buns, Rhode Island Johnny cakes, Minnehaha sauce, Indian corn stew, Yankee tomato relish, snickerdoodles, Baltimore eggnog, roast turkey (like for Thanksgiving) and a host of other mouth-watering recipes. Arthur had been reading them, especially Martha Washington's great cake ('Take forty eggs...'). We had hinted he could write to Dad to tell Americans about Welsh cakes, Welsh rarebit and bara brith. But no; he was only interested in eating. He could have written out the recipe for Welsh cakes: with the flour, mix a little baking powder, nutmeg and butter; add some sugar, lard and currants; mix into a dough with an egg; roll out with rolling pin, cut into rounds; and bake on the griddle on our kitchen range in the living room. Or he could have told Dad how we went with Uncle Noah to catch trout in the Terrig. With its source in the Llandegla Moors, the river was the northern boundary of the parish. The Terrig emptied into the Afon Alun. We walked the two miles across other farmers' fields to a quiet glade and a bend of the river. Uncle Noah waded in, wearing normal boots and trousers, right up to his knees. We watched quietly and intently from the bank, standing perfectly still as he carefully disturbed a boulder. With his other hand at the ready, he swiftly caught a trout as it darted out. He made more catches a short way upstream. Then home with our catch for a supper treat: trout with rashers of bacon. There was so much to tell Dad. But no; Arthur wasn't interested in writing. Only in eating.

And so it was now as we went indoors: 'Say kiddo, what's cooking? Al, choose me something from the *Adriatic* menu.' We play-acted our way through the menu cards of White Star Line steamers and North American hotels: turtle soup, iced honeydew melon, pin money pickles (we liked this one), Vermont turkey with cranberry sauce...

Yes, it was turkey that appealed to us. We had chicken so often. Uncle Noah would come to kill a chicken. He would grab one in the henhouse, grip it by the neck, its wings flapping wildly with a frantic screech, then swiftly the sharp-pointed blade of his horn-handled clasp knife plunged into its gullet; its wings would flap a dying flap as it bled; and he hung it head down outside the wash-house. Later, Mam would pluck its feathers in the back kitchen, with feathers everywhere. (With turkey feathers, we could have made Red Indian headdresses, just like real ones.) And so we had chicken, chicken, all the time. Never roast turkey.

Mam had heard us and came into the living room to lay the table. 'Brawn for tea.'

'I'll have peanut soup...' We reeled off more American dishes.

'Sit down,' said Mam. There was something on her mind.

'And buckwheat cakes and corn-dodgers...'

Mam, depressed, stopped us with: 'Dad says he's not doing so well. It's these new talking pictures.' She had read the letter through while we were out; she picked it up for us to hear: '"...they're all going to the talkies. Audiences are down and that's it. Many theatres are closing down. We may have to cancel the rest of the tour..."' (But somehow he survived, eventually coming home as planned.)

Arthur noisily sipped his tea.

'Drink your tea properly.' Then on with the letter: '"I met Will Rogers at a charity performance. He's been a headliner for years in two-a-day Vaudeville... it's like Variety back home..."'

'What's Variety?'

'Like Chester Royalty Theatre. We'll have to take you to a matinee when Dad's home.' And her eyes returning to the letter: '"...with his name in electric lights...".'

'Cor!'

'"...doing funny monologues and wisecracks in his Oklahoma drawl..."'

'Will Rogers!' I interrupted. 'He's the one who writes in the American papers.' In the cupboard beside the fireplace were old newspapers kept for firelighting. I whipped out two of them. I guessed it must be the same Will Rogers who wrote a daily column, syndicated to many American papers. It was usually on the front page, under the byline 'Will Rogers Says'. It had made his name a household word. He was famous. When the Ford Model A came out, he had been given the first one. He was on American radio every week.

Mam continued with Dad's letter: '"...he uses a lasso to do tricks on stage, wears cowboy clothes and chews gum." Bad habit that.' We had seen a photo of him in a chewing gum advertisement. 'Arthur, eat up.'

'"He can catch a horse with one rope and its rider with another..."'

'Wow!'

'"He's a real showman."'

This description made me search thoroughly for his column. I brought out a pile of papers from the cupboard and found an old one about the previous US President, Calvin Coolidge. Will Rogers, in his humorous way, likened him to a monkey and mimicked his high-pitched Vermont twang. It was in a radio broadcast; he had done it so realistically as to cause nationwide consternation.

'"He was born in Oklahoma..."' This entertainer and humorist had a loud, carrying voice. With his wry, homespun humour and sharp satire, delivered in an off-hand, diffident manner in a Southwestern drawl, he delighted his audiences. He was held in affection, and his wisecracks had become popular sayings.

'"IIe was born in Oklahoma..."' began Mam again, '"where he has a five thousand acre ranch..."'

Bigger than Hope Mountain! And we had nine acres.

'"...with cattle, sheep and 250 goats. He is partly Cherokee Indian..."'

There was something about that too in 'Will Rogers Says'. Oklahoma, before it was thrown open to white settlers, had long been set aside as Indian Territory.

Arthur was puzzled: 'How can he be Red Indian and a cowboy?'

'"...and his mother's mother was half Welsh." Rogers. Sounds Welsh. "He's ten years older than me."' When Mam finished a page she propped it against the milk jug.

'"He has three children and there was a baby that died of diphtheria..."'

'But how can he be a Red Indian and a cowboy? He can't be.'

'"Will Rogers is also a movie star, he's making a talkie, *A Connecticut Yankee at the Court of King Arthur*. Take them to see it when it comes to the Savoy in Mold..."'

'Yes!'

And Mam too: 'I'd love to see these new talkies.' Back to the letter: '"It's the famous book by Mark Twain. Get them to read it..."'

'"I am an American. I was born..."'

'No! You should say like Dad.'

So I began reading page thirty-six again, in my best American: '"I am an American. I was born in Connecticut... I am a Yankee of the Yankees..."'

It was Mark Twain's book about Hank Morgan. Mam had bought it for us when she went to Mold on market day, at Roberts' bookshop by The Cross.

'"My father was a blacksmith." Mam,' I said, looking up from the book, 'like your dad, he was a blacksmith.'

'Who?' she paused as she dusted round the Empire State Building on the mantel shelf.

'Hank Morgan's father from Connecticut. Hartford. Where they make the Colt revolver.'

'This is my Colt,' said Arthur, drawing his 'revolver'. 'Bang, bang, bang...'

'Oh be quiet,' scolded Mam, with little effect.

'I won the West. Bang... Bang...'

'Arthur!'

With Arthur calmed down: 'Who's this Hank Morgan?'

'Brother of J.P. Morgan,' said Arthur, 'the money man who takes your money for the cow in the New York Stock Market.'

'No, no, no. This Hank Morgan, he went back in time.' I had already read half the book, and, excited, I tried to tell the story: 'Back to King Arthur and the Round Table.'

'Morgan. A Welsh name,' she said with growing interest. 'Is he Welsh?'

'Well, nearly, because he says...' I quickly flicked the pages over to find the place: '"...I would utter it even if it was Welsh."'

'A Welsh-American. Perhaps Dad will meet him.'

Dad was always meeting the Welsh of North America. They were everywhere: Montreal; Edmonton, Alberta, with a snapshot of them meeting him at the station; Wilkes-Barre, Penn.; Utica, NY: Wisconsin; New York, NY... oh yes, they were everywhere. They built America.

'Dad's sure to meet Hank Morgan,' insisted Mam.

'No. No. It's a story. It's the talkie film we're going to see. With Will Rogers acting in it.'

'Oh,' said Mam. After a pause: 'He speaks Welsh in the story then.'

'He speaks American English.'

'Oh,' she said, disappointed.

'He goes back in time to Camelot, King Arthur's town, where they speak a funny kind of English, like "Defend thee lord – peril of life is toward", and "sorrowed passing sore".'

'Very old fashioned.'

'It's like *The Book of Common Prayer*,' I said, remembering thumbing through it during the Reverend

Cadwaladr Williams' boring sermons.

'Must be a good book then, if it's like the prayer book.'

'But it's exciting. They had railways in Camelot.'

'All that time ago? But what did King Arthur know about railways?'

'Hank Morgan showed him how to build them.'

Arthur expanded on this: 'Hank invented the LMS Railway and the Great Western. I know. I read it.'

Mam disbelieved him and now she knew he could read she was concerned to see him write: 'Tell Dad about it. Write to him.'

'Hank Morgan built steamships, telephones...'

'He's clever. Of course his father was a blacksmith.' Dad had always said how Mam adored her father.

'And Hank, he marries a girl called Sandy and they have a baby daughter called Hello Central.'

'Hello who?'

'Hello Central. That's what they called her. It's what you say down into the telephone at Beehive when you want to speak to the telephone exchange at Pontybodkin.'

'Hello Central, Hello Central...' Arthur play-acting. 'This is Beehive Stores. Give me Carnegie Hall, New York.'

'Here's your party.' I joined in.

'Hello. How ya bin?'

And laughing I said, 'But you can't speak on the telephone to New York!'

'Well, why not. Tell Dad I want a football with a leather case, so that we can fix our football match. No need to write.'

I returned to the book. 'The knights of the Round Table play baseball all dressed in armour.'

'Like Babe Ruth.'

'Arthur,' said Mam, 'you should be the one reading. Give him the book.' He could read, but he still needed to practise.

But he showed no inclination.

Then I thought of the atlas. 'Tell you what. You find Hartford, Connecticut. Hank Morgan's home town.'

'Okay,' he said, to Mam's satisfaction. 'And I'll find Camelot.'

I went to the bookshelf and opened the atlas at 'North-east USA'.

Meanwhile Arthur recited the doggerel verse that Dad had sent from the Midwest schoolhouse in the hope that he could be persuaded to write it out. Arthur now adapted it to suit the moment:

> 'King Arthur is my name,
> America's my nation...'

'They don't have kings in America!' I protested.

> 'Camelot's my dwelling place,
> And Heaven's my destination.'

'Camelot's not in America. No such place.'

He came over to the atlas, now laid out on the table. After a hesitant start, he identified New York and Buffalo; and Rhode Island, where his little red hen came from. 'New Hev... New Heaven': his finger on New Haven. He pointed up the Connecticut River. 'Here it is. Hartford.' Bubbling over: 'Now let's find Camelot.'

'Camelot's only in legend.' I would have put the atlas away but he insisted.

'Let him,' said Mam.

His finger moved over towards the Hudson River. 'Arthursburg!' he said with tremendous satisfaction. I looked; and so it was: Arthursburg.

His finger now moved up the Hudson, the route Dad had taken to Syracuse, Niagara Falls and Buffalo.

'Camelot! Camelot. I've found it.'

He was making it up, surely. But he insisted on showing me Camelot, yes, Camelot, on the left bank of the Hudson River, not many miles from New York, and about ten miles from Arthursburg. Well well, Camelot a real place: it must be; it was on the map.

I searched in *Pictorial Knowledge* and other books for information about Camelot. Besides being 'the location of King Arthur's palace and court in Arthurian legend' it was 'a place or time or atmosphere of idyllic happiness'. And this, Arthur had found out, was a real place!

'This atlas of yours wouldn't be much cop without Camelot,' he said. Then after a pause: 'I'm going there when I grow up.'

The atlas was shut with a bang.

We could hear the cuckoo. It came loud and clear, up from the wood on this sunny late afternoon in early spring.

'Early this year,' said Mam. 'Very early.' Then suddenly: 'Turn the money over in your pocket.'

'And we'll all be right here in this house, in this living room, this time next year,' said Arthur. 'God's truth. You'll see.' We half believed this superstition that when you first hear the cuckoo you turn your money over so that you'll have money all the year round.

I was idly turning the pages of Volume Six, one of my favourites, with skyscrapers, scientists, musicians and the fold-out model of the Imperial Airways airliner. It vied with Volume Three, about the United States and Canada. In Volume Six was a facsimile of the first English song to be written down:

Sumer is icumen in,
Llude sing cuccu!

'Mam, what's the oldest song in Welsh?'
She did not answer, but began the Welsh song:

Gwcw fach, yr wyti' n fodlon...
(Little cuckoo, you are content...)

Then realising how late it was: 'We'd better get our letters written to get them in the post.'
I began mine, Arthur watching me: 'Dear Dad. Do you hear the cuckoo in...'
'In Connecticut,' said Arthur.
'...in Connecticut...'
'When are you going to write a letter?' said Mam, as she opened her writing pad.
'Dear Jābez,' she wrote. 'Spring is here. Still trying to get Arthur to put pen to paper. The Will Rogers talkie didn't come to the Savoy. Very disappointing. So, I'm taking them to see a cowboy film instead. They've never been to the pictures...'

The electric lights were on. We were tense with excitement at the start of a matinee screening of two American talkie films.

I had looked through the local paper, time and time again, hoping to find the Will Rogers talkie, either at the Savoy in Mold, or in one of the three cinemas in Wrexham, all now equipped to show talking films. Scanning the advertisements, I had seen a British film, *Atlantic*, about the sinking of the *Titanic*. Better not see that, I thought, it would only upset Mam. *All Quiet on the Western Front*: 'the mightiest drama of the screen; with British Movietone News.' No, that wouldn't do. It was about war. 'Coming Shortly: *King of Jazz*.'

'What's jazz like, Mam?'

'Just noise.'

Widow from Chicago; a gangster film; all right for Arthur and me, but not for Mam. There was another gangster film they were making: *Little Caesar*: like Al Capone. And *Broadway Melody*:

'Oh, they can sing as well as talk in the talkies.'

'Sure.'

The Virginian; Sunny Side Up; The Desert Song (more singing); *The Big Trail; Billy the Kid*: about a 'Western gunslinger'. *In Old Arizona* promised 'sounds of action': stampeding cattle, gunshots, etc. There was no sign of the Will Rogers talkie. So it had to be the cowboy film.

We gazed up at the electric lights, counting them. There was a carpet down the gangway. A big safety curtain hung in front of us. Printed on it were advertisements, each in its own rectangular frame. These frames were arranged in regular rows right across the curtain, filling it from top to bottom: Daddies Sauce; Syrup of Figs; Evan Williams

Shampoo; Bovril; Jones Auctioneers; Senna Pods; and 'for your rheumatism' Fynnon Salt...

'We'll read these and then go home,' joked Mam. Arthur took her seriously; he could read them all.

The music started, a band or an orchestra, like a gramophone, but ever so much louder. ('Must write and tell Dad all about it... perhaps we'll get Arthur to write too.') Then the safety curtain was raised. It rumbled up slowly to reveal a huge white screen, much bigger than the Band of Hope magic lantern. The music stopped and the electric lights slowly dimmed.

'Ooh it's going dark,' said Arthur, sitting on the edge of his upholstered tip-up seat. We were in the one-and-nines, the best seats. We heard the projector noise, a brief buzzing and wheezing. Suddenly, from somewhere above our heads, the film's title in big letters and moving pictures flashed onto the screen. It was a man in bed, asleep. He was snoring. It was so loud, so much louder than if he was acting on stage. It came out of a loudspeaker somewhere. Beside the bed was a clock, ticking away: we could hear it. The snore became louder. Suddenly the alarm clock rang. The man stirred; then turned over. He couldn't wake up.

Beside the clock was a telephone, but not a bit like the one at Beehive Stores with its wooden box on the wall, a crank handle to ring the telephone exchange at Pontybodkin, a mouthpiece fixed to the wall and a separate earpiece. The telephone bell rang.

'It's modern,' I said. It was like the one President Hoover had on his desk. We had seen a photo of it.

It rang again. Its bell had a different ring too.

'Higher pitch,' said Arthur. 'Top C.'

The man in bed groaned. He was moving. He put out his arm, clumsily lifted the telephone receiver, and yawned. 'Hello. Hello,' he said into the telephone, still yawning.

'He talks American.'

'Ssh...' said Mam.

'Hello. Hello.' He was half sitting up now, elbow on pillow.

'Funny to hear pictures talking at you,' said Mam.

'Hello...' now wide awake, very grumpy, and annoyed at having his sleep disturbed. 'Hello Central.' Then, more aggressively, with his prominent American accent: 'Who's that on the wire at this early hour? Who's that...'

The bedside clock struck the hour.

'Holy Moses! It's eleven o'clock...!'

We boys laughed our heads off.

This film was only the serial: 'To be Continued Next Week'. The real one was the cowboy film: guns firing, horses neighing, cowboys riding and galloping away to the accompaniment of film music. This was it.

'They went that-a-way!' A cowboy, riding up and drawing his reins. Watching the faces of people as they spoke, we noticed their lip movements didn't quite match what they were saying.

Then a stampede of buffalo.

'Red Indians!' said Arthur. They were hunting buffalo. The stampeding hoofs faded as they moved away into the distance. The Indians had dismounted. Arthur was once more on the edge of his seat. 'They're sending smoke signals!'

Then they all remounted, ever so many of them now. Riding bareback, they made a sustained, high-pitched

'Ah...', but with the fingers of one hand covering and rapidly tapping the mouth, to break the note into a discontinuous, piercing and monotonous noise. This was their war cry. And with whooping and screaming, they galloped away.

'Let's get the hell out of here,' said the cowboy to his buddies. 'It's our last chance!' They mounted and rode away, firing their guns over their shoulders at the approaching, yelling, whooping Indians.

The Red Indian horde came at full speed in full war cry, head-on into the cinema audience.

'Look out!' I yelled.

Arthur ducked.

'It's all right, Arthur, they're only moving pictures,' Mam assured him. But I could tell she was relieved when horses and riders rode away. She didn't like the firing of guns and that piercing war cry.

Arthur was imitating the Red Indian war cry.

'Oh stop it,' said Mam, not for the first time since our Saturday matinee.

But he kept on, his boy soprano perhaps not the same intensity as the talking picture. But repeated often, it was penetrating enough.

Mam was nearing despair: 'If I hear that once more...'

'If I hear that one more time...' said Arthur, impudently, carried away by the American accents of the cowboys in the talkie.

Mam was furious.

He became more amenable when his better nature saw

that he had gone too far. 'Okay Mam.'

To clear the air, I suggested: 'Let's go play Cowboys and Indians.' It would give Mam a bit of peace. So out we went.

'Yippee.' Arthur was now a cowboy on the Cae Cefn range. 'Look! Over there. Smoke signal. By the road to Cymau. Look!'

Of course, in threshing time we would see a real smoke signal: the steam traction engine's puffs of white smoke as the thresher was pulled at walking pace along the Hope Mountain road. The smoke would be a signal to all the small farms of Hope Mountain, Llanfynydd and Uwch-y-Mynydd-Uchaf that threshing was a day nearer and that they would have to pray for a fine day for their threshing.

But now the smoke was make-believe. 'Yes. Smoke signal. On top of Hope Mountain.'

He began singing an American folk song, 'On Top of Old Smoky'.

We had read about Smoky Mountain with its smoke-like mist in a descriptive travel guide booklet Dad had sent from somewhere in the Carolinas. It told of the forced migration of Cherokee Indians from their Smoky Mountain homeland to Oklahoma; and how, on this 'Trail of Tears', very many died of disease, hunger, cold and exhaustion. So the Oklahoman Will Rogers, part Cherokee, had ancestors who hailed from the Smoky Mountain region.

Arthur suddenly broke off singing. 'Cherokees!' he yelled. He made the war cry.

'Charging down Smoky Mountain,' I said, as he continued the sad song.

Along with that travel guide had come a book of American folk songs. When we showed it to Mr Hayes, it was this 'On

Top of Old Smoky' he chose to teach to the class.

'I'll be Will Rogers, cowboy,' said Arthur. 'Bang, bang, bang...'

'Yes, you be Paleface.' (Well, he really was: Mam was for ever saying how pale he looked, and feeding him on cod liver oil, Scott's Emulsion and Virol.) I added: 'I'll be Will Rogers, Red Indian.'

'Yes. You'll have to practise the war cry.' And he proceeded to demonstrate the war cry at his loudest, right next to my ear. It had the tempo of an ear-splitting high-pitched machine gun.

⚬⟨━⟩⚬

'Rwy'n canu fel cana'r aderyn...'

Arthur was back to his favourite song: 'I sing as the songbird is singing...'

And Mam, standing at the dresser, pen in hand: 'Dear Jàbez. Arthur's on top of the stairs, where he sits, always singing. He's "on stage" like his Dad, looking down on the living room...'

'Yn hapus yn ymyl y lli...'
(So happy, unfettered and free...)

His voice filled the house. Mam would always stop dusting or whatever she was doing, and stand momentarily entranced; then, pretending not to listen so as not to inhibit his spontaneous song, her duster would linger and move ever so slowly. And in the rocking chair my eye would stop in mid-paragraph; and distracted from

149

the page, steal a glance upwards as the song came down from the top of the stairs.

With Arthur's song ended, Mam's pen went on: 'I'm having a partition built to shut off the stairs to make the room warm for next winter. Mr Ingman the Carpenter-Undertaker will do it.' Her idea was to have the draughty stairs boxed in with a door at the bottom; and there would be a passage to the back kitchen, which would make our large living room smaller and cosier.

'A dyna sy'n llonni fy nodyn...'
(And this is what keeps me rejoicing...)

Arthur was sitting in his usual place, singing away, ignoring the carpenter's noise. Mr Ingman was sawing and hammering. He paused to listen and look up at him. Then turning to Mam: 'Takes after his dad, eh?'

'Always sits up there, on the stairs, holding his football. Singing.'

Mr Ingman smiled and carried on sawing. Then, pacing up and down to survey the half-completed partition, he paused again to listen to Arthur singing so beautifully. Turning to Mam, and nodding towards the partition taking shape: 'Well, it's going to shut out the singing boy, isn't it.'

'But...' Mam was doubtful, 'but... it'll make this living room warm in winter for them.'

Arthur stopped singing. Clutching his ball, he came down the stairs, and stood for a while, intently watching Mr Ingman at work. He gave his ball a bounce. Then when the carpenter picked up his saw: 'Mr Ingman, d'you use that to make coffins?'

Mr Ingman smiled, somewhat embarrassed: 'Well... yes.' He continued sawing.

And Arthur bounced his ball all the way down what was to be a passage, enjoying the novelty of it.

'Get ready for church.' Mam was upstairs, getting dressed in her Sunday clothes. She had deliberately left the new door at the bottom of the stairs open so that she could call down to chivvy us into getting ready. She was in the church choir, and they were doing *The Crucifixion*. So her preparation for church was more agitated than usual.

I was looking at her copy of Stainer's short oratorio, 'written for performance in parish churches', and 'with hymns for congregational participation.' (Arthur and I sat in the front row of the congregation, where Mam could keep an eye on us from her seat in the choir stalls.) The only other of Stainer's we knew, apart from hymns, was his 'Sevenfold Amen', which Arthur would sing in full voice at the end of evening services.

'Get ready,' called Mam as she came down the stairs into the living room, forgetting to close the new door.

'Hank Morgan, he wants a go-as-you-please church. I'm all for that.' I dreaded the boredom of the Reverend Cadwaladr Williams' sermon.

There was one occasion only when he had held my interest: he gave a history of the parish church. We had gone through the whole of the dreary service and sermon to the last hymn before he remembered that his usual

151

sermon should have been replaced by a talk on the history of the church. In mid-hymn, he suddenly waved his arms about and shouted, 'Stop! Stop!' And he the parson! What if chapel people had been there? What a performance. Cadwaladr was so forgetful. He apologised, and proceeded to put on display in the chancel the old parish chest and other items, including documents which said how, in 1632, the then curate had complained that 'most of the youthes and yonger sorte... play at the foot boole in the churchyard', and 'that th'elder sorte doe commonly fall to drinking....' 'Just like now,' Mam had said as we walked out of the church past the sundial. On that Sunday, in the older part of the churchyard between the church door and the yew, the old headstones themselves had looked more tilted that usual, as if drunk. And Mam had reminded us, her father John the Blacksmith and his bride Mary Ann were the last to be married in the old church before it was demolished, it being 'in a very decayed state, insecure and ruinous'. This was in 1874, with the wedding ceremony in the old tiny church with its roof already partly dismantled. And it was Mr Ingman the Carpenter-Undertaker's parents, Arthur had chimed in (we had heard all this before), who were the first to be married in the new and much larger Church of St Mary.

But now I was immersing myself deeper into the Stainer music copy – Number 18 ('I Came from the Home of the Glorified'), which ends with the five bars, vox angelica, on the organ, and which comes to a climax at the words 'Crucify! Crucify! Crucify!'

I must have said the words out aloud for Arthur asked Mam, 'What's "Crucify"?'

'Croeshoelio.'

'Oh.' And he resumed playing with his ball, not in the least bit ready for church.

'And Arthur, next year you'll be old enough to be in the church choir.'

'Don't want to,' he said sullenly, not taking his eyes off his bouncing ball.

IV
Dad's Coming Home!

'Hurry with your breakfast or you'll be late.' It was a school morning. Then Mam, seeing Arthur was tardier than usual, said, more persuasively: 'Come on, Sunny Jim, eat your "Force".'

There was a postman's knock. 'Mr Marshall!' said Arthur, suddenly coming alive. 'Football for me.'

'You still haven't written to ask for one,' said Mam, going to the door. 'Get on with your breakfast.'

The new partition prevented us seeing who was at the front door. We got on with breakfast, helped with a little play-acting: 'How about a nice little minute steak, buddy, with sugar corn?'

'Yep. Make it snappy. Must get on that train to Noo York.'

Mam came in with a letter with a Virginia postmark. Dad was in the South again.

'Hurrah for Dixie!' said Arthur, his mouth full of cereal.

Mam joined in, trying out her best Southern accent: 'And how goes your tour this time, Mr Jäbez?'

'He's a regular fella, yes sir.'

'This is your first visit to Virginia in so long.'

'Open the letter,' demanded Arthur, bubbling with excitement.

'Later. Or you'll be late for school.' Then back to her Southern accent: 'Eat your breakfast, honey-chile.' And as she propped the unopened letter against the 'Force' cereal packet: 'As you-all know, Mr Jäbez sang for us on his last tour. Tonight we enjoyed his performance more than ever.'

We clapped: 'Hear! Hear!'

'They say "Give him the glad hand."'

'...So, ladies and gentlemen, raise your glasses: we toast Mr Jäbez.'

'But it's Prohibition.'

'Not if you know where...' Arthur slouched over the breakfast table; he attempted a slow, menacing huskiness a world away from his high-pitched, rapid speaking voice: 'Not if you know where to get the liquor.'

'Come on. On your way to school.'

'Oh please,' pleaded Arthur, straightening himself and attempting to reach for the letter. 'What does Dad say?'

She relented. 'All right. Just a quick look.' As she opened the letter, we sat still, cereal spoons in hand, eyes fixed on the sheets of notepaper coming out of the envelope. '"...three more weeks' engagements in Virginia..."' There was a newspaper cutting, and '"...in the barbershop, a coloured boy shines your shoes, and you pay him a nickel.... Then we return to New York..."'

There were motorbuses in New York now. And lots and lots of motor taxicabs and masses of cars.

'"The flags will soon be out on Fifth Avenue; President Hoover is taking part in the Empire State Building opening ceremony."' The ten million bricks and the one thousand miles of steel wire were all now in place, put there by the three thousand workmen building one storey per day. And the Quaker, engineer and self-made millionaire President would, we assumed, be going up in the elevator, up into the sky, a quarter-mile high!

'And from the top he'll fly home to the White House by airship.' Airships were Arthur's abiding interest. He had even read a newspaper article about the flights of the *Graf Zeppelin* and others.

'"At last this tour's coming to an end. Carnegie Hall Monday 13th. Agent says it's going to be a sell-out." Ardderchog!' (Excellent!) said Mam.

'Gee! Nice work if you can get it. Made a nice dollar. Dad?'

'"Then next day I sail home..."'

We cheered. Mam in her excitement nearly knocked over her cup of tea.

'Dad's coming home!'

'Whoopee!'

She pushed the teacup aside to make room for her elbow on the table, holding up the letter and placing another page against the cereal packet. '"We've booked on the new ship, *Britannic*, arriving Liverpool morning of Monday the twentieth." Mark the calendar,' she said, turning round towards the calendar on the wall.

'With a great big mark,' I said to Arthur, already with pencil in hand at the calendar.

'Not this week...' – his finger was on the date – '...not next week...' his voice rising to a crescendo: '...but the week after that: Dad's coming home!'

We cheered again.

'There...' he marked a big cross with thick strokes, 'Twen... tieth,' and returned to the table, all ears for the rest of the letter.

'"When you write, don't send it to my agent, Redpath Bureau in Chicago. We shall be in New York two nights before we sail, so write to Hotel Chelsea..."' She paused to turn the page. And, emphasising Dad's underlined words: '"... 23rd Street at Seventh Avenue."'

'How can a street be at an avenue?' asked Arthur.

'"Mark Twain was there once."' Writing his famous book, perhaps.

'King Arthur was there,' said Arthur, 'and his knights. Must be a palace.' Well, Hotel Chelsea had four hundred rooms. Like Buckingham Palace? Or like King Arthur's palace in Camelot after Hank Morgan had modernised it with the electric light and things.

We already knew a great deal about New York, 'the world's second city', from postcards, letters and what we had heard when Dad was home. You could ride round Central Park in a horse-drawn Victoria. In the Park was a bandstand. There was Grand Central Station, with its magnificent roof full of stars; and the old, noisy Elevated Railway on Third Avenue. Broadway was the centre of things, with electric light signs: the white, green and red making a jumble and bursting like a bubble. Men spat and smoked cigars. There were speakeasies. On the street plan Dad had sent was Carnegie Hall. And Pennsylvania Station; not all that far from Hotel Chelsea, the Victorian Gothic building with wrought-iron balconies, at 23rd Street at Seventh Avenue.

'But how can a street be at an avenue.' The hotel address puzzled Arthur.

157

'"I'll be right glad to be home with you and the boys. Jäbez. And for the boys, kiss, kiss, kiss."' Mam showed us the kisses. '"PS. This bon voyage card came this morning."'

Out of the envelope came a card with 'Bon Voyage' in gold letters with a picture of a modern, streamlined steamer with low funnels, steaming full steam ahead (Dad coming home at speed!), on a purple sea and a blue sky. Mam admired the card's pink ribbon; and Arthur studied closely the picture of the black ship with a long trail of smoke, coming home three thousand miles. Inside was the message: 'March 1931. From Elmer, Martha and little Emily.'

'Americans,' surmised Mam. 'Expect Dad knows them.'
And, printed inside:

> Here's wishing fun for you
> On a voyage sunny and blue...

'What does "Bon Voyage" mean?'

Explained Mam: 'Have a lovely voyage all the way home!'

We shouted 'Hurray!' and then again and again, all the way out of the house and down the fields on our way to school. And once in the school playground our unspoken words would be: We've got a dad too – and not just on the back of picture postcards. We'll show 'em...

But when we reached the stile we couldn't resist climbing up into the sycamore tree. We would spend a short spell chipping and cutting away at the bark with our pocketknives – just for a few minutes. We had neglected our carving. The branches swayed and creaked slightly with our weight. A gentle breeze blew through the trees. The birds were singing. It was a sunny, spring morning. We had to finish these initials before Dad came home – a surprise for him. And a surprise for Mam too.

I paused to give my arm a rest, and glanced up at the blue sky through the upper branches not yet in leaf: 'Don't forget we're on our way to school.'

'Yes. We'll get on with it,' said Arthur, purposefully. 'Get it finished.' He proceeded to cut away at the bark with furious intent. These initials were to be many inches high, cut deep into the trunk, with thick lettering.

We had a spell of wild energy. 'You chipping away like that makes me see stars,' I said.

Arthur answered, without deviating from his vigorous work: 'Yes. Stars. Forty-eight of them. On the Stars and Stripes.'

'Oh yes. Old Glory. "I pledge allegiance to the flag... and to the republic for which it stands."'

Then rhetorically, with a wave of his arm which nearly made him lose his balance, Arthur took up the oration: '"One flag, one nation, one people, indivisible...."' And with mock weeping: 'Indivisible; I can't do long division...'

'"...with liberty and justice for all."' It was the pledge which American schoolchildren say, hand on heart, standing facing the flag draped above the blackboard, at the beginning of their school day. Dad had written it out and sent it as a writing exercise for Arthur. Arthur could declaim it, but he wouldn't write it.

He now broke into song, to the tune of 'God Save the King'. (We had stood, at the end of the talking picture at the Savoy, for the National Anthem, with George the Fifth himself flickering on the screen.) But Arthur's words were: 'God save George Washington...'

'No. He's dead.' He began again with the same tune:

'My Country 'tis of thee...'

I took up the second line, 'Long live our noble king....', and Arthur battled with 'Sweet land of liberty...' To help the confusion we added, 'Roll-him-on-the-belly with a rolling pin'; and a further verse; 'Long live our old tom cat, Feed him on bacon fat...'

Then Arthur, more seriously, and adapting the words somewhat, sang lustily:

'Land of my father's pride...'

'Like Land of my Fathers,' I said, interrupting.

A moment or two later our hard-working pocketknives were accompanied by: 'I've got an engagement for you at the Chicago World's Fair. Then a month all the way down to Noo Orlins. Leave Chicago on the Illinois Central...'

But Arthur broke into song again, in full voice on the top notes: 'From ev'ry mountain side, Let freedom...'

'Oh gee!' he sighed. 'When do I sail home? Book me a cabin on that new liner *Britannic*.'

'Okay chief. You'll have guaranteed smooth crossing in six days.'

And we set to again, furiously cutting and chipping the letters into the bark of the trunk of the tree.

After a minute or two: 'We ought to be going. School time.'

'I'm goin' to finish it.' And protesting: 'I'm goin' to finish it. Before Dad comes home.'

'Okay, King Arthur.' Another pause. 'Did you know there was a President Arthur?'

'No... then I'll be President.'

'His full name: Chester Alan Arthur.'

'No... well I never! And he didn't live in Chester.'

Arthur was now into the third verse of 'My Country 'tis of Thee':

> 'Let music swell the breeze
> And ring from all the trees...'

'I'm going to sing it for ever, for ever and ever and ever...'

'Amen.'

'Yes. Amen.' And he began orating again: 'I pledge allegiance to the flag... his only begotten son...'

'You've got it all mixed up...' I said, laughing. Then, leaning sideways to look at the intials A.T. taking shape in the bark: 'Say. King Arthur... you should carve K.A., King Arthur.'

'Okay, whiz kid. You are Al... Al Capone, Public Enemy Number One.'

'Number Nine. I'm nine. You're only eight.'

The train whistle blew.

'We got to run,' I said as I clambered down, jumping off the lowest branch. The train, our clock, was rumbling along the single-line track curving through the marsh.

'Come on!' I called back to him as I hastened down the tunnel through the wood. 'Right now!' But he was absorbed in the job in hand. 'Or we'll be late. Very late.' Then a few paces farther down the shaded path I turned and shouted: 'The train is always dead on time...'

⋯⊰⧓⊱⋯

'King Arthur and the Knights of the Round Table lived in Camelot...'

Mr Hayes kept his promise to read to the class the legend of King Arthur. But as the lesson proceeded, he skilfully broke off from time to time from the main story to weave into the lesson a mixture of myth, literature and history. We heard about the *Mabinogion*, the old Welsh tales collected in the Middle Ages: Gwenhwyfar (Guinevere), Bedwyr (Bedevere) and Gwalchmai (Gawain). We heard of Brân, the god of battle and courage, and the patron of bards and minstrels. He was the brother of Branwen, the Venus of British mythology. Perhaps King Arthur, the legendary king of the Britons, was a later version of this god Brân. (Arthur was late; he was really missing something.) We heard of King Arthur's twelve battles, culminating in a victory at Mt Badon where, with a cross on his shield, he killed 960 of the enemy single-handed! (Arthur would have been spellbound by all this magic and enchantment.) Much of this was legend, but perhaps there was a real Arthur who led the Celts against the heathen invaders. Then at the Battle of Camlann, Arthur fell, mortally wounded, and was borne away to the mythical land of Avalon.

These events were in the Dark Ages, before they built Offa's Dyke, which ran by Wmphre the Gamekeeper's cottage. (This earthwork, built by King Offa of Mercia –

162

roughly the English Midlands – was to become the traditional boundary between England and Wales.) It was the time when the Welsh language began. There was sorrow at the passing of the *Pax Romana*; chaos and slaughter in the land were brought by the invading heathen. Arthur would come again to rescue the people from death and destruction; and so grew the myth of his second coming. And his spirit – his name deriving from a word meaning 'The Black One' – was believed to reside in the crow; and so medieval folklore held it was taboo to harm that bird. But through all the plunder and killing of the Dark Ages, said Mr Hayes, Wales was never conquered.

We had recently learnt by heart the poem by Eifion Wyn, 'Paradwys y Bardd' (Poet's Paradise), and had written it out in a handwriting lesson. The poet speaks of Wales, a fair, enchanted land; a thousand heroes, bold – descendants all, of knights in Arthur's court of old: Llin marchogion Arthur.

It was at this line, during that handwriting lesson, that Arthur had quickened the pace of his pen; instead of labouring, he was inwardly enthusing. And he had finished it, a reasonably fair copy. Perhaps, thought Mam when she heard, he would write to Dad yet.

The class now recited all twenty lines of this poem. Mr Hayes followed by saying that myths tell us hidden truths and were 'about time and eternity', but he forgot to explain what 'eternity' was. Then he told us about Moel Arthur, a pre-Roman hill-fort in the Clwydian Range. It was 1500 feet high, and higher than Hope Mountain. We could see Moel Arthur, Moel Famau and other peaks of the Clwydian Range from Hope Mountain on a clear day. They were to the west, over the boundary hedge with the hawthorn tree.

The setting sun lit their sharp outline. The small, steep-sided, circular Iron Age hillfort at Moel Arthur, where some Romano-British pottery had been found, could have been occupied and used right through to King Arthur's time. Perhaps the old Camelot of King Arthur wasn't just a place in legend, said Mr Hayes, but a real place, and maybe it was here, not many miles away...

Mr Hayes stopped. Both he and the class looked towards the door. The brass doorknob turned slowly with a squeak. The door opened a few inches. In squeezed Arthur, shutting the door gently. We sat in silence, watching him walk towards Mr Hayes, his boots resounding on the wooden floor.

'Where've you been?'

'Up a tree sir.'

'You'll be caned next time.'

He walked to his place.

Mr Hayes picked up the story book, looked round the class to make sure he had our attention, and continued: '"...and the Knights of the Round Table were knights of chivalry. They helped the weak, and they were bold; they rode fine horses..."'

'Please sir,' interrupted Arthur, his hand shooting up, 'they rode on bikes.'

The class broke into laughter. 'You're right,' I whispered. 'In Mark Twain's book. You bin reading it?'

'Ya, sure.'

Mr Hayes cleared his throat. It subdued the laughter of the class and our whispered chatter. 'Listen,' he said sharply. '"The Knights all wore shining armour..."'

'Please sir...' Arthur's hand up again. 'Where d'you keep your hanky when you've got armour on?'

'Just listen to the story.' Mr Hayes tried to hide his smile behind his hand.

'Sir, you could use your sleeve.'

Yes, Arthur had been reading Mark Twain.

'I sing as the songbird is singing...'

The last lesson of the day. We were all in full voice in the Big Room, with Mr Hayes at the piano.

He stopped us. 'Arthur: on your own.'

Arthur sang:

'So happy, unfettered and free...'

At the end of the verse Mr Hayes said to him, 'You will be singing a solo in the school concert.'

A smile came over his face.

'Now sing the refrain.'

After the refrain, he sang the second verse in Welsh:

'Rwy'n gwenu fel gwena y seren...'
(I smile like the star of the morning...)

Mam, full of excitement, was standing by the dresser, pen in hand. And many, many years later, when this letter came to light, I recalled how she had then decided to send us to bed first: '...just a line for them to post in Pontybodkin. You'll get it before you sail...'

We lay in bed much too excited to sleep. The bedroom door still open, Arthur called down the stairs, 'When are we going to the hairdresser with Uncle Noah?'

'Go to sleep.' The new door at the bottom of the stairs was left open so that she could be sure we were going to sleep and not staying awake, talking. And her letter went on: 'Instead of cutting their hair in the wash-house, Noah is taking them to Mold to the hairdresser by the Market Place – the first time ever – a special treat <u>because Dad's coming home</u>.' The letter was spattered with words underlined.

'Mam. Which train will we catch?'

'Saturday,' came the impatient reply up the stairs, her mind on her letter-writing: 'More photos for you. Haven't they grown! Georgie Jones took them on Cae Cefn; Arthur holding his ball.' We stood upright in this photograph, wearing identical jerseys, ties and socks. 'He's dying to have a proper leather-case ball...'

'Mam,' called Arthur again, 'd'you think Dad'll bring me a football?'

'Perhaps, if you write a letter.' No doubt prompted by this pleading, the letter continued: 'Arthur mad about football, as if life is too short for anything else...'

And Arthur, to emphasise his heart's desire, added: 'I've got forty-seven cigarette cards of footballers. And Dixie Dean.' He only needed three more to complete the set.

No reply came. She was absorbed in her letter; 'And he will be singing <u>a solo</u> in the school concert, and <u>you'll be home</u>. He sings beautifully, like an angel... he takes after <u>you-know-who</u>... and we'll give him the opportunities and spare him the early struggle you had... he'll make our dream, yours and mine, come true. D'you remember how we used to walk up through the wood in the summertime – not the tunnel, that other path – from the Glee Singers rehearsals...' It was a long, rambling letter.

We settled down, drew the bedclothes over us and gazed at the candlelight flickering on the ceiling, talking in undertones:

'D'you see what I see?'

'What?'

'Cracks on the ceiling.' The window, with its curtains and roll-up blind down, was beyond the brass rail at the foot of the bed. Above it the ceiling cracks were more pronounced. 'They make a map.'

'Mm... Yes.' Arthur propped himself up on his elbows.

'I can see Florida. Sticking out over there.'

'No. Lake Michigan. Well. They're the same shape, nearly.'

Our bedroom had an iron bedstead with brass knobs, a dressing table with mirror, a marble-topped washstand with jug and basin, a copiously illustrated, multi-coloured but faded bilingual Lord's Prayer in its gilt frame at the head of the bed and a pair of much smaller picture frames with head-and-shoulder animal sketches in charcoal, one a dour bulldog and the other a solemn cat, looking straight down at us with Victorian disapproval from above the fireplace. But these familiar furnishings faded as a whole new world came sailing into our candlelit bedroom. We cast our eyes round the huge expanse of ceiling. The cracks in the plaster made maps of anywhere we chose: Mississippi, Long Island, Newfoundland...

'No, it's not Newfoundland. It's an iceberg.'

Then Arthur called out louder, with excitement: 'I can

see a ship's funnel.' It was above the wardrobe. 'Smoke coming out. *Britannic!*'

Mam had heard. 'Blow out the candle and get to sleep.'

I leaned out of the bed, blew out the candle, settled down again and drew the bedclothes over my shoulder.

'Dark!' whispered Arthur with a mock shiver. 'Ooh... I'm going to stay asleep till the *Britannic* comes in.' A mock yawn. 'Say, big fella, wake me when she docks.'

'Okay, soldier.'

His mock snore reverberated round the large, high-ceilinged, dark bedroom.

A little light filtered up the stairs from the living room. Mam, with her poor eyesight, had the paraffin table lamp on the dresser beside her, the writing pad directly under it: '...they're so excited with you coming home. Arthur can't keep still a moment, but I can't get him to write to you...'

'By golly,' said Arthur suddenly, 'we're going on board.' Then propping himself up again: 'Mam,' he called, 'are we going to see the ship?' We had been to Liverpool so many times: *Laurentic*, *Newfoundland*, *Nova Scotia*, *Adriatic*... sometimes to Gladstone Dock (on the Overhead Railway), sometimes to the Princes Landing Stage, and not once going on board. 'Mam,' he called more insistently, 'are we going on board the ship?'

We lay perfectly still, listening for her answer.

Then, after a few moments: 'Yes. And go to sleep.' But her voice was hardly raised above normal, as her pen dipped into the ink bottle and scribbled away: '...and we musn't forget this time to take them aboard...'

'Great ship, *Britannic*.' We rambled on about this new 27,000 ton liner, the steadiest afloat. She was built by

168

Harland and Wolff, like so many of the White Star ships, for the Liverpool-Belfast-Glasgow-New York run. She could carry 1500 passengers. Her picture in the daily paper had shown two squat funnels, very modern; her fore funnel was 'there to make her look right', said the caption. A one-funnelled ship was thought to look odd, and under-powered. One half of this dummy funnel had been made into a smoking room for the engineers and the other half held water tanks. The cheapest fare on this, Britain's first trans-Atlantic passenger motor ship, was £19. On board was a cinema with the talkies. When she set sail on her maiden voyage the BBC broadcast a commentary on a ship's departure for the first time, with announcers, wireless engineers and microphones. She would be returning, and Dad would be on board! Plans were afoot to give her an official welcome when she arrived back in her home port of Liverpool; and we would be there!

'Yes, great ship!' We were far too restless to lie down to sleep. '*Britannic*,' said Arthur suddenly, aloud. And began singing the refrain of 'Rule Britannia'. But the first line 'Rule! Britannia!' was followed by 'Two tanners make a bob', which he quickly changed to 'My two bits make a bob...'

'Ssh...' I put my hand over his mouth. 'Mam's writing to Dad.'

But our quiet, excited chatter was unsubdued. When we grew up, we would go to the States on the *Britannic*! And Arthur's two bits in his money box would help pay the fare.

'Oh... yes,' said Arthur aloud, forgetting himself.

We lay perfectly still a moment, wondering if Mam had heard, as we looked towards the pale light from the table lamp flickering up the stairs to our open bedroom door.

We listened intently, heard her cough ever so quietly and what could have been the scratch of her pen: 'Katie Jones Dressmaker came to measure me for a new suit with the new higher hemline. With it I'll wear the necklace you once sent me from Minneapolis. And I said it must be ready for the day...'

'Mam,' called out Arthur, 'will we go in the Beehive taxi motor car?'

But she was carried away: 'I'm buying a cloche hat. I'll get rid of that one with a black crow's feather – I've had it for years – since Arthur was born. And Arthur has your eyes. D'you remember him clutching your hand tight when he was a baby, always laughing...'

'*MV Britannic*: Motor Vessel,' I whispered. 'Runs on diesel oil.'

'What's diesel oil?'

'Like your cod liver oil.'

'Ugh.'

'It makes her go. She sails miles and miles on one spoonful.' In fact, the newspaper report said her trial voyage had shown that for each ton of the ship's weight only a thimbleful of diesel oil was needed to take her one mile. Her equipment must have included a thimble, I thought. And I had visions of her engines being fed with thimblefuls once every mile for three thousand miles.... Anyhow, she was most economical and would revive the Liverpool-New York route, now suffering from the big decline in emigration to the New World. Liverpool had cause to be proud, and had great expectations of her.

'...and I'll buy a new dress when I get to Wrexham, crepe-de-Chine perhaps, and silk stockings.' There was a slight commotion. We stopped our subdued chatter. Then we heard her say 'Oh!' aloud. And reading this letter decades later, it was obvious what had happened: 'Sorry about the blot. And I keep telling the boys – mind the ink bottle, and I'm having my hair bobbed. The boys will be wearing their new suits. You won't recognise us...'

'Super ship, *Britannic*. Not even Hank Morgan could invent diesel engines.'

'We'll see the engines. And Dad's cabin...'

'And the ship's wireless.'

'And swimming pool.' Arthur raised his voice with excitement: 'And the ship's orchestra!' He placed his fists to his mouth to make a trumpet, and out aloud toot-tooted – it was 'Rule Britannia' again, this time the opening bars.

'Ssh...'

But Mam did not hear: '...and with this new ship the crowd to meet you on the Princes Landing Stage will be like Armistice Day, *and we three will be there*. Goodnight Cariad.'

After the trumpet outburst, I quickly got up, tiptoed in my bare feet across the cold linoleum and quietly shut the bedroom door. As I snuggled back under the warm bedclothes, deep into the feather bed: 'We've got to go to church tomorrow.'

'Ugh!'

We turned over to sleep, tired out by our over-excitement. Arthur yawned: 'Wake me when that ship comes in.'

'Arthur. Take your cod liver oil before you go to church.'

Mam was busy at the sewing machine. Climbing trees

or other play often led to ripped trousers which had to be patched. We were changed into our best suits ready for church.

Arthur watched the whirring and ticking sewing machine intently. 'It's a Singer!' And immediately sang down the scale in tonic sol-fa: 'Soh fah me ray doh...' Then up the scale, attempting some words: 'Stitch in time saves nine...' We learnt tonic sol-fa at school, but at home music was in staff notation; we didn't have lessons, music copies were just all around. But now it was Mr Hayes' tonic sol-fa, and somehow Arthur's singing voice transformed the whirr of the sewing machine into an accompanying musical instrument. In the beginning was the word... (and the word was Welsh), but for Arthur, in the beginning too was the song, the voice modulating the word. Or, as Mam put it, he could sing before he could talk and walk. Not that any notation could possibly tell a singer to sing the way Arthur sang. There was no possible means of showing, with notes on a stave, that it could be sung like that – it came, intimately, from his heart and voice. No con amore, dolce, vivace, on the music score – no mere words in print – could indicate how. His voice and the notes he sang were so clear you could almost touch them. His song lingered on after he ceased singing, like when you pluck the harp, the strings play on: your hand has left the strings, yet the notes haunt the ear, inwardly – the tune now in the minor key, poignant, unchanging, perpetual; seemingly unending; then dying away... leaving a moment of stillness, before the jolt back to the day's routine.

'Arthur,' repeated Mam, 'take your cod liver oil before you go to church.'

But he ignored her. He had now taken his money box down from the mantelpiece. He was shaking it, turning it this way and that. Perhaps he was getting out a penny and a ha'penny to buy a stamp for his letter to Dad, to get that leather-case football.

A few days previously an unusual photo had arrived. It came from a college in Nova Scotia where Dad had been singing. It was a snap of a football team, with goalpost and college buildings in the background. And there was Dad in makeshift football kit, standing in the back row of the group, about to play with the students in an informal football match. It had been sent – this was some months after Dad's visit there – by one of the students direct to us. So Dad hadn't seen it. Arthur looked at that snap hard and long before propping it up on the mantel. The player sitting cross-legged in the centre, front row, was holding the ball. Yes, a leather-case ball!

Recently too I had hinted that having a leather-case ball would strengthen his plea to Mam to allow boys to come up our fields to play a football match, reminding him he could be Dixie Dean. (The real Dixie Dean scored eighty-two goals in one season!) But now I said nothing, for Mam's attempts to get him to write had become one long, constant nagging, nagging, week in week out, without effect. In any case, far from getting out a penny-ha'penny to buy a stamp, he was concentrating on the shillings compartment of his money box, peering into it and trying to extract a coin by pushing back the spring catch over the slot with his fingernail.

'What are you doing with your money box?' Then Mam said, with satisfaction, 'Oh, church collection of course'.

'Hank Morgan,' I said, 'when he was a boy, saved his

pennies and gave buttons to the missionary.'

'Then he was a bad boy,' she quickly retorted.

'And in Camelot he made coins with King Arthur on one side and Queen Guinevere on the other. Cents, nickels, dimes...'

'A dime; ten cents,' said Arthur. He was intrigued by the fact that it was like 'dimé', the colloquial Welsh for halfpenny, though pronounced differently. 'Wonder if Hank Morgan knew that... and they had quarters in Camelot,' he said, still shaking and manipulating his money box. 'I've got a quarter...' he gave his money box a violent shake. 'In here. Where's my pocketknife?' Out came the knife from his trousers pocket; and pulling out its blade: 'I'll use this to slide it out.'

'Same size as a shilling, and worth about a shilling.'

The blade was no sooner into the slot and the right coin dropped out of the shillings compartment on to the table. 'There. A quarter. Dad gave it me. Twenty-five cents.'

'What are you going to do with it?' asked Mam, puzzled.

'It's American,' I said in support, 'no good for church collection.' It was for spending in America. When we grew up, it would be the twenty-five cents to take us up the elevator, to the top of the Empire State Building. Or ride the Subway. Or the trip by ferry to the Statue of Liberty. Or buy peanuts to feed the pigeons in Times Square. And there was Coney Island... 'No good for our church collection,' I repeated.

'You'll see.' He put the coin with his knife into his pocket. 'It's real money. Quarter: two bits.'

'I'll race you down the tunnel through the wood.'

'No,' said Arthur, a little breathless, for we had already run down our fields. We sat on the stile for a few moments to recover. 'Plenty of time for school. Let's leapfrog down.'

'No. We'll play Hide and Go Seek.'

'No! That's sissy.'

'Okay then. We'll leapfrog.' So we climbed over the stile, taking a quick look at our still-unfinished carved initials on the sycamore tree above it. Our leapfrogging took us halfway down the tunnel till we were completely out of breath.

'I'm going to peg out.' Arthur collapsed on to a grass bank, sprawling himself out.

A bird sang close by: a cheerful, sweet, warbling song.

'Listen! I heard that bird before.' It was like the bluebird I read about. 'It's your bird: "I Sing as the Songbird is Singing". Listen.'

He sat up. 'Yes.' For a few moments he listened. Then, looking around: 'There's our secret path: the Indian trail.' Jumping to his feet, he made his Red Indian war cry.

'Yes. The Redpath.'

'Where we picked nuts and saw the shoot.'

'Yes.'

We pushed through the undergrowth, determined to go beyond the small clearing where, that autumn, we had gathered nuts and had been caught up an oak tree while the shoot was nearby. The narrow, overgrown path turned and twisted, downhill. At a steep bit, Arthur got down on all fours. Suddenly, the ground levelled out at the lower edge of the wood.

I was leading. 'We've come to the marsh. Hm. Dead end.' The path seemed to stop abruptly at the water's edge. We heard a gentle splash of water and a waterhen's call, and looked up to see a pair of them swimming rapidly away from us.

'There's the railway!' But a stretch of marsh water, bulrushes and boggy ground lay between us and a black railway gate used for animals crossing the line. Beside it was a smaller gate to which our own 'secret path' led. It had obviously once been a well-used path, and from this railway gate it would be possible to get to the Sion Chapel and on to Pontybodkin. But a barrier now lay immediately ahead.

'We've got to cross the marsh. Follow me. We'll try going by those bulrushes.'

We inched our way, testing for solid ground as each foot went forward. Suddenly there was a big splash behind me; Arthur's foot was in the water up to his ankle. He moaned; and momentarily stood on one foot, not knowing where to step next.

'Come on.'

'The water's deep.' But he eventually caught up with me. We reached firmer ground.

'We'll sit on that railway gate and watch the one o'clock train.'

'Good idea.'

'And then if we run we'll get to school on time.' We clambered up and sat on the top bar with our legs dangling down, looking at the shiny rails of the Mold-to-Brymbo branch line, the track curving with the marsh on either side. 'We'll see her come round the curve.'

'Doing sixty miles an hour.'

A railwayman was standing by the cast-iron railway notice, a little distance away on the other side of the track.

He had his back to us and didn't appear to be aware of our presence. Wearing a white apron over his railway uniform, he was painting a 'Warning' notice, black lettering on white. 'What does it say?' Arthur subdued his voice so that the man wouldn't hear us.

I tried to read it: '"Warning... Purs... uant to..."' It was difficult from a distance. '"... and in accord... ance with... not... with... standing any... thing contained here... in... to the contrary..."' I gave up. 'Can't understand railway English.'

'Ha,' said Arthur teasingly. 'You can't read.'

'It's in Welsh too.' This was clarity itself; plain Old Testament '"Na wna...":' Thou shall not... trespass on this line.'

'We're not trespassing on the line,' said Arthur, all innocence.

'Ha ha. Forgive us our trespasses.' (It should have been 'Forgive us our trousers': we had sat on a small streak of wet tar on the top bar of that five-barred gate; but when we were home later, Mam didn't notice.)

'We're not trespassing on the line,' insisted Arthur. 'We're only... looking at it.'

'That's right. If we trespassed, we'd cop it. Go to jail.'

'Sent up the river.'

'Yes. To Sing Sing. And we'd have to pay a big fine.'

'I could pay the fine,' boasted Arthur. Then remembering the signwriter and subduing his voice: 'I got piles of dough. I'm a millionaire.'

'You ain't got no money.'

'I have, I have...'

'Say bud, are you kidding?'

'I have, I have...' he chuckled.

'Show me. I come from Missoura kid, show me.'

'Okay.' His two hands came out of his trousers pockets and he held out his fists: 'Which one's got the money?'

'That one.' A light slap on one fist. 'Show me the do-re-mi.'

'Dead right.' He laughed: 'Pop bottle top'.

'Oh Geez!'

Arthur looked thoughtfully at his bottle top and fingered its jagged rim. 'If I put it on the rail, the train would run over it, flatten it out, and make it flat as a penny.'

'For church collection.'

'Yes.' Then after reflection he added: 'But I got real money. Guess again.'

I slapped the other fist.

'Dead right again. A quarter. Two bits.' And began chanting: 'Two bits, four bits...'

'...six bits, a dollar' – I joined in.

'Four of these, and I'd treat you to a dollar dinner, with steak.'

'Bah. It's a dud. Let me look.' He handed it to me.

'Mm... looks genuine.'

'Course it is.' Then I looked again at the coin: 'George Washington. The first President. Called "Father of his Country".'

Arthur started humming the Welsh National Anthem.

'Ssh...'

'Well, "Father of his Country": "Land of my Fathers". See?'

'He'll hear you,' I said under my breath, nodding towards the signwriter. Then watching him at work with his paintbrush: 'Bet he can't sing.'

'Yes he can,' said Arthur in a high-pitched, chirpy, excited voice. 'Everyone's got a voice, so everyone can sing. Bet he's in the Coedllai Male Voice Choir.'

I turned the coin over. 'An eagle. Look.'

'Yes. Great.'

'"United States of America. Quarter dollar."' I gave Arthur a poke on the shoulder with my forefinger: 'It's the one you didn't put in the collection.'

'I'm going to put it on the rail.'

'You're not!'

'Yep. Flatten it out into a super oval shape.'

'But... but... you can't! It's worth a shilling; would buy a penn'orth of monkey nuts twelve times over; or mint imperials. It's... it's no chicken feed!'

'No... it's peanuts,' said Arthur with a laugh. But remembering the signwriter, he stifled his laugh with both hands to the mouth, almost losing his balance on top of the gate.

'But... but... it's worth a shilling!'

'You put the pop bottle top.'

'Mm?' I hesitated. 'No.'

'Don't chicken out.' Then, more persuasively: 'Lovely oval shape. Think about it.'

'Er... but I've got a penny.'

'That'll do.'

My hand delved into my trousers pocket. Slowly, out came the penny. I examined it carefully. The king. George the Fifth... with his neat, trim beard. Britannia on the other side. Strange how you don't notice details on coins you handle every day. '"*Dei Gra Britt Omn Rex...*"': don't know what it means. It's Latin. What they speak in Buckingham Palace. Funny, we can read the American one, but not ours.'

'But wait till Hank Morgan's been to work on it. Let me see.' He tried: '"*Fid... Fid...*"' I finished it for him: '"... *Def Ind Imp*".'

'Deaf imp – that's him,' he said, looking at the king's head. 'He won't hear the train. Come on.' He jumped off the gate. 'Let's put them on the rail.'

'Okay.' Still reluctant, I followed. At least Arthur wasn't flattening a silver dollar or a five-dollar gold piece like those Dad had shown us.

In a jiffy, the two coins lay side by side on the smooth surface of the rail, and we were back on the gate. He didn't see us. We spoke in undertones.

The signwriter was still concentrating on his task, a painstakingly slow job – he would need a very long time to paint all that railway English in tiny letters. Impatiently we leaned forward, looking in the Brymbo direction, but the curve of the line and the hedge beside the track prevented us seeing more than a few yards.

'Train's late.'

'No. Never late. It'll be by the Pant-y-Stên Level Crossing any time now.' This was a mile away, near Wmphre the Gamekeeper's cottage and Offa's Dyke, where the line entered the marsh.

Restlessly, Arthur looked about him. Turning towards the marshy ground behind: 'Let's pick marsh marigolds for Mam sometime, on our way from school. And go home up our secret path.'

I began humming softly the opening bars of 'Dawn of Love'.

That set Arthur off in full voice:

'I'm living o'er...'

'Ssh... He'll hear you.'

He began again, sotto voce, barely audible:

'I'm living o'er the mem'ries
Of my childhood days now gone...'

He stopped. 'No.' Grinning, and jabbing a finger towards the coins on the rail:

'I'm looking o'er the two bits
I am putting on the line
To change into an oval shape
Which is beautiful and fine...'

We laughed quietly.

'I betcha my coin'll be a better oval shape than yours.' Then he said after a pause: 'Aren't the rails smooth and shiny.'

'Yes. Four trains a day.' The one-coach passenger train to Brymbo had four miles of track – through the marsh, over a viaduct, curving through steep-sided cuttings deep in the rock, over high embankments, and entering Brymbo over a high bridge by Brymbo Parish Church with its peal of bells. It returned thirty-five minutes later: the steam locomotive's tender first.

Arthur was becoming very impatient. 'I'm going to put my ear down on the rail to listen. Tell if she's coming...' He jumped off the gate, landing on the ground with a thud, and tripped lightly towards the track.

'No!' Belatedly, I realised the danger. 'She'll come suddenly round the curve.' But he took no notice. 'Come off the track,' I yelled.

He crouched down on the ballast stones beside the rail. 'She ain't left Brymbo yet. I'll put my ear down...'

I could swear I heard the faint whistle of the distant train. 'Arthur!' I called sharply. 'Come off...'

'I'll be able to tell if she's reached the level crossing.'

'You can't hear that far. Even if you press your ear hard to the rail. It's a mile away. Anyway, she might come ahead of time. And come round the bend like crazy. Get off the track!'

He pressed his ear close. 'She's leaving the Brymbo Depot now.' He was completely unconcerned with the danger: Brymbo was out on the prairie or some place, and we were on the railroad track by the marsh called Lake Michigan.

I clearly heard the train whistle and the distant rumble of the train wheels. 'Arthur, come off the rail!'

'She's by Pant-y-Stên now.'

The pounding wheels of the train approached with a continuous deafening screech of the whistle. 'Arthur! Get off the rail!'

He suddenly darted away from the track. The rail vibrated and sagged as the powerful wheels passed over. The rush of air nearly unseated me off the gate. 'Phew!' said Arthur. And as he leapt back on to the gate, breathless: 'I'm with you brother!'

The train receded into the distance. We looked at each other. Quietly and hesitantly, we climbed down. We paused to look at the signwriter, still painting with his back to us. We walked gingerly with quiet footsteps towards the track. The ballast stones made it difficult. We paced up and down, a few steps at a time, searching, for the coins had jumped off the rail.

'Found mine.' My penny was near the rail, leaning against a wooden sleeper. 'Look. Perfect oval shape. George the Fifth squashed out with a long nose.' And the back of his head stuck out, like Mam's hair in a bun. 'Perfect oval shape.'

'Mm? It's poifect. Poifect.'

'Where's your two bits?'

'Can't find it.' He continued his search, now and again crouching down to take a close look in among the ballast stones. I looked thoroughly on the inner side of the rail, but to no avail. 'We've got to go.'

'Can't find it.' He was becoming tearful.

We searched in vain.

'Come on. We'll be late for school.'

'Can't find it.' He paced up and down in despair. Tears were running down his cheeks. He kneeled on the wooden sleeper near where we had placed the coins, and tried to look under the rail itself.

'It's late,' I said, moving away. 'Come on.'

'I can't find it.' He was heartbroken.

'Come on. We've got to run.'

'I can't find it...' he said again through his tears as I sped away. 'I can't find it...'

The classroom was a hum of children reading quietly, with Mr Hayes sitting at his desk. It was Silent Reading.

Suddenly the hum stopped and everyone looked up towards the door. The brass doorknob turned slowly once again. The door opened, a few inches. In squeezed Arthur, shutting the door gently. We sat in silence, again watching him make the noisy journey across the wooden floor towards Mr Hayes' desk.

'Why are you late?' Mr Hayes was sharp.

'Lost some money sir.'

Subdued titters from the class; they stopped abruptly when Mr Hayes opened his desk and brought out the cane.

'Hold your hand out.'

The cane swished three times as it came down on the palm of the hand; Arthur winced; involuntary gasps came from the class.

He walked to his place, while the hum of children reading quietly resumed. Pressing his hand to his chest, he gently rubbed the palm against his jersey, and then held it awkwardly with fingers curled in; then with hand close to mouth, blew gently into the palm. He opened his book with the other hand.

'Right,' said Mr Hayes at the end of the lesson. 'Close your books.' Our books were collected and put away in the cupboard. 'Look up.' We sat attentively.

Mr Hayes announced that the electric light was to be installed in the school. Those children living in some of the houses well below the railway station had it already, and on the great day they had been allowed to go home early to see the electric come on. Next day they had pronounced it 'Champion!' And: 'It hurts your eyes at first and you don't need matches to light it.' 'Like daylight,' said another. Perhaps it would be like what Hank Morgan put in Camelot. Or like the Broadway electric light signs, the white, green and red making a jumble and bursting like a bubble. The school, said Mr Hayes, would be wired in the holidays, in time for the school concert. Arthur would sing under the electric light. Another surprise for Dad.

Then, when we stood ready to go out to play, Mr Hayes said: 'This afternoon Miss Robinson, our student teacher, will take you on a nature walk.'

'Oh...' whispers of joy from the class.

'Arthur,' added Mr Hayes sharply. 'Stay in playtime...' he paused and mellowing his tone somewhat added: '...to practise your solo for the school concert.'

At playtime everyone in the yard was excited at the prospect of a nature walk. I loitered in the cloakroom. Standing with my ear to the door, I heard Mr Hayes at the piano and Arthur singing, his voice soaring on the high notes.

We were supposedly lined up in order, ready to depart, but the loud chatter was something Mr Hayes would not have tolerated.

'Please miss...' his voice raised, Arthur was trying to make himself heard. Then more to himself. 'Oh gee....' He mustered enough voice to be heard above the noise: 'Please Miss Robinson Redbreast...'

The din continued.

'Well, children...' Miss Robinson had too weak and hesitant a voice for the job in hand. She had an English accent. 'Well, children... do come along.'

The rabble moved off, out through the school gate and up towards the wood. It was early spring. Those of us walking near enough to our student teacher heard through the chatter the instruction to note the signs: the flowers opening, the leaf buds, the birds building their nests...

Arthur and I were at the front of the line, and unconsciously our footsteps led the column up the tunnel in the wood.

'We gonna see our own farm,' I said to Arthur. 'Well, well...'

We reached the stile, our student teacher walking near us and not quite leading. Eventually we climbed our fields and came round to the back of the house.

'This field is Cae Cefn,' said Arthur, with a loud voice, addressing his audience. 'Square, miss. Six sides. Wanna see elk, moose, prairie dog? Some prairie, huh?'

The cow was in Cae Cefn. As our noise approached she raised her head and, displeased at being disturbed in her grazing, hurriedly walked away with a loud, long moo.

'That's a buffalo.' And turning and raising his voice to the following crowd: 'Am goin' to ride him in the rodeo at the state fair. Giddy-up. Giddy-up. Oh, no good. He's a Tennessee walking horse.'

'Bringing all those children!' Perhaps we'd been too optimistic – or just didn't give it a thought – in thinking Mam would not notice a whole class of children walking all over our fields. Nor did announcing that the electric was coming to the school divert her: 'I hope you didn't trample through the hayfields.'

'Oh no!'

'That's not the way to get a good crop of hay.'

'Oh no.'

'We have very little left in the hayloft. And it's three or four months till the next crop.'

That would be in the summer: haytime, when Price from Tir-Paenau on Hope Mountain would come again to mow. We would be turning the hay with pitchforks, gathering it into haycocks, loading it on to Price Tir-Paenau's haycart, filling the hayloft and building a haystack in the stackyard by the gate into Cae Cefn. And, like previous years, with Price's two horses Bess and Punch pulling us up the slope, riding high on top of the last hay load home. There would be just one sad moment: when the mowing machine would go too close to the hedge and we would see some of the hedgerow flowers cut down.

Mam was worried about this next crop. 'We'll have to keep the cow out of the hayfields soon, or this year's crop will be a poor one. Mustn't have people trampling.' Her mind was on that rabble of children; she did not mention the student teacher; it wouldn't have been surprising if she hadn't noticed her.

'We kept to the path, all the way back to school down through the wood.'

And Arthur: 'We didn't even show them our secret path.'

'Oh? Where's that?'

'It's where the men came to shoot pheasants,' said Arthur.

'Oh...?' Mam was suspicious.

'Where...' agitated, I was trying to allay her suspicions. 'Where we picked nuts,' I said hastily.

'Yes, that's right,' said Arthur, coolly. 'Where we picked nuts.'

'You keep out of the wood.' She was thinking of the dangerous old mine workings deep in the wood. 'If you want to play, bring children here.'

Perhaps Mam had said this without sufficient thought, for Arthur immediately seized on it. 'Yes!' His eyes lit up. 'We could have our football match.'

'On Cae Cefn.' Trampling Cae Cefn didn't matter; it was the all-purpose hen run with washing line, where we played most of the time. 'Football match on Cae Cefn.'

'Gee. Great! Great!' At last our Wembley Cup Final football match, that Arthur and the boys at school had planned and talked about for so long. Then Arthur, with a change of mood: 'But I haven't a proper football, a real leather-case ball...' He was resentful.

And Mam, for the umpteenth time: 'Why don't you write to Dad to ask for one?'

'Ugh.' He sulked. 'Don't want to.'

'You've still got time before he sails home – if you do it straight away.'

'Yes, why don't you?'

'Ugh.'

'Well, you write, and you can have your football match.' Mam, it seemed, was prepared to tolerate the lesser evil of a horde of boys trampling over our fields – even risking the hayfields – if it could be used as a bait to get Arthur to pick up his pen. 'Write, and there'll be a football match.' She sounded quite firm. And to clinch the issue: 'That rubber ball will do till you get a real one.'

'I want a leather football. Right now.'

He sat at the living-room table, quietly sulking, with his arm on the table and his head resting on it. He sat there for fully half an hour. I suspected that the message was finally sinking in.

Meanwhile I was in the rocking chair, reading, and Mam busy in the back kitchen. She came in and, at a stroke, swept away the sulks and the reading: 'Get out of doors. It's a lovely spring day.'

When I opened the front door we could hear the birds singing. Calling from the door: 'Tell you what, let's show Mam our secret path.'

'Mm?' Arthur was now at the window, propping up his chin, his nose pressing against the pane. He turned to me, his enthusiasm lighting up his face. 'Yes! Let's!'

'Come on then,' said Mam, carried away, and completely forgetting her repeated warnings to keep out of the wood. Still, going with her was different.

Taking a route other than our usual – across Cae Cefn, down the slope, passing the well, the spring bubbling with the water glistening in the sun and looking magical – we were down the fields in no time, showing her a particular hedgerow where later in the year we would be picking wild strawberries. We showed her our 'horse'. Of course we had no horse on our farm and our stable had been empty since Grandfather's day; in her childhood, reminisced Mam, there was always a pony and trap. But our 'horse' was a young oak in this same hedgerow. When a sapling it had been bent so that now its young trunk had grown into a shape that was easy to ride horseback as we ate our wild strawberries.

We walked through the bracken near the edge of the wood. A rabbit was sunning itself. Then through the bluebells. 'Ooh,' said Arthur, running ahead, 'let's pick some to send to Dad.'

'But... they'd be dead...'

'Oh Arthur,' said Mam as we caught up with him. 'Your tie. Look how you've screwed it up. Come here.'

Spring was in the air. Besides the bluebells, there were

the wood anemones with their nodding white flowers, making a carpet in the wood. Primroses, especially on the grass banks along the wood's lower edge, would soon be out in profusion, and Arthur would pick a bunch for Mam on the way home from school. We would see the occasional hare darting along the edge of one of our fields. Or a hedgehog would slowly cross the path near the stile. Warblers, tits, thrushes, and the owl at night. And high in the sky, ravens and buzzards. Sometimes a spotted woodpecker. And in the wood itself, the oaks, the ash, beech and hazel; the sun making patterns between the trees. After a windy day, we would gather firewood. The days were lengthening, it was spring, and we were on the way to show Mam our secret path...

Down the tunnel. 'This way,' said Arthur when we reached the gap leading off into the heart of the wood. He was ahead, with Mam bringing up the rear. Then, as he stopped to trample down some undergrowth: 'You don't know our secret path.'

'And it's a short cut too. Down to the railway.' We carefully avoided mention of putting coins on the rail.

We pushed forward, brushing through the undergrowth with twigs snapping; down the winding path, bypassing the small clearing where we had once gathered nuts. We helped Mam at the very steep bit.

'Oh,' she said, stopping. 'I haven't been this way for years. Hasn't it got overgrown.'

'What? You... you know about this path?'

'Yes.'

'Oh! We thought it was our secret path! And you knew all along.' We couldn't hide our disappointment: denied the joy of revealing our secret.

'We used to come home this way, Dad and me. In the summertime. From rehearsals with the Glee Singers.'

'Oh, we thought...' began Arthur, feeling let down.

'It was somewhere along here we... well; Dad asked me to marry him.'

We were hardly listening, so full of disappointment: 'You've known this path all along.'

'We thought it was our secret path.'

'It was our secret path too,' said Mam, taking Arthur's hand for him to lead her forward. And as we pushed on downwards: 'It was somewhere along here we... we first thought of you.'

'Before we were born.' Arthur looked puzzled: 'But how did you know I was going to be born before I was born?'

I stopped to tie my bootlace.

'How did you know I was going to be born...' repeated Arthur as he and Mam moved on ahead, now out of sight beyond a sharp bend where the path rounded an oak tree.

We reached the lower edge of the wood and the marsh. The water lapped gently, and waterhens swam about, slow and contented.

'Let's have a picnic sometime, American style.'

Chuckling, Mam said, 'It would be nice, but...'

'By the marsh. Like Chicago – a picnic on the beach on Lake Michigan.'

'...but there's never any time...'

'Well... we'll come anyway. Make it July 4th... and Mam, you bring the kids dressed in Sunday shirts.'

'And I'll win all the races,' said Arthur.

Reluctantly Mam had to spoil our flights of imagination: 'Really, this is no place for a picnic. It's getting late. We'd better hurry back.'

191

On our way up, we promised to show her our other secret: on the sycamore tree. She sat on the stile to rest.

'Look. Up there.' We showed her our initials carved on the tree, done with the pocketknives from *Adriatic*.

'And your initials.'

'And we're going to finish them,' insisted Arthur, 'by the time Dad gets home.'

'Well. Fancy, you didn't tell me about it.' And turning to Arthur: 'You'll have to tell Dad – write to him...'

'No, no, a secret,' said Arthur quickly and evasively, 'to show Dad when he gets home.' We explained that they had to be finished in time, and we wanted to work on them there and then.

But Mam insisted it was late. 'Both of you: bring the cow. I'll go and get tea ready. Put her in her stall; give her bran. And go easy with the hay.' She went on ahead, leaving us to round up the cow. And calling from a little distance up the path: 'Arthur, get some Indian corn to feed the hens.'

I took the cow into her stall and tethered her.

Arthur went in at the barn door and straight up into the hayloft where he could pitchfork hay down to the cow. He was singing his own version of The Lord's Prayer: Our Father, which art in the hayloft... bum, bum, bum, bumbiddi bumbiddi bum-bum... He called down: 'How much d'you want?'

'Send down plenty.' The cow raised her head and jangled the chain round her neck. Swoosh! Down came a pitchfork of hay straight in front of her.

'There,' I said, as she gave an appreciative, quiet moo. I patted her on the back. Then calling up to Arthur: 'A bit more.'

I could hear his footsteps on the hay. Up there the swallows were twittering. They were back. The great-grandfather who had built Pen-y-Wern had thoughtfully put round holes in the hayloft shutters, big enough for these insect-eating birds to enter, build their cup-shaped nests in the rafters, rear their young, and keep down the insects.

'A bit more,' I called again.

'Okay. Coming down.'

And down came another pitchforkful.

'Ah, that's plenty for you.' I gave the cow another pat.

'Awh!' It was Arthur. He hurried down, his boots heavy on the wooden steps, and came round to the cow's stall. 'Bird droppings straight in my eye.' He gave his half-shut eye a wipe with his sleeve. And said to the cow, who was a little disturbed by his rushing in: 'How'd you like bird droppings in your eye, you old moo-cow? Going to watch our football match? Be the referee?'

'We don't know if we're having one yet.' I was trying to be tactful, to ease his realisation that the letter had to be written. 'You've got to write to Dad first.'

'Sez you.'

'Look,' I confided. 'I've put my oval-shaped penny up on the ledge...' I pointed to the ledge above the cow's head. He climbed on to my shoulders to have another look at it. 'And when we find your two bits, we'll put it there too.'

'Yes,' he said in an excited undertone, as if planning when our next search on the railway track would be. 'Yes. Great. Great.'

'Arthur, it's time you fed the hens.'

'Okay,' he said cheerfully, and out he went.

Broody hens would soon be sat on their clutches. Fluffy little chicks would hatch out three weeks later, the broods venturing onto Cae Cefn following the mother hens. And Arthur would have to feed the chicks four times a day on stale bread crumbs broken up fine and mixed with finely chopped up hard-boiled eggs.

'Alun...' Mam took me into her confidence as soon as Arthur was out of the door: 'If you write to Dad now, perhaps he will. There's still time.'

'Yes.'

'Encourage him. It worked to get him to read.'

'Yes.' I put the writing pad and inkstand on the table.

Arthur breezed in a few minutes later. 'Rhode Island Red missing again.' Only recently we had seen her cluck-clucking the loudest and leading the flock away to the far end of Cae Cefn. Mam had to shoo them back towards the henhouse. Another time, her dark reddish-brown feathers were all ruffled, as if she'd been somewhere she shouldn't have. Grubbing and pecking where she wished, and the others following, she knew where to find the best worms. And if the cockerel was leading the flock, digging up the worms for the hens, Little Rhody was sure to be the first to come running up. You never saw her laying eggs in the henhouse like the others. Or hatching out a brood of chicks. 'Little Rhody' – Arthur was a bit depressed – 'She'll turn up.'

After a pause, in which his gaze studiously avoided the writing pad: 'Mam. When shall we have our football match?'

'When you write,' she said tersely.

'"Dear Dad..."' I began my letter. We agreed to keep as a surprise the coming of the electric light to the school in time for the school concert. (But the electric would never come to our remote farm, thought Mam. Yet in America, they had electric machines to wash dishes, sweep the carpet and milk the cows.) As I wrote, I repeatedly glanced towards Arthur out of the corner of my eye to see if there was any response. '"We showed Mam the secret path... the one where you thought about me... before I was born..."'

'Put "How did you know I was going to be born before I was born?"'

'Hm, you write it. Anyway, you're only eight and I'm a year older than you, and we didn't know each other then because you weren't born. You write it.'

He came and sat in a chair beside me at the table. I pushed the inkstand to be within his reach in case he picked up a pen. But he made no move. So I continued writing, quietly. Then, breaking off: 'Did you know, when Will Rogers was born in the Indian Territory, a doctor would bring you into the world for two dollars a visit?'

'Well,' said Arthur thoughtfully, 'put "Did you send for the doctor?"'

'I've put that.' And continuing the letter: '"...and did you get a birth certificate to say I was coming?"'

'What's a "birth certificate"?'

'Well, it's... it's like a school attendance certificate, to say you didn't miss coming.'

Mam added: 'Or a Band of Hope Certificate, to say you're home and dry.'

'Oh,' said Arthur. Then, to me: 'You came first.'

'Yes,' said Mam, 'with a book and a pen in your hand.'
Arthur laughed.

'And you,' she said to him, 'you were born singing.'

'Like a ship's fog horn,' I said, suppressing a laugh.

'No. I was born with a twenty-five-cent cigar.'

'You weren't.'

'I was. To make smoke signals.' He gave a piercingly loud Red Indian war cry.

'Oh stop it,' said Mam sharply, quite put out by the shrill, penetrating noise. Then turning to me: 'And don't you ask for a football for him. He's got to write.'

'Bah...' Arthur was defiant.

'Since Dad's been away,' said Mam with mounting anger, 'you haven't written once.' And she reminded him of some of the presents Dad had sent: a Red Indian peace pipe made of red stone 'catlinite', after a visit to an Indian Reservation; a jacket each, American style, with four pockets and a zipper (a great novelty, this) down the front; small specimens of gold ore from a gold mine in the Rocky Mountains... the list was endless if we included those that came out of his suitcase each time he arrived home. Then there were the balsa wood model aeroplanes with elastic to drive the propellers, posted from Philadelphia ('Philly': 'City of Brotherly Love'). We had raced them across Cae Cefn until Arthur's crashed into the clothes line. They were not biplanes like Imperial Airways' Heracles, but monoplanes like the one in the snapshot of Will Rogers standing with his fellow Oklahoman, the aviator Wiley Post. (Later, Wiley Post was to fly his monoplane round the world.) And other snapshots were of Dad under a palm tree in St Petersburg (Florida), fishing with rod and line in Newfoundland, having an American picnic, standing beside a Ford Model A with its Illinois number plate.... They were arranged on the mantelpiece, behind the model of the Empire State Building and the money boxes, and propped against the big mirror. They were only removed (into an old biscuit tin) to make room for the latest to arrive. Picture postcards: they came all the time, each with Dad's message on the back. And Arthur thought of nothing but football – and he hadn't written to Dad once. Not once.

'Arthur,' I said, trying to be conciliatory, 'if we had a football match, we could ask Jack to come and be the referee.'

He was sulking now: 'Haven't got a proper ball.'

'It's football, football, football all the time!' said Mam in a rage.

She recovered enough to say, persuasively, that Jack would bring more cigarette cards for him. But to no effect.

After considerable sulks and silence, I said, 'Come on, don't dilly-dally.'

He turned on me: 'Oh gee, button up your lip.'

This made Mam lay down the law one more time: 'You can have your football match on Cae Cefn if you write to Dad.'

I pushed the writing pad in front of him. 'Come on. You gotta write a letter.'

'Oh shucks,' he snarled.

'Get on with it.'

'Drop dead, bighead; your head's as big as Birkenhead.' Then really bad tempered: 'Drop dead, you...'

'Now then,' said Mam. 'Don't talk like that.' We were making no headway. Just the reverse.

'You... you goddam son-of-a-bitch...'

'Arthur!' Mam was shocked. 'Who d'you think you

are?' It was hard to say whether he was being serious or play-acting: 'You're the lowest man on the totem pole.'

'Humph, bet you can't write at all.' I took the writing pad away.

'You don't know nothin'. Smart ass. You wanna get wised up.'

'Hm. You've got the screaming meemies.'

'Oh Gawd Almighty... You're a screwball...'

'Arthur, how dare you...' Mam tried to restrain him.

'...Quit you, doggone you. I'll smash you to smithereens...'

'Arthur!'

'You bloody...'

'Oh shut your mouth,' I said.

'Gurche, you couldn't sing... you're not even good enough to sing in a honky-tonk.'

'You're trying to cop out.' I was riled. 'I'll hold your hand to write it.'

'You... schmuck...'

'Stop it, stop it, both of you!' burst out Mam in a mixture of anger and tears. 'Quarrelling like this and Dad coming home. What would Dad say? Oh...' she sighed heavily, and collapsed into the rocking chair, distraught.

We both fell into silence. I fingered through the pages of the writing pad, uneasy in the tense atmosphere. Arthur sat, slumped in his chair, motionless and glum.

At last said Mam: 'Let's have the record on,' and got up to walk to the gramophone. Then, before even touching it: 'Alun. Show me again.'

I walked over, and demonstrated: winding, the speed regulator on 78, switching on the turntable, putting the needle in the groove... then stood back to let her do it.

'No, I can't,' she insisted, just as she had insisted before. 'I'll always let you do it.'

The record began:

I'm living o'er the mem'ries...

'Oh, thank goodness we've still got Dad.' She heaved a sigh of relief.

By now Arthur had quietly walked over to watch the gramophone record spinning round. He surreptitiously placed his finger against the speed regulator, making the record go round at slightly too fast a speed. The singing voice slurred up to sing faster at a higher pitch.

'Arthur! Don't...'

'The talking man on the talking machine – he's running.' Arthur was back to his normal self.

'Oh, oh, there's something wrong.' Mam with her poor eyesight had not noticed. And, agitated: 'What do we do? What do we do?'

I put the speed back on 78: 'There. Like that.' The singing voice reverted to normal.

'I don't understand it.' She was unhappy with anything mechanical.

'Easy.'

'I'll always leave you to put it on.'

'It's easy.'

'No. I won't touch it.' She was adamant. 'No, I'll never be able to do the gramophone on my own. I'll always let you do it for me.'

The song drew to a close.

The final note, that top G, had hardly finished when Arthur and I broke out clapping.

'What's the clap for?' asked Mam, happily.

'Encore. The greatest tenor in the world.'

'No,' said Arthur. 'The greatest... on earth!'

'Well,' said Mam, smiling and now completely at ease, 'put the record on again then.'

V
Grief

A parcel arrived with a New York postmark.

'Football for me, I bet.'

Well, the parcel was just about big enough – shoebox size. The ball would not be inflated of course. It would be like the one we saw displayed in its box in a sports-shop window in Wrexham, complete with pump. Mam took off the outer cover. Inside were two smaller parcels wrapped in brightly decorated paper. No football obviously. Unwrapping the first revealed a book: *Pocket Dictionary of American Words*. 'You know American words already the way you go on,' said Mam, handing it to me.

Arthur waited for the other to be unwrapped, his impatience already turned to disappointment.

'A writing case. For Arthur. Oh, lovely. Look: a caribou-skin writing case.' Opening the two press studs revealed writing paper, envelopes, an array of pens, a small ruler and a packet of pen nibs.

'You could write a really good letter to Dad,' I said, cautiously.

He was silent.

I tried to catch his reaction but there was no hint. 'And you could use words out of my new little dictionary: American words. Let's see now...' I flicked through the pages and, as usual with a new book, looked at some of the last pages first. '"Whiz kid." Say kid, you're a whiz kid.'

'Huh,' he said with a contemptuous glance towards the book, 'that's not much cop.'

I persevered, turning over the pages, trying to find words that would capture his interest: *showboat* (show-off), *shyster* (shifty person), *slowpoke* (slowcoach)... we knew some, like *smart ass* and *stumblebum*. I turned over page after page – words, words, words: what is more fascinating than a dictionary? And the same words with different meanings in different countries: *vest* (waistcoat); *suspenders* (braces); *undershirt* (vest).... It would be fun making up sayings: You wear your vest over your braces! Or your suspenders over your vest! Two languages: well, not quite. I was temporarily lost, forgetting I was trying to get Arthur interested.

So I set about making up things to say, using nothing but American words, to try out on him. 'You're a bum (tramp).'

There was a glimmer of interest.

'You're a booby, so I'll put you in a booby hatch (asylum).' No. That was a bad choice. 'Want a popsickle (lollipop)?'

'Yeah, sure.'

He came over and sat beside me at the table, trying not to show he was looking at the new dictionary.

'"Cute." You're cute. Clever guy. Want... to read some? "Guess." I guess... I guess you're a cute whiz kid. Huh?

How about writing to Dad and saying you're a cute whiz kid footballer?'

He made no move.

'Tell him you're a regular guy.'

There was a glimmer of a smile.

'Dad'll buy you a real football,' chipped in Mam, 'and bring it home with him.'

'And we could have our football match with your rubber ball straight away. As soon as your letter's posted. Then when Dad's home, another match with the new leather-case ball...'

He didn't say a word.

I strode over to the mantelpiece. The photo from the college in Nova Scotia, showing Dad about to play in a soccer football match, had stayed on the shelf for a very long time. Arthur had often taken it down to gaze at and ponder over; replacing it on the shelf in a more prominent position. I picked up the photograph. 'We could have a football match like Dad,' I said, with half an eye on him. 'With a real leather-case ball – like this one in the photo. When Dad brings it home...'

Still he made no move.

'And a football match with your rubber ball now – as soon as your letter's posted... use your new writing case...'

It lay on the table. He had hardly looked at it.

My eyes searched around the room for something else to entice him; almost in despair I chose a book from the bookshelf at random and opened its cover. It was Mam's *Messiah*, with her father's copperplate signature 'John Roberts, his book, April 8th, 1872' inside the cover; and Welsh words meticulously handwritten above the printed

English for many of the choruses. Written with a broad-edged nib, it was clear and legible, with beautiful letters correctly formed, the thick and thin strokes properly in place, yet it was handwriting of character. 'Just look, Arthur. How you could do lovely writing...'

But it was no use.

Back again to the new dictionary, rather than give up. 'Plenty of words here: look.' It was said more in desperation than anything. '"The Big Apple: New York."' Not a glimmer of interest; it seemed hopeless. In despair I turned over pages, and was about to abandon the attempt – it was past hope. But I flicked over to the letter P: '"Pantywaist",' I read, laughing.

Arthur grinned. 'Let me see.' He read the entry: '"*Pantywaist*: a sissy."' And he slapped me on the shoulder: 'That's you! A sissy!'

We laughed. Scores were even. And 'Pantywaist' had tickled our fancy.

There was a long pause.

'Gi'me pen.'

Mam quickly brought the inkstand over from the dresser to the table. 'Be careful. Don't spill it.'

He opened his new caribou-skin writing case, selected a penholder and took out a brand new nib. He dipped the pen deep into the ink bottle with such force that the ink came up the pen holder and on to his finger tips.

'Be careful.' The ink was running down the outside of the bottle. 'Put the blotting paper under it.'

'Humph.' He was reluctant to start.

'Come on,' pleaded Mam. 'You must post it today. Dad sails home on the fourteenth.'

'It'll just get there in time.'

'No hurry. No hurry. I'll send it by airship. From big Pontybodkin Head Post Office.'

'Oh come on,' said Mam, as he just sat, making a dot pattern on the blotting paper. A pause. 'Well, address the envelope first. Put: "Hotel Chelsea..."'

'But the airship goes to the mast at the top of the Empire State. I'll send it to the Empire State Building.'

'You can't. Dad doesn't stay there.'

'Come on, Arthur,' appealed Mam. 'Dad will just have time to buy your football. Let's see...' She walked over to the calendar. 'Evening of the thirteenth, before he sails on the *Britannic*, he's at Carnegie Hall...'

'That's it,' said Arthur decisively. 'I'll send it to Carnegie Hall. The Stage, Carnegie Hall...' And, turning to me: 'What's the address, bud?'

I didn't know without looking up the plan of Manhattan.

'I'll put "Big Apple".'

Mam tried to force him: 'Put Hotel Chelsea, 23rd Street at Seventh Avenue...'

He sighed; defeated.

Slowly, the pen began scratching the envelope.

'Oh good,' she said, encouragingly.

He muttered as he wrote: '"...23rd Street at..."' Then burst out: 'But how can a street be at an avenue?'

'Oh just put it,' said Mam, losing patience.

'How can a street be at an avenue?' But eventually the envelope was written.

When he came to the letter itself he was still argumentative. Then to put it off yet again: 'I'll use invisible ink: dip the pen in lemonade.' (This was something we had read about. You put a little lemonade in an egg cup. Dip your pen – it must have a clean, new nib – into this 'invisible ink'. Leave it to dry. Then to reveal what you have written, hold the sheet of paper in front of the fire. After a few moments the writing becomes visible in a dark brown colour.) 'Yes! I'll use invisible ink!'

'The day you write a letter,' said Mam, with a sigh of despair, 'will surely be a red-letter day.'

Then Arthur, with a quizzical look: 'Red letter...?' And suddenly raising his voice and bubbling up: 'That's it! I'll use red ink.'

'Well,' she said, resignedly, 'there's the red ink bottle.' He took out another new pen holder from his new writing case, put into it a new nib, unscrewed the top of the red ink bottle on the inkstand and opened the writing pad in its case. He began, with the pen scratching dreadfully, muttering to himself: '"Pen-y-Wern, Treuddyn, Near Mold, Flintshire, Wales, Great Britain..."'

'You don't have to put all that.'

And raising his voice and writing with a flourish: '"...The World, The Uni... verse!"' He was talking big; with his address as long as a transcontinental railroad. Then clearing his throat: '"Dear Dad..."'

'You haven't put the date.'

'Let him be,' said Mam to me in an undertone.

He wrote, with a quiet mutter. I occasionally took a stealthy look over his shoulder. He began slowly, filling up the loop of every e and every o: a splodgy mess. Some of his ps and gs were more like crotchets and quavers. In all, the ruled notepaper was like a messily copied-out sheet of music, in red. He had done far better handwriting for Mr Hayes.

He paused and looked at his pen. 'It scratches.'

'Well use a pencil.'

'Needs sharpening.'

I was about to sharpen a pencil with the pencil sharpener in the base of the Empire State Building replica, but he continued writing.

Mam sidled up to me, and whispered: 'Put this penny-ha'penny stamp on the envelope for him.' I took the stamp, licking it as I watched over his shoulder. He paused as if from exhaustion, slumping back in the chair with the pen stuck behind the ear. After a respite he took his pen and licked the nib as if it were a pencil point. Realising his mistake, he wiped away the spot of red ink on his lip with his sleeve and plunged the pen deep into the bottle. Once more ink overflowed and dribbled down on to the blotting paper. He resumed writing.

'Oh, a blot.'

'Tut, tut,' said Mam, clucking her tongue. 'Never mind, just use the blotting paper.'

'Oh what the heck, I'll dip my pen in the blot...'

'No, you'll make a mess.'

He used his pen to stir the ink blob on the paper as if he were stirring water colours.

'Ty'd o'na, cariad. Come on, love.'

Mam had appealed to his better nature. He pressed on with his letter.

'Shall I go with him to Pontybodkin?' We spoke in whispers.

'Yes, make sure he gets it in the post.' Then she realised it was late and I still had to go to the well. She suggested I went as far as the stile to see him on his way.

The letter caught the evening post.

207

We were up in the sycamore tree, cutting away at the bark with our pocketknives for all we were worth. 'My letter...' said Arthur, not pausing in his concentrated effort, 'my letter, it's halfway there by now.'

'Nearly.'

We worked furiously. Then, after some time, Arthur exclaimed: 'Finished!'

'Me too. Just about.'

He raised his left leg to rest it along the branch, with the sole of his boot pressed against the tree trunk. Leaning back precariously to admire his handiwork, he had to grab a nearby branch with an outstretched hand to stop himself falling. He put out his chest and said, 'Done to a T.' The letters A.T. and J.T. were complete, carved deeply into the bark. We were both A.T., and J.T. served for Mam as well as Dad. It halved the work, having the same initials.

'And these initials,' boasted Arthur, 'are going to be carved on this tree for ever. We'll show them to Dad the first day he's home.'

'Yes,' I said laughing, 'and Dad'll say...' (it was an attempt at imitating Dad pretending to be cross) '..."Who's carved my initials up there?"'

'And I'll say; "A Rocky Mountain goat. No. Racoon."'

'No. Billy the Kid.'

'No. Big Foot. Big Foot! I'm fierce!' He bellowed.

'Huh, you bellow like a buffalo.'

'I don't. I'm a grizzly bear.' And he growled.

There was a lull, and the mention of grizzly bears reminded me of our playground song, 'The Bear Went Over the Mountain'. We adapted the words:

'The bear went over Hope Mountain,

The bear went over Hope Mountain,
The bear went over Hope Mountain,
To see what he could see...'

'Huh,' said Arthur, breaking off before the end of the last line. 'What would he see?'

'What? Up there? On top of Hope Mountain? Well... Horeb... little Horeb Chapel.'

'No. He'd see Camelot. Camelot's on top of Hope Mountain.'

I told him not to be silly.

'But...' said Arthur, pausing for reflection, 'what would he see, far, far away on the horizon, looking from the top of Hope Mountain?'

'Mm... The Mersey. Yes. The *Britannic* sailing in. He'd see Dad coming home.'

And we gave a cheer, and put hands to our eyes to shield them from the light as we spied out towards the horizon; or, like a captain on the bridge, peering into a make-believe telescope to scan the seas. Well, you could see the Mersey from the top of Hope Mountain, but only on a clear day – it was twenty-two miles distant as the crow flies over the Dee Estuary and the Wirral Peninsula.

Arthur switched to trumpeting 'Rule Britannia', and I battled simultaneously with 'To see what he could see...'

'Huh,' said Arthur, 'you sing like a Red Indian nose flute.' Then, after pausing a moment, he went back to his own song:

'Rwy'n canu fel cana'r aderyn...'

swelling to the top of his voice:

'Yn hapus yn ymyl y lli...'

I relaxed and listened to him sing, filled with wonder and delight. It was the same when he sang in the house: for a few fleeting moments all the daily humdrum – even all the knowledge in *Pictorial Knowledge* – did not matter. The words of the song – mere verses under the music – were beautifully transformed. Now, out in the open air, he sang the song to the end. And, I thought, he would be singing it in the school concert, with the electric light. And Dad there to hear him!

After an interval in which we gazed up at the blue sky, still visible because the trees were only just beginning to come into leaf, I said, 'Time we went home.'

'One more thing.'

'What?'

'You'll see.' Arthur took out his pocketknife again, and with slow deliberation pulled its blade out of its holder. He chose, from the branch hanging overhead, a short piece of newly grown stem and cut it off with a sharp cut. Then he whittled away, ending up with a straight three-inch length. He loosened the soft, new green bark: 'Easy to do on a new-grown piece... see? Dad showed me.' Then he chipped one end carefully with his pocketknife: 'You shape the mouthpiece... then a notch here... half an inch from the mouthpiece... there. A whistle for the referee.' He put it to his mouth, and with a mighty blow into it, produced a short, high-pitched, weak, peep-peep of a whistle.

'They wouldn't hear it.'

'Ugh.' Then, cheerfully: 'We'll get Jack. He'll be referee.' Adding with a boast: 'And I'll be Dixie Dean.'

Cae Cefn was Wembley. Jack was on the touchline, an indeterminate line that started somewhere near the washhouse and skirted the nettles by the old pigsties. On the other side of the pitch the touchline followed the clothes line. The ground there fell away steeply, which made it fine for roly-poly on summer days, but now effectively marked the limit of play. Behind the opponents' goal was the overgrown hedge with the hawthorn tree: the neighbouring farm's hayfields beyond it. The goalposts were piles of boys' jackets. Arthur's rubber ball had been booted about in a match that had lasted all afternoon with neither team scoring the victorious goal. Jack had given up being referee from sheer exhaustion.

'Come on, Dixie Dean...' shouted Jack.

Arthur had practised all that morning for this afternoon match, dribbling round the clothes line post. Out on the field he had placed a large bucket, tipped over on its side, and from thirty yards he shot the rubber ball straight into it. We had taken the cow out of Cae Cefn to be out of the way, and as she settled down to browse quietly on the scanty grass near the rabbit warren, Arthur had passed the ball neatly and squarely between her legs; running behind and round her to retrieve the ball and score a goal again, low and accurate. The old placid cow moved forward at a contented pace, unconcerned, her legs and body a moving goalpost. He had practised shooting at goal against the wash-house wall. Then a marathon, dribbling the ball right round the boundary of our nine acres (I went with him, taking a book, for it was a warm, sunny morning) – through the ferns, shooting at goal when we

211

came to a gate, heading the ball at the trunk of an oak tree, his singing of snatches of songs alternating with his dribbling, until we had been right round, back through the farmyard to the dairy to gulp down a jug of thirst-quenching buttermilk. That morning, too, on Cae Cefn, we had heard the peal of bells from Brymbo Parish Church four miles away (a wedding, or just bell-ringers practising?), audible when the warm wind blew gently from the south through the gap between Hope Mountain and the hills and heather of Uwch-y-Mynydd-Uchaf. The shape of the hills themselves directed their resonance upwards to us at Pen-y-Wern. But Arthur was intent on his ball that morning. Back in the house he had swallowed down his food quickly: he wanted to be ready out on Cae Cefn before all the boys came up the tunnel through the wood. 'Calm down,' Mam had said, 'or you'll have the cow in calf before we know where we are.' And when he dashed off: 'Good gracious me, you don't want to lose a moment of your life, do you?'

'Come on, Dixie Dean...' shouted Jack again. He now stood where the touchline met the nettles, watching Arthur dribble the ball past the big boys of thirteen and fourteen from our elementary school. All those boys, the neighbouring farmer had said, they'll ruin the grass. 'It'll do it a world of good,' Mam had replied with a smile. The grass was greener that afternoon.

The play was heading towards the opponents' goal. Arthur, eight years old and nearly nine, the centre forward in the thick of the play, was the smallest player on the field. The ball was up in the air.

'Head it into goal!' shouted Jack. 'All you need... goal!' Arthur had scored.

'Hurray! We've won! We've won!' The cheers from the winning team drowned Jack's voice.

'All you need, Dixie,' persisted Jack with his usual chortle, 'is black curly hair like the real Dixie Dean – and a real football.' But our Dixie had fair curly hair and a pale complexion. Jack raised his voice, for Arthur and some of the boys were some distance away, trying to retrieve the ball from near the hawthorn: 'Arthur, all you need...' But he broke off, took his watch out of his waistcoat pocket, realised it was late and turned to me: 'Well, I must be getting along.' He said goodbye and walked towards the Cae Cefn gate, singing 'My Blue Heaven' in his non-musical, raucous voice.

The boys all drifted off home. I went to help Arthur find the ball. We trod down the nettles. I got a thorn in my finger.

'Where is it? I've lost my ball...' Arthur was distressed. 'Where is it?'

The red sun was low in the sky and shining through the hedge. Soon it would set behind Moel Arthur and the other peaks in the Clwydian Range and Mam would be saying: it's late, it's milking time.

'Where is it?' said Arthur, tearfully. 'I've lost my ball...'

Suddenly a hen clucked loudly in the lower branches of the hawthorn tree. 'It's the Rhode Island Red! Little Rhody!' exclaimed Arthur with delight, forgetting his lost ball for a moment. He pushed forward. The broody hen was sitting on a nest she had built. She flapped her wings and clucked loudly to keep us away. Arthur quickly turned and ran towards the house, calling loudly and excitedly, 'Mam, Mam, the red hen is in the hawthorn tree...' I stayed by the tree, standing well back, watching her. She had settled back on her nest. The sun's rays shone through, with a shaft of light on her dark, red-brown feathers.

Mam came running up with Arthur, and in his excitement he disturbed the wayward hen again. She had laid a clutch of eggs; six brown eggs. 'Come on, Little Rhody,' he said, stepping forward towards the nest.

'She's going to hatch them out here.' Mam pulled him away. 'Don't shoo her. We'd better leave her. Leave her.'

'But I want to find my football.'

'Oh we'll find it.' Mam watched for a while as we pushed farther into the nettles under the tree and the overgrown hedge; and then she walked back to the house.

We searched and searched, nettled and scratched. Then I saw it. Arthur's face lit up with joy as he plunged forward to retrieve it. 'I can... I can just reach it.' And, picking it up: 'Oh... it's busted. Look.' He was nearly in tears.

'Ah, it's got a thorn in it.' The ball was flat and limp, as if a pitchfork had plunged into it.

'It's busted.' He was in tears. 'My football's busted.' We walked disconsolately back to the house. 'It's busted... I haven't got a football....' He was sad beyond all comforting.

In the house, I opened the door of the spench, the glory hole under the stairs, and threw in the rubber ball, now a punctured, useless thing.

⋯⋯⋯

Arthur sneezed.

'Bless you,' said Mam: 'Sneeze on Monday, sneeze for

danger. Hope you haven't got a cold.' Then after a pause in which she noticed Arthur looked none too well: 'Fagged out, aren't you. You haven't taken your cod liver oil.'

'Don't like it,' he said weakly.

'You do look pale. Washed out.'

'My legs ache.' He sat in the rocking chair, his body sapped of life.

'You're tired out with all this football. No strength left. I shouldn't have let you play for so long. Worn out...' and she went on, blaming herself.

'My throat's sore.' He could hardly speak.

'We'll get you to bed. Straight away.' I helped untie his bootlaces and take him to bed.

I boiled the kettle, filled the hot water bottle and took it upstairs.

'Put your head down on the pillow. Come on.' Mam tried to comfort him as he gave yet another sharp, ringing cough.

'Pain in my neck. Here.' It was swollen.

'You're really ill.' Mam was agitated. He was feverish.

'It hurts.' He was barely audible as he coughed again. 'Can't breathe.'

'Lie down.' He seemed reluctant to put his head down on the pillow, despite his weak condition, wanting to keep himself alert for any excitement. 'There,' said Mam, tucking him properly into bed.

Then, weakly, he attempted to move his head. 'Will we meet the captain on the *Britannic*?' He moved under the bedclothes, as if he should be out and about.

'You lie still.'

'Will we meet the...'

'Yes, I'm sure we will.'

'We didn't before.'

'Yes, Dad will fix it.'

After lying still a few moments, he moved his head again, with something disturbing and troubling his mind: 'I want Dad... I want Dad...'

'When Dad is home, he'll come and kiss you goodnight.'

'I want Dad, I want Dad...'

Quietly I went downstairs to see to things like putting coal on the fire.

Mam hurriedly followed. 'Alun,' she said, taking the coal scuttle out of my hand, 'go down to Pontybodkin. Straight away. To the doctor's surgery. Ask him to come at once.'

The doctor was an Englishman. The way he spoke reminded me of that man in the Sunbeam motor car, who, with his wife and little girl, had stopped on the Tyrpeg to ask us the way to Corwen. 'I'm new around here.' He was jovial. 'So this is Penny Worm.'

'Pen-y-Wern,' I corrected. I sat on a chair beside the gramophone, with the cat on my lap.

'He's anaemic, doctor: so pale in the face.' Mam was worried, yet so relieved he had come.

'Don't assume because he's pale he's anaemic.'

The cat meowed.

'Hello Puss.' The doctor came over to stroke the cat. 'You want medicine too?'

'He's really ill, doctor.' Mam moved towards the stairs. 'Will you come up?'

'Right.' In his professional tone: 'Lead the way.'

As soon as they were out of the room, I chuckled quietly to the cat: 'Penny Worm!' I stroked her. She purred.

Suddenly she sat upright in my lap, then, turning towards the gramophone on the table, stood with her front paws on the table's edge. She meowed. 'No, we can't play the gramophone now. We've got to be quiet.' She looked intently at the record on the turntable. I raised her up in my arms: 'Want to see the dog on the record?' She purred, stretching her neck forward, making it difficult to hold on to her. She meowed appealingly. 'Well, all right, I'll just let the turntable go round and round, and you can watch it.' I switched it on. Her eyes were glued to the revolving record. It made a continuous rumble, and the emptiness of it struck me; the dog listening to his master's voice a mere blur. Then she stretched out a paw. 'Here!' I said sharply but trying to keep my voice subdued. 'Keep your paw off. You'll scratch it. It's only a picture of a dog going round and round.' She meowed again. 'Cat wants to chase dog, eh?' Her head darted to and fro as her eyes followed the revolving dog. 'Pwsi, you'll make yourself giddy.' I switched off the turntable.

'There. Sit quietly.' She relaxed, a bundle of contentment, purring softly, her paws tucked in; her body warm on my legs. I stroked her head and back and she yawned, then purred loudly, completely satisfied with herself.

They were coming down the stairs, the doctor's hurried and heavier footsteps leading. 'We must get him to Meadows Lea Isolation Hospital immediately. I'll get the ambulance to come. Right away.'

'He's dangerously ill Jack...' Mam was very distressed.

Jack had heard, and had come to see if he could help. 'Oh dear, oh dear...'

'There's no hope for him, Jack. No hope.' The shock and suddenness of the news had struck Mam with such intensity; she was stunned.

'This is bad news.' Jack was at a loss for words.

'Mrs Williams Beehive brought the telephone message from the hospital. And Mr Williams will be here soon with his taxi to take me to the hospital...'

'Oh dear. Shall I... shall I stay here with Alun while you're...?'

Mam was preoccupied. After a few moments she said, 'It was kind of you to come.'

Jack had in his hand a little parcel wrapped in brown paper. 'Look... I... er... I brought this for the boys.'

'I must get ready.' She wondered what to wear to visit the hospital. I couldn't go; I wouldn't be allowed in.

I whispered quietly to Jack as he handed me the parcel: 'What is it?'

'Mr Williams will be here with his taxi any minute.' There was really no time for Mam to have a change of clothes.

'It's a record,' said Jack to me. 'Wrong time to be bringing you a record...' he glanced towards Mam '...a time like this.'

'Oh... I'll just throw my coat on...'

'What's on it?'

Jack unwrapped the brown paper and took the record out of its paper sleeve. 'It's... er... this new American singer.'

I looked at the label: 'My Blue Heaven': Jack's favourite song. '"Sung by Bing Crosby."'

'Not a singer like your dad. A crooner.'

'What's a crooner?'

'Jack will play it on the gramophone for you...' Mam was tidying her hair and putting on her hat before the big mirror above the mantelpiece. And, moving the Empire State Building to one side for a moment to give herself a better view, she said: 'He'll stay with you while I'm at the hospital.'

'I'll cheer him up a bit. Let's wind up the gramophone.' A man's voice, light and pleasant, floated out, singing with lots of slurring. He was accompanied by what Jack called a jazz band. It had a great deal of jarring brass. The record captivated Jack.

'I shouldn't be long.' Mam was not aware of the playing record: 'It's not far, is it, Meadows Lea?' Meadows Lea was at Pen-y-ffordd, seven miles distant – through Pontybodkin and Pontblyddyn... we would be passing near it on our way to meet Dad off the *Britannic*. Then more to herself she added: 'Perhaps I should put on a better pair of shoes.'

There was a knock on the door.

'Oh it's Mr Williams, he's here with his taxi.' She had only taken a stride or two towards the door when we heard the latch of the door open.

'I've let myself in.' It was Mrs Williams Beehive.

'Oh... Mrs Williams. Come in. Is Mr Williams there?'

Mrs Williams shut the door quietly, and approached Mam with a grave look on her face. 'Jane... they telephoned again from the hospital. Jane...' she spoke softly with a slight tremor in the voice: 'I've got some very bad news for you.' She closed up to Mam, taking her hand: 'Mae Arthur druan wedi marw.'

'Oh...' Mam sobbed quietly. A tear fell down her cheek.

'Come and sit down...' She led Mam to the rocking chair and drew another chair from the table to sit close. She put her arm round her.

Mam sobbed with her head resting on Mrs Williams' shoulder. Mrs Williams said little to her: words don't count for much, they lose all meaning when you are left desolate, devastated; Arthur snatched away like that. No words of consolation can compensate. Mrs Williams Beehive knew, for she had lost a son aged nineteen, killed in 1918 – her only child. An older woman, she knew how to cope. She just let Mam cry on her shoulder.

The gramophone had played on, the revolving record with a stranger singing; it came to the end of the song. And Jack, to divert my attention and cheer me up – it was his way – nervously tried to smile and had quietly joined the closing bars. The record finished with a brief, loud passage by the jarring brass accompaniment.

Mam, with Mrs Williams sitting beside her, sobbed for what seemed like ages, with tears. I had never seen Mam cry before.

'I felt sorry for Mrs Williams Beehive... having to come to tell us,' said Mam.

'Yes.'

Mrs Williams left soon after Jack, but she had offered to stay the night, and pressed, saying it was no trouble. But Mam would have none of it. Jack, too, had said he would call early tomorrow evening.

'We must send a cable to Dad.' Jack or Mrs Williams Beehive could have seen to it, but Mam, before they left, was too distraught to think of it. And the cable had to be sent straight away; Dad was sailing home tomorrow.

'How d'you send it?'

'Through the Post Office. You'll have to take it. I'd better write it out.' She walked over to the inkstand on the dresser, tore out a page from the writing pad, and wrote: 'April 13th.'

'Oh...' she paused. 'Tonight he's at Carnegie Hall. What time is it?'

'About nine o'clock.' This was no more than a guess.

I could not remember hearing the last train. It felt past bedtime. It had been a long day: milking as usual, coal on the fire, water from the well, the oil lamp lit... it had been dark some time since Jack left. It was a Monday in the Easter holidays. 'If it's now nine o'clock... remember we're five hours ahead of New York.'

'He'll get it before he goes on stage. Poor Dad.' She dipped the pen in the ink, and muttered to herself as she wrote: '"Hotel Chelsea... 23rd Street at Seventh Avenue, New York, USA."' And sobbing quietly: '"Arthur... dead. Jane."' She took her handkerchief out of her sleeve, removed her glasses and wiped away the tears running down her cheek.

'It'll be teatime there.' I tried uneasily not to notice her tears.

'Here you are.' A tear had fallen on the notepaper, causing a slight smudge. Without glasses, she didn't realise, so it did not upset her, 'Take it to Pontybodkin Post Office.'

'But they'll be shut.'

'Go round to the back door.' She was now a little more like her normal self, though very agitated. 'Knock hard. I know it's late. Take this pound.' She opened her handbag to take out her purse, found it wasn't there, searched the dresser, shelves and coat pocket, and eventually found it on the mantelpiece close to the Empire State Building. She took out and gave me a pound note, something I handled very rarely. 'I don't know how much it will be.'

I put on my coat. 'It's dark.'

'Take Arthur's flashlight. Oh…' her sobs returned, but she was sufficiently in control to open the door and send me on my way.

Down the fields, over the stile by the sycamore tree, down the tunnel, the beam of light on the uneven path immediately in front. It was a moonless night. 'Tu-who…': a staring owl; otherwise the wood was unusually quiet. Along the wood's lower edge with the primrose banks alongside the path and the marsh below, past the school gate, along the short length of mineral line to cross the Brymbo line by the railway signal, on to the Hope Mountain road by the Sion Chapel; then by the station and the level crossing, a downhill straight stretch of the Tyrpeg, the flashlight shining on the unpaved footpath, and not a sound except my own footsteps. My left hand was in my coat pocket, clutching Mam's piece of paper with the pound note wrapped in it. I had walked to Pontybodkin so many times, but never before in the dark.

'Nos dawch!' said someone, a 'goodnight' said with reproof and surprise that a child should be out alone in the dark so late. It was near the bridge, the 'pont' of Pontybodkin, and the Post Office was opposite.

The house and Post Office were in total darkness. I ventured round to the back of the house. A dog barked vigorously and bounded forward, but was held back by its chain attached to its kennel. The dog's bark brought a flickering light – a candle or an oil lamp, with shadows moving about – to the curtained kitchen window, a woman's voice telling the dog to be quiet, and the sound of the back door being unbolted.

The cable was on its way.

Hywel delivered the papers as usual: *Liverpool Post*, *Y Faner* (The Banner) and the *Chester Chronicle*. And the *Children's Newspaper* and *Cymru'r Plant* for us.

'Schoolboy dies...' began the headline.

'Why didn't I call the doctor earlier,' said Mam through her tears, and not for the first time. Yet how could that be? The doctor couldn't have come earlier.

I folded the paper with the report uppermost: '...nine-year-old Arthur, the eldest son of Jabez Trevor, the Welsh tenor...' Eldest? Arthur was only eight. I was the one who was nine. I was older. (I was somewhat hurt and a little resentful; puzzled that a newspaper could get it wrong.)

'Why didn't I call the doctor earlier...'

'...died of diphtheria at Meadows Lea Isolation Hospital...'

The hymn was 'Llef' (Cry):

O Iesu mawr! rho'th anian bur...
(Come, gracious Lord, descend and dwell...)

We stood, in our usual place, except that Mam was not in
the choir, but with Mr and Mrs Williams Beehive and me
in the front pew.

Mr and Mrs Williams had come for us in their taxi, and
we had followed the hearse, the car moving at walking pace
up the Tyrpeg, passing Beehive Stores, Britannia Inn and
the iron stile post crowned with an iron crown. We passed
through the village; a column of people all wearing black or
a black armband, walking behind, among them Mr Hayes
with the schoolchildren. It was a motor hearse, not horse-
drawn like that for Gwilym Gwern-y-Llyn; black and silver
with glass panels to show the little coffin inside. The bell
tolled: it would be Mr Marshall the Post, the sexton, at the
bell rope behind the pulpit. People stopped at the roadside
as we passed, the men taking off their hats and Glyn Ty'n
Llan his cap. The hearse stopped at the church gate, where
stood the Reverend Cadwaladr Williams, prayer book in
hand. Mr Williams Beehive, Jack, Georgie Jones and Uncle
Noah carried the coffin shoulder high, led by the Reverend
Cadwaladr, along the gravel path towards the church door.
We followed. The bell tolled, closer and louder, a compelling
summons: a dark-toned tinny bell slowly tolling; thin,
metallic, sombre. We followed the coffin up the aisle to our
pew. The coffin was placed in the chancel, between the
choir stalls with the men on the one side and the women on
the other, where Cadwaladr once put the old parish chest
when he talked about the history of the parish church. The
choir stalls were full with a lot of new people, mostly men.
The bell tolled: sounding quieter now we were in the

church, until the organ began the 'Dead March' from Saul; the organ bellows worked by the new electric. The church had been fitted out with the electric lights, and a special one fixed to the wall by the pulpit so that Cadwaladr wouldn't lose his place in his notes during sermons.

There was something different about the singing. At first I thought: why was it so bad? Well Mam wasn't in the choir, but in the pew with us. And Arthur wasn't singing. The congregation was full, like harvest festival with flowers. Why had everyone come to church? The Reverend Cadwaladr was at the organ for this one hymn, besides conducting the service. Suddenly a glorious swell of voices... then I knew: the men were the Coedllai Male Voice Choir, Dad's choir, in the choir stalls and overflowing into the congregation. What were the Coedllai Male Voice doing here?

When we came to the last verse, the first and last notes of this hymn tune were the same as that of the tolling bell. Had it always been so? I had heard the tune and the bell before, but not to notice. Mam had been sobbing, handkerchief in hand. But she bravely sang through her sobs to join all those supporting male voices. The Reverend Cadwaladr led the coffin to the graveside. His surplice was clean and white; the whitest white surplice in the world, Arthur would have said. It made Cadwaladr's slight stature large, like a ship in full sail, sailing down the Mersey in the olden days. And we, line astern, just there to see her off: Fare thee well, the Princes Landing Stage.... It's not the leaving of Liverpool that grieves me...

Oops! Cadwaladr stumbled on the uneven path, and paused momentarily to adjust his thick specs. We walked along the path – it must have been difficult to carry a coffin – close by Great-grandfather's grave with the low iron railings. Cadwaladr's ankle-length black cassock brushed the grass. Weaving slowly, we passed through this older part of the churchyard between the porch and the yew. The old gravestones – the churchyard drunks – leaning forward and sideways and narrowing the winding path, made the passage even more difficult.

The open grave was by the low churchyard wall next to Glyn Ty'n Llan's field. Cadwaladr's wide-sleeved surplice again billowed in the breeze. Why does he wear a nightshirt, Arthur might have said. It was spotless white, anyway. There was much shuffling of feet on the grass. No one spoke; but birds sang a little distance away as the hushed crowd gathered round.

Cadwaladr intoned: 'Dyn a aned o wraig...' Man that is born of a woman hath but a short time to live... but Arthur wasn't a man. '...ac a dorrir i lawr...' ...and is cut down, like a flower...

There was a subdued lowing of bullocks. A few heads turned to see Glyn Ty'n Llan's livestock come to peer over the low wall; then, unconcerned, quietly turn away, swishing their tails, back to their grazing. Beyond was the green of Hope Mountain. From the churchyard, it looked so far away. The coffin was lowered, slowly, down to the bottom. Did Cadwaladr remember to fasten the lid properly? He was so forgetful, '...yr m ni yn rhoddi ei gorph ef i'r ddaear...' ...we commit his body to the ground; earth to earth.... Why did Mr Marshall the Post have to throw handfuls of dirt down on the coffin? '...lludw i'r lludw...' ...ashes to ashes.... Ashes? But ashes are in the fireplace, not here. '...pridd i'r pridd...' ...dust to dust; in sure and certain hope...

226

We bowed our heads, the men holding their hats. Led by the Reverend Cadwaladr Williams we spoke The Lord's Prayer: 'Ein Tad...' Our Father, which art in heaven, Hallowed be thy Name...

Cadwaladr's prayer book was now closed, and hidden by the folds of his surplice. His voice in the open air had resonance: 'Thy kingdom come. Thy will be done...'

I mouthed the words as I watched the bullocks slowly and quietly edge their way back towards the churchyard wall.

'...in earth, as it is in heaven... Give us this day our daily bread...'

Past their feeding time perhaps. But no. The livestock, noses on the low wall, were attentive.

'And forgive us our trespasses, As we forgive them that trespass against us...'

Well, they broke into the churchyard, once.

'And lead us not into temptation... deliver us from evil...'

Above the chorus of speaking voices Cadwaladr spoke out with clarity: 'For thine is the Kingdom...'

Once more my downcast eyes wandered towards the churchyard wall, this time to the wreaths propped up against it. From the corner of my eye I could just read the inscription card attached to one of them: 'From Mr Hayes and Scholars'.

'...glory. For ever and ever. Amen.'

'I won't need to mend Arthur's shirt any more.' She sat at the sewing machine on the table. The jarring noise of the machine stopped. 'There you are. That's yours.' She turned to put my shirt over the arm of the rocking chair. I had brought out Mark Twain's book, and was now in the rocking chair thumbing through it. It was an attempt to find something to say which would console or at least divert her from her sobbing. Perhaps bringing alive the silent words on the printed page would work. I noticed the book used the word 'vest' for 'waistcoat'. There was a list of all the things Hank had invented: 'Hank Morgan invented a sewing machine in Camelot: a Singer, like yours.'

But she busied herself around the room, still sobbing, doing nothing in particular, preoccupied, handkerchief out frequently.

'And a phonograph. Dad says that's American for gramophone. And they sometimes call it "Victrola".' On page 365 was a whole list of modern benefits Hank had introduced into Camelot for King Arthur's people: schools, colleges, newspapers, telephones, steamships and railways. (But not aeroplanes: Hank Morgan couldn't have known about them, living in Connecticut in the 1880s before he travelled back in time to Camelot.) 'And the electric light,' I added, looking up to see if my effort was succeeding. She sobbed: 'I won't need to wash and iron his clothes any more.'

'And he built a railway from Camelot to London with dukes and lords working it. With their armour on!'

'You must tell Dad...' she said, half-smiling, as she tidied the mantelpiece. She picked up Arthur's money box, and painstakingly dusted it, then rubbed it to make its silver metal shine. With her forefinger, she pushed back the spring catch over the slot of the shillings compartment. She smiled to herself; for a moment her sorrow banished. Fondly and carefully she put the money box back in place on the shelf.

Pretending not to notice, I said hurriedly: 'And Hank, he wanted to send explorers to discover America.'

'You must' – her sobbing returned – 'you must tell Dad all about it.'

I turned the pages over rapidly, pausing only to look at the many Dan Beard illustrations. The cat, lying on the rag rug in front of the fire, got up, stretched, and came over to rub against my legs, wanting attention.

'You'll have to feed the cat now. Arthur's job.'

Hurriedly, before she had time to start weeping again: 'Hank Morgan wants to be first President of Camelot. Like George Washington.'

But she only sobbed more loudly.

So, more insistently: 'But they want a royal tomcat to be king, and call him King Tom the Seventh, by the Grace of God, King.' I had forgotten this bit, and laughed aloud. It was in the same chapter forty. 'A royal Magnifi-Cat!' Then trying to get through to her: 'And Mam, Mam... his highness says "Me-e-e-yow-ow-owow...!"' I looked up, hoping my cat imitation had had the desired effect; but my laughter stopped abruptly. She was in tears. I ended lamely: 'A royal tomcat with tights on.'

A few moments later, through her tears, she said: 'You have two pocketknives now, haven't you. And his pencil case...'

I flicked over more pages, found something funny to tell her, but her sobs and tears were continuous, a refusal to be comforted. More pages, more tears. Then, chapter twenty-seven, about Hank giving King Arthur a haircut: '"I inverted a bowl over his head and cut away all the locks that hung below it."' I laughed.

'Children do die – such a waste of a young life. But...' There was some anger in her voice: 'But why one of mine? Why?'

Hank Morgan and King Arthur were travelling incognito. 'Mam, Mam,' I persisted, 'King Arthur travelled disguised as a farmer, and Hank Morgan said, "Call yourself Mr Jones".' I laughed softly to myself, enjoying the book all over again. 'But he doesn't know anything about farming...'

'One of mine.' She moved away, supposedly to dust the windowsill. 'Why? Why?'

'He... he thinks...' I tried to raise my voice: 'He thinks plums come out of the ground. And onions grow on trees. And he visited a blacksmith...'

But she sobbed, and spoke with catches in the voice: 'He'll come back... he'll come back, won't he...?'

'You know, a blacksmith, just like your dad. Just like your dad, always singing, always full of fun...'

'Why did it have to be Arthur? Why? Why?'

My attempt petered out: 'And the blacksmith called King Arthur "Brother Jones".'

'...when there are so many older people... who've had a life to live? Why?'

I renewed the effort, remembering how Dad had always said Mam was so like her father in her ways. Mam thought the world of him. 'You know, Mam, like your dad, a blacksmith...'

Upstairs in a big trunk in one of the spare bedrooms was a rolled-up piece of parchment paper, locked away along with other family documents. This was her father's articles of apprenticeship, all curly and wouldn't lie flat.

It proved he had been a blacksmith. Often Mam had recited to us:

> ...The smith, a mighty man is he,
> With large and sinewy hands...

She knew the Longfellow poem by heart from her schooldays:

> ...Toiling, – rejoicing, – sorrowing,
> Onward through life he goes...

His speciality was ornamental ironwork, and the elaborate iron railings in front of one of the Nonconformist chapels were his handiwork. He was honoured, with his name carved on the chapel's foundation stone (and he a churchman!): 'This stone was laid by John Roberts.' But to everyone he was John y Go, John the Blacksmith, liked by everybody, the always full-of-fun John, blacksmith like his father, a church chorister, and so generous he would give away his last penny. To Mam the ring of the hammer at the anvil; the forge, the bellows, the shaping of metal – these were the sights and the sounds of her childhood, her memories constantly recounted. Taid (Grandfather), she would say, showing us a photo of him at work wearing side whiskers and leather apron, worked from six in the morning till six at night: the loud and resonant clang of metal on metal, the white-hot iron hammered with sparks flying, then plunged into the cold water trough with a hiss and a cloud of steam. And always repairing children's iron play hoops but never accepting the penny charge. Obviously Mam had adored her father.

'A blacksmith,' I repeated with as much emphasis as I could, but still to no apparent effect.

'Why? Why?' she went on. 'Arthur's gone, and I'm still here...'

'A blacksmith, Mam. Like the US President's father – he was a blacksmith too.'

'...It's wrong. It's wrong.'

I momentarily withdrew, leaning back in the rocking chair. Then I thought about the knights, and leaned forward again, quickly turning pages to find the place. 'Hank Morgan doesn't have any armour, but he wins every time. He uses his lasso, just like Will Rogers.'

'I miss his voice.'

Looking around the room, all was empty; his boots were near the cupboard by the hearth, one boot on its side. And in the other rooms, the blinds down – for days now... the house was dead.

There was a long uneasy pause. I felt defeated.

'It's wrong,' she insisted again, but not with quite the same intense feeling of injustice; this time there was hesitation as if for reflection. The anger and tears had run their course. She turned: 'But I must be brave.' There was more than a glimmer of a smile as she looked at me. 'And I've got you.'

'"A Republic is hereby proclaimed"': reading aloud to keep up the momentum before she had time to relapse. 'What's "Republic" Mam?' (Well, I knew really; I was playing the pupil, perhaps she would play the teacher.)

Our eyes met, and she smiled: 'You're wonderful really. Tell me how the story ends.'

'"Whereas the King having died and left no heir..." King Arthur died.'

'I expect he was old.'

'And Hank Morgan's little baby girl, Hello Central, she dies.'

This was on the wrong tack, so I quickly added: 'And Hank Morgan goes to sleep at the end...'

'Arthur's... gone to sleep, really.'

'...and sleeps for thirteen centuries. Well I think he does. And wakes up in modern times.'

But I was becoming unsure of myself. I clung to the book like an anchor, with both hands, my grip holding it tight. People didn't die in books, or if they did, they came alive again. In my confusion, I forgot what was real and what wasn't. Perhaps Arthur was only pretending to be dead: just play-acting like when we quarrelled over writing his letter to Dad; his play-acting could be so real. Yes. He was play-acting: Arthur, playing the part of Arthur himself. Or like Hank pretending at the beginning of the story to be a magician like Merlin, and so saving his own life when he was due to be executed. Hank, because he had studied science (like the science in *Pictorial Knowledge*, Volume Six), is able to foretell an eclipse of the sun. And so King Arthur makes him Chief Minister. Yes, Arthur, like Hank, only pretending. He's dead but he won't lie down... no, he's alive but he won't get up... I'm with you brother! Yes, like Hank, only pretending... only pretending...

Or perhaps Arthur really was dead. Why didn't Mam kiss him better? I was confused... my hands still gripping the book, I moved one hand to the arm of the rocking chair and for a moment clung to it for dear life. I would look up all the volumes of *Pictorial Knowledge* but even they couldn't tell you everything. Anyway, Hank at the end fights a terrible battle and is wounded, and Merlin's spell makes him sleep. And in his sleep he returns to modern times. But in a postscript on the last page he really does die: in his sleep. I couldn't tell Mam all this; she wouldn't understand. So, recalling an earlier episode, I said to her, 'In Camelot, they sing "In the Sweet By and By", like Band of Hope.'

'That flashlight's yours now.'

Then after a while (I was getting too immersed in Mark Twain's *A Connecticut Yankee at King Arthur's Court*, oblivious of the passage of time): 'You'd better go to bed, it's getting late. If only Dad was home. I dread the night. If only Dad was home.' She fetched a candle holder for me from the back kitchen and lit the candle. 'Goodnight, cariad,' she said as she kissed me.

'Goodnight.'

'And take the box of matches.' She placed it on the candle holder. 'The draughty stairs might blow it out. It's a cold, windy night.' True enough: as I approached the new door at the bottom of the stairs (it was open wide, as usual; we never quite got the habit of shutting it, perhaps because of Arthur's way of sitting up there, singing), the draught down the staircase nearly blew out the candle. I climbed the creaking stairs quietly and slowly with one hand cupped to protect the flame. 'Mind the bedroom curtains,' she called up after me. 'Keep the candle well away.'

The hinge of the bedroom door creaked horribly. I placed the candle by the bedside, undressed quickly, jumped into bed and blew it out. An owl's screech came up from the wood. The wind blew up again and rattled the window. I sobbed a little, telling myself it was because I was cold. To keep warm, I doubled up my knees under my chin and at the same time pulled the pyjama bottoms down over my feet. My sobs wouldn't go away; I put my head under the bedclothes so that Mam wouldn't hear...

⚬⟞⟨⟩⟜⚬

'Oh!' I woke with a start. I had been asleep. For how long? But was I really awake or still asleep?

It was the gramophone playing; it had wakened me. Dad singing that quiet passage:

> I want you in the evening
> When the sun sinks in the west...

I rubbed my eyes and propped myself up on my elbows. She had the gramophone on! How? But... but she didn't know how to put it on!

> I want you in the night time
> When the whole world is at rest...

Then the few bars of the piano accompaniment on its own. She might break it – with her poor eyesight she might let the needle scratch the record. She had insisted she didn't know how to do the gramophone...

But it played to the end. I relaxed back into the bedclothes. Shortly after, the new door at the bottom of the stairs opened (she must have shut it so that the record wouldn't wake me), her quiet footsteps came up the creaking stairs and light from her flickering candle came through the crack in the bedroom door. She was coming to bed. When she was at the top of the stairs, I distinctly

235

heard her mutter to herself, as she wept softly: 'Jäbez; ty'd adre'. (Jäbez; come home.) Her bedroom door shut quietly.

The wind rattled the window again. Tired, I turned over and went to sleep.

Feeding the cat; water from the well; feeding the hens; coal on the fire; fetching and feeding the cow; milking time; meal times, with an empty chair at the table...

Mam wept about the house continuously; she took off her spectacles and tried to wipe them with her far-too-moist handkerchief. In the evening, she turned into a statue for what seemed like ages: stunned; absent-minded; staring a blank stare into the distance. I lit a candle and walked down the passage, stopping briefly to prevent the draught blowing it out. Through the back kitchen into the wash-house, where I placed the candle on the windowsill, so that its light shone across the backyard to the coal house. I filled the coal scuttle and brought it in.

Another night of weeping.

People came. One morning Mr and Mrs Williams Beehive came with Jack. While Mrs Williams was in the house with Mam, the men stood outside near the front door. They were talking, careful to be out of Mam's hearing. It was about diphtheria – the symptoms: swelling of the neck and throat; throaty voice. Up and down the country, local outbreaks of the disease occurred from time to time. It was infectious; one of those boys playing football could well have been a carrier. (The two men were talking quietly, unaware I was standing just inside the door, listening.) It was a disease that spread rapidly through the body, taking a hold without you being aware: it paralysed the throat, making swallowing difficult; it damaged the heart; sight became blurred; muscles of arms and legs became paralysed... breathing became very difficult: if the disease hasn't taken too great a hold and the child is taken to hospital in time, they can put a breathing tube into the front of the windpipe.... (They dropped their voices; I could not hear it all.) 'It attacks the larynx – that's where the vocal cords are.' I turned round, with my back to the doorway, and quietly and absent-mindedly closed the new door at the bottom of the stairs. Still full of talk about diphtheria, Mr Williams and Jack had now wandered off towards the barn to see what outside jobs they could do. I took a pace forward into the open doorway; but hesitated, wondering whether to join them or join Mam and Mrs Williams Beehive in the back kitchen. Instead I just stood – looking out towards Hope Mountain, and because the men were now some distance away from the front of the house, out in the yard, they no longer thought it necessary to subdue their voices: '...the child chokes in the end...'

Other people came. They would say: 'It's God's will', 'Time will heal', 'God has a reason' and 'You'll get over it', which only brought Mam more angry tears and 'But you haven't lost Arthur!' It was Mrs Williams Beehive who came every day, but she gave no advice; she was the bedrock of comfort. And in the evenings after she had left, tears streamed down Mam's cheeks once more, bringing no relief.

Another day. She was a little like her normal self; making a determined effort to keep a hold on herself: 'Ever so many things to do before Dad gets home. Mustn't sit down and cry.' She knew she had to bear up and not despair. 'I'll tidy the garden a bit. Will you take the sickle and cut down the nettles by the old pigsties?'

'Yes. I've been to the well...'

'Oh. I'll fill the tea kettle then.'

'...and fed the hens. I'm going to fetch the cow.'

VI
MV Britannic

The cow was in the lower field, not far from the stile. 'Milking time!' She raised her head and began walking towards me. I gave her a pat: 'But you stay here a while, by the sycamore tree, while I...' I plunged my hand into my jacket pocket and brought out a piece of cow-cake. 'Here you are.' She gave a brief, appreciative moo, and put out her big tongue. I placed the cow-cake on it; she rolled her tongue round it and drew it into her mouth. Moving away I called: 'Won't be long.' Then I ran towards the stile, looking back at her as I climbed over.

Down the tunnel, running as fast as my legs would carry me; turning off into the secret path. Brushing through the undergrowth, scratching my legs; birds taking flight as I approached; twigs snapping. Leaping down the steep part where Arthur had found it easier to scramble on all fours. The lower edge of the wood and the marsh: a waterhen swam rapidly away. I paused, breathless: now... how to cross the marsh? Yes, by the bulrushes.

Through the gate and on to the ballast stones of the railway track... no train this time of day. I paced up and down, breathing heavily; standing still a moment to get my breath back. I searched and searched; if I looked carefully, I might find it. We put the coins on the rail... just here... opposite the railway gate. If I look very carefully, I might... then, after a few minutes: no, I'll never find it. No. No use looking any more. No sign of it. Taking a last look on the inside of the rail, I ran my hand along the edge of a sleeper: I'd better go. No use.

Still crouching by the rail, I looked up with a start: heavy footsteps were walking towards me, giant boots crunching on the stones a little distance away, closing in. The railway signwriter! He was still here. He had seen me. I straightened up to run. But he smiled. Paint brush in one hand, he delved with the fingers of the other into his waistcoat pocket, under his white overall. He brought out something, stopped in front of me, held out his palm and said: 'Dyma fo'.

'Er...' I was overwhelmed and overjoyed: 'Oh! Diolch, diolch yn fawr...' Thank you, thank you very much... I ran a few paces away, and, in my confusion, stopped to call back to him: 'Diolch i chi.' And as I ran towards the railway gate, almost tripping on the ballast stones: 'Thank you, thank you very much.'

Through the gate; clutching it tight in my fist the whole time; across the marsh, sinking up to my ankle in my haste; elated, I ran and ran up the secret path: 'Arthur! Dyma fo...' here it is! Panting; brushing up through the undergrowth in high spirits, up the steep part, grabbing the end of a low branch with my spare hand to pull myself up: 'Arthur! Arthur!' Breathless; I tripped and grazed a knee: 'Arthur! Arthur! P'le wyt ti...?' Where are you...?

At the stile I broke into tears: exhausted, wretched and thoroughly miserable. The flattened coin was still clasped in my hand; tightly gripped, its sharp edge had cut the skin; it clung to the palm, both coin and palm clammy with perspiration. I tried, with moist eyes, to look at it. Instead, I put it into my trouser pocket and wiped away the tears with my other sleeve.

The cow mooed and walked slowly towards me. 'You've waited for me.' I was choking back the tears: 'Only you to talk to now.' It was late afternoon; a distant cuckoo sang somewhere in the wood, but its far-carrying song sounded quite close. 'Listen. Turn the coin over in your pocket. It ought to cheer you up.' She understood. More tears; then, recovering a little: 'Why didn't we ever give you a name, like Daisy or Blodwen?' She swung her head round.

'Well, you're in good shape anyway, licking your back.' She gave another moo. 'Patiently waiting for me.' And taking her into my confidence: 'You mustn't tell Mam I've been crying. Or that I've been down the secret path to the railway. You mustn't go down there to those railway trains.'

She took a pace or two away, and turned her head as if beckoning. 'Oh, you're going to take me home.' And as her hooves began to tread the way up: 'Oh, all right then...'

We reached the farmyard gate. Patiently she watched me shut the gate, and only moved off when she saw I was following. She knew her way into her stall. As I tied the loose chain round her neck, she swung her head round to lick the back of my hand with her long rough tongue and looked at me with her huge eyes.

241

'Here you are.' I gave her plenty of cow-cake. And then, softly, leaning over her: 'Don't tell Mam. And you must stand very still for Mam when she's milking. She's... she's upset.' She munched away, quiet and content. 'You will, won't you.'

I was leaning on her with my left forearm on her back. My other hand was in my trouser pocket fingering the flattened coin with its edge no longer milled but very sharp. I brought it out to look at it. With tears welling up: 'Want to see it? Look. Lovely oval shape. Two bits. Worth a shilling.' I held it in my outstretched palm in front of her face. 'A quarter.' Her nose touched my hand. 'No, not a quart! You can't drink it! A quarter. Twenty-five cents. It's a coin,' I chuckled. 'A silver coin.' She mooed quietly as her nose pushed into my hand. 'No, you can't eat it!' I held the thin coin between finger and thumb: 'George Washington, look, with a long nose.' And laughing through tears: 'Squashed out long! Just like George the Fifth on my penny.'

With one foot against the cow stall's partition, and one hand on the cow's back, I could just raise myself sufficiently to reach the ledge above the cow's head where we had put the flattened penny. 'There,' I said as I climbed down, 'the quarter is now with the penny.' Tearfully: 'Don't tell... don't tell. Let me put my head on your neck... where it's warm, and give you a hug...' But my arms weren't long enough to go all the way round her big neck. She turned her head round, her heavy breath warm on my face.

⚬⚬⚬

'You've been a long time.'

'She was in the bottom field,' was my timid excuse as

I shut the door, 'by the sycamore tree.'

When I walked sheepishly into the room, she noticed straight away: 'You've been crying.'

'No. It's a cold...' I sniffed. And in confusion: 'No... it's all... right. Well, it was the cow... she tossed her head... and her horn caught me on the arm. Here.' I held up my elbow.

'I've never known her do that before. The gentlest cow we ever had.'

'It... it wasn't deliberate.' I sniffed again.

'If you've got a cold, where's your hanky?'

'Well,' I said with some truth at least, 'it's the catarrh.'

I sat in the rocking chair. This revealed my knees, prominently, for the chair faced the light from the window: 'Why, your legs are scratched. Where have you...' she was trying not to be cross, 'where have you been?'

'It's nothing.'

'But how did...'

'The cow...' I began, not very convincingly, 'she broke through... into the wood... and I had to get her out.'

'Well she's never done that before.' Mam was trying to hide her disbelief. 'There's nothing for her to eat in the wood. She wouldn't go in the wood.'

One lame excuse led to another: 'I went to play with...' the words were hard to bring out, 'to play on my own... in the wood... and... and because it was a windy night, there'd be broken branches, so I thought I'd collect sticks for firewood.'

She did not believe all these lies. That I could see. But instead of being cross: 'You must be careful not to go out like that, you'll catch a cold and get yourself ill.' Her sobs were welling up again: 'I've only got you now.' And broke into tears.

Seeing her cry made me completely forget my escapade through the wood down to the railway. 'Mam, don't cry. Dad'll be home soon.'

'Soon?' Through her tears, barely audible, she sobbed: 'Not soon enough.'

'Well, perhaps... perhaps he'll come quickly by Imperial Airways.' After all, the aeroplane, like the wireless and the telephone, was one of the Seven Wonders of the Modern World. I had to say something to counteract the sobs and the tears. 'They'll build a floating aerodrome halfway, with a wireless, and... Dad will be able to send us a message to say he's on the way home.' I was recalling what I had read in the newspaper some time previously. M. Bleriot, the first man to fly the Channel, had forecast there would be a regular airline service from New York to London, like the one between London and Paris, in about ten years. Arthur and I would then be eighteen and nineteen years old, I had thought at the time. It would be done, M. Bleriot had said, by having giant floating aerodromes for refuelling mid-Atlantic. They would be anchored in the sea and fitted out with powerful wireless to help guide the airliners. 'And Hank Morgan will invent it...'

'I'll have to sort out his things.'

'If Hank could travel 1,361 years back to King Arthur's time, he could travel forward, only forty years, to now. And invent it.' Then seeing her sobs, I reflected: no; Hank Morgan's only a story.

Her sobs went on, unabated.

I hurriedly took out a volume of *Pictorial Knowledge*. 'Dad might come by airship from the Empire State Building. Marvellous things, airships.' (We had not only read about them, but had planned, when we grew up, to go to the States by airship.) The *Graf Zeppelin* had hovered over Wembley to watch the Cup Final. The R100 had been to Canada and back. 'Airships travel fast; Dad could be home in four days. He'd be home by now.'

But then there was the *R101* crashing, killing forty-eight people. The newspapers had been full of it: '*R101* battles with storm' ran the headline. (It was a Monday morning paper, with Arthur reading the football results: '"Everton 7, Charlton 1." Dixie Dean's scored another two goals.') There were pictures of the airship's twisted metal. Dead bodies were laid out on the ground. They were taken to a village schoolroom. The village people brought their white bed sheets to cover the bodies. It was the maiden voyage of the 'Titanic of the Sky', the world's largest airship, 777 feet long, able to cruise at sixty-three miles per hour, and 'as safe as a house' they had said. Her crew had blue uniforms with '*R101*' in gold; and there was a promenade with celluloid windows, sleeping cabins, dining room, elevator, wireless room and an all-electric kitchen. She had diesel engines, each of 650 horsepower; five of them, to drive the propellers. The airship had left England on the 'all-red route' to India: 'Godspeed' they had said as she left her mooring mast one dark night – some of her crew using their flashlights at her windows to flash back 'Goodbye'. Caught in a rainstorm, lurching out of control, she staggered over Normandy; there was an explosion and a vast sheet of flame lit up the sky. She crashed into a beetroot field near Beauvais. King George the Fifth was 'horrified' to hear of the disaster. French policemen searched for more bodies – all found burned in the wreckage of the worst air crash ever.

245

No. Dad had better not come home by airship. 'Why doesn't Jābez come home?' Mam now distraught; almost angry.

'But he's on his way. On the *Britannic*.'

'He's far away...' She walked towards the window, and looked vaguely out. Then turning round: 'and... I'm here... on my own....'

'The *Britannic*,' I said again with as much emphasis as I could, 'the great new ship.'

'On my own... and this happens.'

'The *Britannic*, with diesel... er...' I hesitated, thinking of the *R101*'s diesel engines; 'perhaps they weren't so good after all... with diesel engines,' I made myself say, enthusiasm faded. Then recovering: 'She's called *Britannic*. You know, like "Rule Britannia". Hank Morgan, he built steamships, but they weren't much good. If Hank travelled forward in time, we could take him to see the *Britannic*, a great modern ship.'

'Well,' said Mam, her tearful anger mellowing, 'you'll be able to see the ship, if not Arthur.'

I picked up the daily paper, delivered about midday by Hywel. (No children came except Hywel; diphtheria was contagious – who could blame them, keeping children away.) I found the shipping column: 'Shipping News: Arrivals and Departures.'

'It says "*MV Britannic*; expected time of arrival, 10am, Monday." On the morning tide.'

'I wonder if Dad got the cable...'

'Yes, must have.'

'...before he sailed.'

'Yes, of course he did.'

'He may not. Oh dear....' And back came a flood of tears.

'He may not know... he may not know Arthur's dead. We may have to... break the news to him.' Collapsing into a chair, breaking down, hardly audible through her weeping she sobbed: 'Why did it... why did it... happen to me? God... has given me up...'

⟞⟡⟝

I remembered to put the pencil stub in my trouser pocket just before bedtime. It usually lay on the mantelpiece, and Mam used it to write the grocery list to give to the Co-op man. The stub was quite blunt; so I gave it a few turns in the pencil sharpener in the base of the Empire State Building replica. I could have borrowed one of the new, shiny pencils out of Arthur's pencil set – the one that came with the Empire State Building – but I wanted a pencil small enough to be out of sight in my pocket.

Earlier, when Mam was out milking, I had rushed upstairs to place under my pillow the writing pad and an envelope out of Arthur's new caribou-skin writing case. I hurried down and out again in time to take the cow back to the field. I had always wanted to learn to milk, but the hands of a nine year old are not big enough; I was glad now I couldn't, for doing things like milking diverted Mam from her grief. Otherwise it was weeping: sobs; tears; never-ending, day and night. Especially at night. I had to do something.

Undressed and in bed, the lit candle beside the bed and pencil stub in hand, I took out the writing pad from under the pillow and wrote the address 'Pen-y-Wern' at the top of the page. How to begin? Dear Reverend? No. I propped

247

myself up more comfortably, the jerk making the bed springs grate: must do it quietly. I began: 'Dear Cousin the Reverend Thomas. Please excuse pencil, writing in bed with candle...' I stopped to search under the pillow for the envelope, and decided to address it before it slipped out of sight into the bedclothes: 'To the Rev. Thomas Trevor, Tennessee-the-Monkey-State, USA.' I wrote 'URGENT' in the top left-hand corner. By fastest ship: *Majestic*? No, she was the biggest. 'By Fastest Royal Mail Ship.' It would need a penny-ha'penny for a stamp. I would get them out of my money box, using my pocketknife. Now the letter itself: 'Please write to Mam, if not too busy with monkeys. Will you write in Welsh?' Perhaps he couldn't. 'If you can.'

I fought to keep back the sobs; they made my hand unsteady, 'Will you write to Mam because...' because... because? How to word it? I stifled my sobs; a tear fell on the envelope lying on the bedclothes; I hurriedly wiped it with my pyjama sleeve. A sigh, searching for words to write. No. It was no use. The letter wouldn't get there in time. Why, oh why didn't I think of it before? (In the last few days I had lost track of the calendar, forgetting to cross off each day, day by day.) The letter would take a week to get there. And another week for him to write back. And Dad would be home long before then. I shut the pad with the envelope inside and put it back under the pillow; I placed the pencil stub on the candle holder and blew out the candle. My head down on the pillow, a tear or two of joy now confused with those of sorrow, I drew the bedclothes over – and thought, in better spirit: Dad will soon be home: just a few more days. Dad'll be home: and then – it will be all right; it will be all right...

'Here she is!' It was the deep, prolonged boom of the *Britannic* coming in. She hove into view, out in the estuary, nosing her way towards us.

At the Princes Landing Stage, it was only Mam and me. The wind blew off the river, seagulls swooped. The crowd chatted excitedly, craning their necks. Then the ship's boom again, this time nearer, the ship looming large and the crowd's chatter swelling up with some cheering.

'Keep back from the edge of the landing stage,' said Mam as I edged forward to get a full view.

'White Star Line all right.' You could tell from the colour of her two squat funnels. Then her boom again, a loud deep note, now close. 'Why the long blast Mam?'

'What does it matter so long as she's bringing Dad home?'

She was very close now. Tug boats were in attendance, chug-chugging away with their high-pitched whistles and lines aboard at bow and stern, to manoeuvre her into position alongside.

On the landing stage were decorative streamers; red, white and blue bunting and Union Jacks; a few Stars and Stripes too. All put up for this special occasion: the return of Britain's first transatlantic diesel motor ship to her home port. The streamers were trailing in the high wind, flapping above our heads. Farther along was a small dais, cordoned off. Near it was a band, assembling their instruments ready to play.

She was going to tie up. Lines now linked her to the shore. Passengers were gathering on her promenade deck. 'Look out for Dad,' said Mam. 'But keep back from the chain fence along the edge.'

249

I hadn't wandered more than a few paces when a sharp command from a stevedore made me jump: 'Stand back there!' He had the Liverpool accent; a Scouse accent, said Mam.

The ship slowly sidled closer to the landing stage, inching her way, narrowing the streak of water between ship and shore with its floating refuse, oil and mud, the oily water lapping against the ship's side. At our level was the vast expanse of her side with long rows of port holes, an occasional head looking out from one or two of them. Above, the crowded promenade deck was close enough now for us to hear the returning passengers' cheers and shouts to the waiting crowd on the landing stage.

The stevedore had walked along the front of the crowd to press them back and was some distance away, but his sharp, Liverpool voice carried above the excited crowd: 'Clear away from the gangway.' With the rattle of a winch, the gangway was lowered, and the welcoming crowd pushed back even more.

On the promenade deck the passengers were pressing against the rail, scanning the shore to spot their friends and relations. And on shore, standing alongside us, were a small group of people who suddenly erupted and waved frantically when they saw their dear ones on board. The cheers, waving and general excitement grew as more and more people recognised each other across the narrow water. All the men waved their hats.

The Lord Mayor, wearing his robe of office, was now standing on the dais with one or two other important people. He spoke through the confused noise and uproar: 'We welcome home... this fine new ship...' he paused, a little carried away by the excitement all around him.

'...after her maiden voyage...' His voice, a Lancashire accent, was slightly distorted by the public address system, '...this fine new ship back to her home port of Liverpool.' An immediate cheer and some handclapping from the crowd standing near the dais.

Then the band struck up with 'Rule Britannia'.

'Mam, it's not a patch on Coed Talon Silver Band. Not even a proper band: it's got tiny, squeaky little flutes and piccolos.' It was the Band of His Majesty's Royal Marines.

Above the hubbub and band-playing, the man in the group near us bellowed across the water in a very English voice: 'Johnny, welcome home!'

'Wave your hat,' said the woman with him. Then she shouted and waved towards the ship: 'Johnny, we're over here.' But her voice was lost in the confusion of cheers and chatter, the band-playing and the hoots of tugs and other river traffic. Even the tune of 'Rule Britannia' was barely recognisable against the competing emotional tumult.

'Can you see Dad?'

'No.' All 1500 passengers must have been on the promenade deck now, those in front leaning over the rail, waving and looking down at us, and many more behind them trying to get a glimpse, their heads barely visible to us ashore. Perhaps Dad was behind somewhere. 'Can't see him.'

'Must be somewhere...'

The English people next to us suddenly waved frantically. 'He's seen us,' said the woman. 'Johnny,' shouted the man, 'we've got great news for you!'

Mam told me to walk up and down the landing stage. The ship's promenade deck was quite a length, and so too was the stretch of crowd, many deep, fronting it. 'See if you can... but keep away from the edge.'

I paced along the front of the crowd, away from the band, occasionally bumping into people, my eyes fixed upwards towards the promenade deck. There was no sign of Dad. I moved farther along. No sign anywhere. I reached a point opposite where the promenade gave way to the ship's open deck and the mooring ropes towards the stern; and turned round to retrace my steps.

'Are you meeting your papa too?' It was a small girl.

I was taken aback; my eyes had been fixed on the passengers and she had emerged from the crowd behind me.

'Er... meeting my who?'

In the welcoming crowd a little distance away was her mother: 'Molly, don't wander too far.'

'Vewy well, Mama.'

The din was deafening, but another Englishman standing behind shouted: 'Did you have a good voyage?'

And the woman with him called: 'Where's Babs?' Then, after a pause, in her normal voice and bubbling with excitement: 'Oh there he is.'

Something had amused the crowd: a wave of chuckles rippled through it. 'Oh look,' said the little girl Molly. 'Look at the baby with its toy. A white furwy seal. Waving it over the ship's wail.' The baby (this must have been Babs), tightly grasped by its mother, was leaning over the ship's side, holding its soft toy out at arm's length over the water.

The crowd's amusement suddenly turned to 'Oh....' The baby had dropped the 'furwy seal', a long drop into the water below. I dashed forward to the chain fence at the edge to see it hit the murky water; stared at its white fur sinking, enveloped in the blackness of the lapping water between ship and shore.

'Hey, lad, stand back there!' It was the sharp voice of the stevedore. I guiltily retreated.

'Gone.'

'Ah...' said Molly.

After a pause: 'I'm going to see the ship. Going on board.'

'How jolly.'

'Is your father on board?'

'Yes!' she said with a slight giggle. 'Fwightfully exciting. My papa's an architect.'

'Did he go to 'Merica to build skyscrapers?'

'Expect so.'

'I'm going to meet the captain.'

'Oh, spiffing!'

'Spiff... ing? What's that?'

'Molly dear!' The kindly voice of Mama called from her place in the crowd behind the front row. 'Do come now.'

'Wightiho, Mama, I'm coming.' And turning to me: 'Cheerwiho.' She merged into the mass of people.

Fancy talking like that!

Back to Mam. Her first words were: 'Have you seen him?'

'No.'

I searched the other way, towards the bow, without success.

'Where can he be?' Then pensively: 'I wonder if he knows...'

On the promenade deck directly opposite us, new faces appeared, taking turns to wave from the ship's rail. My eyes searched, watching every movement and every new face. An occasional glance at Mam: would she bring out her handkerchief, begin sobbing, thinking she would have to break the news? Finding him there at the rail would rid her of this mental anguish, and she would smile and wave and shout across the narrow water like all the others, and not cry with all the people around. Not that the crowd would notice: their chatter and cheer quite drowned the band.

'There he is!' Dad had one arm over the rail, waving. He had already seen us: only the two of us... involuntarily he half-turned, away...

'Where?' Mam was smiling, her arm raised ready to wave.

'Next to the...' I pointed with one hand and waved with the other and Dad was trying to wave back.

'Passengers...' began an announcement over the public address system, perhaps from the ship; then suddenly the voice went dead – there was a brief burst, a jarring, grating noise, suddenly throttled.

'Where?' said Mam again, her eyes fixed on the faces where I pointed; but her eyesight never was good. Then: 'Oh! I can see him!' She waved. Then suddenly stopped: Dad had his handkerchief out, and seemed to turn aside....

'Passengers...' the distorted voice of the announcer began again, 'Passengers... about to... to disembark....' It was drowned in the hubbub.

Mam sobbed a little. 'I wonder if he knows. He can see it's only the two of us. He must know.' And very softly: 'Mae Dad yn crio.' Dad tried to wave again with his other hand. I waved back once more, but my hand stopped in mid-air....

The band was now playing with great verve. They could have been the Coed Talon Silver Band after all; they played with such sparkle and liveliness. It inspired the crowd to join in singing, amateurishly, when they reached the end of the refrain:

254

...Britannia rules the waves,
Britons, never, never, never...

But before the final note, the singing crowd broke into a
tumultuous cheer, for the first passengers were about to
come ashore.

We shuffled slowly with the crowd towards the
gangway. Passengers were now stepping on to the landing
stage. There were huge piles of luggage and porters
hurrying. 'Passengers for Customs,' said a uniformed
official, 'move along this way please.' And in the milling
crowd just ahead was the little girl Molly's Papa. He
picked her up in his arms. Into the Customs shed they
went, Mama, Papa and Molly in the middle. Dad would be
down the gangway soon.

The hug and the greeting: the joy and the tears...

The cable (it arrived, we learnt later, just before the
evening performance in Carnegie Hall) had said 'Arthur
dead'; no mention of diphtheria. Dad had spent the six-
day voyage wondering, wondering... an accident? On the
railway track? The old coal mine shafts deep in the
wood...?

Almost immediately a Customs official came to take
Dad by the arm, to avoid the queue for Customs. He led
us through a side entrance. There was a minimum of
formality; Dad wasn't even required to open his suitcases.
I recall little of the Customs shed for my eyes were misty
with disappointment: we were going to see the ship... we
were promised; we really would see the ship this time.

Formalities over, we walked out and to the ferry and
Mr Williams Beehive's taxi car, Mam now safely on Dad's
arm. I followed behind, dragging my feet a little: but we

were going to see the ship, I whimpered... I want to see the ship....

Dad was home.

Some days later I noticed a brand new football, 'Junior Size', had been put in the spench under the stairs. There it stayed, uninflated, its bright, shiny leather case in its cardboard box.

'Alun, fetch the cow.' Mam was back to her real, cheerful self. And Dad did all the outdoor jobs to be done.

He was home more often now. It was Depression, and engagements were fewer. No more eleven performances per week as in the busy times before the coming of the talkies. Now, when on our way to Liverpool for him to begin another tour we passed the Cammell Laird Shipyard in Birkenhead, all was quiet. The White Star Line, once one of the world's biggest and most prosperous shipping companies, was near-bankrupt and was merged with Cunard. The *Laurentic* was laid up; and the great *Majestic* with many others, went to the breaker's yard. The economy-conscious *Britannic* continued to cross the Herring Pond, but no longer with emigrants to the New World. The Depression had forced the USA to impose severe immigration restrictions. Dad found it difficult to get or extend his work permit; his spells abroad were shorter.

'Alun, feed the hens.' Mam, happier now with Dad home more often, was for the most part utterly unaware of the Depression, until it was brought home with the closure of the local colliery.

Thirteen million unemployed in the United States, a

quarter of all the workers – the worst depression the world had ever seen. President Roosevelt found 'one third of a nation, ill-housed, ill-clad, ill-nourished'. When nominated for the Presidency he had said, 'I pledge you, I pledge myself, to a new deal for the American people'. Al Capone, gangster-millionaire, ran soup kitchens in downtown Chicago, and was cheered when he went to watch baseball games. Prohibition, its laws openly flouted, went out when President Roosevelt came in to the White House. Dad's cousin in Tennessee was unemployed; that was the last we heard of him.

'Alun, we need water from the well': Mam was dusting the Empire State Building on the mantelpiece, its shiny copper-coloured metal reflected in the big mirror. But the real one on Fifth Avenue and 34th Street was called, said Dad, the Empty State Building; while men on the sidewalk, shivering and hungry, sold apples. The mast for mooring airships above its 102nd floor was never used.

Jack brought his records to play on the gramophone: 'I'm Forever Blowing Bubbles'; 'Two Lovely Black Eyes'; 'Happy Days are Here Again'. Some of them, instead of a dog listening to his master's voice, had 'Columbia' with 'Magic Notes' in gold letters and two golden semiquavers. He brought another Bing Crosby record, 'Brother, Can You Spare a Dime?'. The needle always used to stick in the groove where the singer sings about building a tower.

Will Rogers was dead: killed with his fellow-Oklahoman, the flying ace Wiley Post, in an air crash in Alaska. But Mark Twain was very much alive in his books; I read *Huckleberry Finn* and all the others.

A couple of years later we left our farm Pen-y-Wern to live in the village, on the Tyrpeg, not very far from the church.

Dad sang for the last time in his sixties, at the unveiling of a plaque in memory of Mr T.G. Jones – T.G., the old schoolmaster and conductor of the Coedllai Male Voice Choir. It was in the Big Room of his old school.

'What did you sing, Dad?'

I didn't need to ask; it was the Roger Quilter setting; and it was Mam in song – singing around the house in an elderly but still firm voice:

> 'O mistress mine! where are you roaming?
> Journeys end in lovers meeting
> What is love? 'tis not hereafter
> Then come kiss me, sweet-and-twenty...'

'Sweet-and-twenty? But Dad, you're sixty-six....'

'Youth's a stuff will not endure.'

VII
Coda

Twenty-five years after the *Britannic*, I was in Carnegie Hall, with its gold and red plush interior, its steep staircases to many seating levels. It was 1956, the bicentenary of Mozart's birth. The Philadelphia Orchestra was conducted by Sir Thomas Beecham, his commanding figure with its neat, trim beard was very imperial; as imperial as King George the Fifth on the penny. The hall was packed. The seventy-seven-year-old Sir Thomas had provided himself with a lightweight chair on his rostrum. During the pauses between the movements of a symphony, he rested for a few moments. His considerable bulk sank onto, and overflowed, the chair. It swayed precariously with one leg perilously near the edge of the rostrum, while the conductor's arms were spread out on the brass rail. He smiled graciously down at the 3000 in the audience. The chair swayed again: would the empire fall? No. He stood erect once more to raise his baton to continue the precise and accurate playing of the Philadelphia.

After the interval came the *Jupiter Symphony*. I had read the commentary on this symphony beforehand, in the glossy brochure on the series of Mozart Bicentennial Concerts: 'masterpiece... unequalled synthesis... themes presented concisely and coherently... and the extended coda unsurpassed.' The usual spiel.

The symphony was drawing to a close. I got up and walked along the aisle, telling myself I wanted to be out before the crowd. But the baton that took us through the final pages was that of the leading exponent of Mozart. And perhaps the commentary was right. So I hesitated... and turned to look at the stage, not really seeing what I was looking at. Then to the marble stairway. I hesitated again; the closing bars of the coda: tumultuous and rapturous applause. I tripped on a step and hurried down into the street and traffic noise: the New York of the nineteen-fifties. People were scurrying, others strolling along the crowded sidewalk: tourists clicking their cameras. I turned the corner and went down Seventh Avenue, while the traffic lurched off from the traffic lights. It was late afternoon. Now... where am I going?

'Excuse me.' My words were lost in the rush, noise and swift strides.

But a passerby answered: 'Sorry, I'm a stranger here myself.' A Midwest drawl.

'Just keep right on.' This was unmistakably a New Yorker. 'Twenty... twenty-three blocks down.'

'Er... how far?'

'Mile and a half, I guess.'

'Thank you.'

'You're welcome.' Then raising his voice, now a little distance away: 'Goin' to walk? Gee!'

56th Street, 55th, 54th... Manhattan, this island city of rectangles! 53rd... 52nd... block after block, the din and the clatter...

'It's a great life, if you don't weaken.' The drunkard drained his hip flask and hiccuped. He was lying near a subway entrance. People stepped over him, quickly, adroitly.

A policeman sauntered up, flexing the fingers wearing the knuckledusters, and twirling his blackjack in the other hand. 'Step on it, you lousy...' but his curse was lost in the crowd. The drunk, a youngish man shabbily dressed, staggered to his feet and shuffled along, brushing against hurrying people, lips moving, stopping to talk to his own reflection in a store's large window. He dragged his feet past a line, four abreast, waiting to enter a motion-picture theatre. 'Will Rogers Junior...' said the posters and neon lights in front of the house, 'stars in *The Story of Will Rogers*.'

The traffic halted with a screech of brakes. I had reached Broadway and Times Square. Dusk was falling. The somewhat drab daytime appearance was giving place to The Great White Way of night time: a blaze of light and life, a brash glitter. 'And here's little old Broadway, gee, what a dazzle!' a lady holidaymaker said to her escort.

'Taxi!' The hotel doorman called for them. A yellow cab drew up and stopped violently with squealing brakes, narrowly missing pedestrians stepping off the sidewalk.

'23rd Street,' said the holidaymakers. The door slammed shut and the taxi rapidly accelerated away into the stream just moving off from the traffic lights with a discord of car horns. Pedestrians were now moving along the sidewalk at an indifferent pace – the sightseers of Times Square at Manhattan's centre, jabbering crowds gaping at expensive store windows and cheapjack shops, watching the famous cigarette advertisement puffing out 'smoke', and the moving electric news sign. Everything was noisy and congested. Passing near scores of theatres, movie houses, the *New York Times* building, under the flashing neon lights, I stopped and stared. Hotels, with the Stars and Stripes flying over the awning, restaurants and honky-tonks: the centre of the Big Apple, the City of Skyscrapers, the Empire City, Noo York....

'Verily I say unto you the Lord's day is at hand....' A Salvationist was addressing the indifferent crowd, standing beside a Salvation Army band resting their instruments. He prayed: 'Our father who art in heaven, direct our feet towards thee...' A turbulence immediately rippled through the feet on the sidewalk – they moved more rapidly and purposefully. The band struck up with a selection of Moody and Sankey. The quickened pace on the sidewalk came to an abrupt halt when lights changed for the cross-town traffic. Pedestrians waited.

'How's Joe?'

'Oh, he's getting ahead.'

'Well... must move on...'

The lights had changed again and now the cross-town stream halted with engines running, windows open and a car radio blaring: '...for just five dollars you too can have this beautiful bust of Mozart... The Dow Jones climbed to a record high...' But the radio announcer was lost in the atmospheric crackle, the grating of gears and a crescendo of impatient car horns. Then away they went, surging forward with tyres squealing.

A barrel organ, with a monkey on a leash and begging bowl on the ground, played a succession of tunes from the twenties, one hardly distinguishable from another in the din of traffic and sidewalk chatter.

Snatches of conversation flitted by among the moving crowd: 'That's a whole different ball game...' 'Made any dough?' 'If you're smart enough... yeah. Big problem...' 'That's a lot of applesauce...' 'It's not so bad at that...'

Past the giant neon sign: 'CHEVROLET'.

'Peanuts, roasted peanuts,' called a street vendor. A smell of roasting came from the grill on top of his push cart. 'Peanuts, roasted peanuts.' A jamming of brakes; the streams of cars suddenly came to a crushing, resounding halt with a chorus of horns and angry voices. A newsboy: 'Extra! Extra!'

'Hold it!' A press photographer, his camera clicking with flash.

I veered away from the commotion towards the kerb then walked on at a hesitant pace, looking vaguely for street signs.

'Keep right on.' Another New Yorker. 'A couple of blocks beyond the Cable Office.'

'Thank you.'

'Mighty glad to help.'

I now took a fairly quick, determined stride: 39th Street, 38th, 37th...

'Have fun...' said one to another at the street corner as they departed their separate ways. A salesman was outside his store; out on the street to entice customers in: 'For two hundred dollars, for two hundred dollars, the latest super record player... phonographs, radios... bargain prices...'

'Say honey...' A somewhat elderly couple were strolling past. 'Say honey...'

'Yes, Martha,' said the man for the hundredth time.

He was grey haired and rather stout. Then he recognised a face in the crowd, a much younger woman, and gave her a jovial greeting in his loud, carrying voice: 'Hello, look who's here!'

The younger woman approached: 'Martha! Well... how ya bin?'

'Everything okay?' said Martha, no longer nagging, having given her a hug, and smiling.

'I guess so.' Then the younger one, her arms over both their shoulders, to the man: 'Gee, I like your necktie. Swell guy.'

The crowds on the sidewalk were much thinner now, and the traffic less hurried; appearing more distant. I took a few uncertain paces towards the trio.

'Gee, there's a Limey. Tell by the way he walks.' It was the man's carrying voice, loud even when subdued. My footsteps had intruded.

'Excuse me...' I began, hesitating, and approaching a little nearer. But an old, old man, sitting on a stool on the sidewalk, was playing a musical saw, forcing my attention away from them.

Meanwhile the trio, like all New Yorkers, were anxious to help:

'Where you goin' Mister?'

'Can we help?'

'Who you looking for?'

Odd they should say that...

But the musical saw captured my whole attention. The old man on the stool a few paces away had one end of the saw anchored between his knees. As he bent the saw with his left hand, he drew his bow with the other across the saw's edge to produce an eerie musical sound but not exactly tuneful, like a slurring and sometimes wobbly, high-pitched human voice singing 'Ah...'. It was made all the more mysterious by the excessive slurring of the notes as he bent the saw, creating an atmosphere that was disturbing, uncanny and ghostly. Then a recognisable tune; the weirdness disappeared and it became exquisite, less unnatural and more sublime. A familiar tune! I began humming as he played, taking a few paces nearer. He was quite old with a grey untidy beard and a quality suit gone shabby and frayed at the cuffs. The tune ended with a tremendous slur up to top G.

I placed a coin in his hat and wandered on.

'Keep right on, beyond the Five and Ten.' It was the man with the loud, carrying voice, calling after me; or so I thought. Awkwardly I looked round to acknowledge his help. 'And turn left into 34th Street.' But his helpful New Yorker voice was probably directed at someone else. Then, to Martha and the younger woman, in his normal voice as he looked at his watch: 'Holy Moses, it's a quarter of.'

I entered the ticket office from 34th Street, consulting the visibility notice (then realised it was dusk anyway) before buying a ticket. I counted out the right coins and placed them on the counter. As she counted the money, the lady cashier said brusquely: 'Er... foreign coin.' She handed back the offending coin.

'Mm? Oh, I beg your pardon... it's a shilling. Er...'

'You need a quarter.'

'Yes. Er...' Fumbling among my nickels and dimes:

'Here we are. Same size. So sorry.'

'Oh don't mention it.' She gave me a friendly smile as she handed me the ticket. 'Elevator straight ahead.'

'Thank you.'

'You're welcome.'

The express elevator to the 80th floor and a slower one to the 86th floor Observatory.

I had been up in the daytime in the heat and humidity of the previous summer, to find somewhere cool and to see the magnificent panoramic view which stretched for fifty miles on a clear day; a quarter of a mile down below the streams of cars were like miniature toys. I had peered down, pressing my head against the protective wide-mesh steel fence. The promenade deck then was crowded with noisy, excited Sixth Graders from a Long Island elementary school on an end-of-term school trip into the city. Before they left, their teacher had checked their names: Zukowski, Luttenberger, Lopez, Irrazari, Zeilerbach, de Santis, Socrates, Rattazzi... Jones....

But now it was evening. And although the city lights were on, from the almost deserted open promenade deck there was still some of the half-light of dusk: the sky red over New Jersey. Small gusts of wind were buffeting the building. The only other people on the open platform were a young mother and her two small boys. They were hardly aware of my presence.

'Come on,' said the harassed Mom, anxious to depart, 'or I'll never bring you to the city again.' The two boys were huddled round the telescope.

'Come on.'

'Okay Mom.'

'Oh, okay,' said the reluctant shorter one.

266

'And don't talk with your mouth full of peanuts.'

But they hardly took their eyes off the instrument. 'Won't work.'

'Let me, let me,' said the impatient second one, pushing to get his eye to the telescope.

'Come on. It's going to be well past your bedtime.' But Mom had completely lost their attention. The telescope had captured their interest instead.

'Oh, you have to put in a coin.' The second boy looking at the instructions: 'Place... d... d... dime in s... sl... slot and... and... open-rate.'

'Operate. You can't read.' And trying to push the other away, a coin ready in his hand: 'Gi'me. Gi'me... you can't read.'

'I can, I can.' The impetuous younger one now reading rapidly: 'Place-dime-in-slot-and-oper... rate.' He pushed in his coin. 'Gee! I can see Europe.'

'Don't be stupid. Europe's way over the horizon. Too dark, anyhow.'

'Come on,' said Mom yet again. But the telescope held their interest until she added: 'Or we'll never get to the Yankee Stadium tomorrow.'

'Gee, let's go!'

'Dad says I'm going to be Babe Ruth when I grow up!'

A heated argument began. 'I knock the ball out of the lot every time I step up to the plate.' The younger one proceeded, empty-handed, to demonstrate his prowess, pushing his baseball cap back on his head.

'You hit nothin' but foul balls.'

'I'm goin' to be the hometown slugger. Play in the big leagues. Play for the Yankees and win the World Series.'

'You'll be slaughtered.' One started chasing the other.

'There's no time to play tag now,' said Mom, to no effect. Then, exasperated: 'Come on! Don't forget we're going to see that ship too.'

'Yeah,' said the younger boy, stopping his chase to peer through the steel fence: 'I can see her now, coming up the East River.'

'The *SS United States*,' said the other contemptuously, 'is too big to come up the East River.'

'She arrives tomorrow,' said Mom, taking a few paces towards the doorway, 'and the day after we'll have a guided tour on board.'

'Great. Great,' said the excited little one. 'We'll see the world's fastest liner. Not today. Not tomorrow, but the day after.'

'Hooray!'

Mom called from near the souvenir stand: 'Come on!'

'We're coming, Mom.'

'Okay.' The younger one slouched as they went in through the doorway. 'Let's go hit the hay.'

I strolled over to take another look through the protective fence, down the canyon below at the myriad of toy cars. From this distance up, they could all have been Model Ts and Chevrolets. Then, heard distinctly through the city noise, a long, deep, sustained note: an ocean liner coming up the Hudson.

Later, I took the subway downtown to the Cunard office at 25 Broadway, and booked a cabin on the Queen Mary home.

I would go back to Pen-y-Wern and take a walk over

the fields and down through the wood. And because it would soon be summer I would see the wood warbler among the beeches and the jays screeching in the oaks. And the little wren with its short tail in the hedges between the hayfields. There would be caterpillars on the birch trees; and in the autumn near those same birches, red toadstools dotted with patches of white. (A birch branch is good to swing on.) In the autumn too, the bright red berries of the cuckoo pint under the hedge; and the winged seeds of the sycamore, twirling round as they fell, blown by the wind. The young sycamore tree by the stile would be big and fully grown. On the hedgerows spiders' webs would be heavy with dew, glistening like jewels – like Mam's necklace from Minneapolis. Spring would come again: meadow buttercups; daisies, coltsfoot, gorse; cowslips in the fields; wood anemones; honeysuckle scent widespread on the hedge; hawthorn in Cae Cefn; yellow pimpernel in the wood below: all in glorious bloom – and the cuckoo would be singing! (In our fields just next to the wood we had seen a badger once, coming out of its set.) Nine acres of fields, banks and hedgerows, stretching steeply down to a wood a mile long and half a mile wide. Primrose-covered banks, wild rose in the hedge, bluebells in the wood and foxgloves; hazel catkins like lambs' tails. Wood pigeons and pheasants after acorns in the oaks. Yes, perhaps I would see a pheasant: a pheasant, with its beautiful chestnut-brown plumage with green, black and purple markings, its dark green head and long tail; and, seeing it close, the scarlet round the eyes and tufts behind the ears. The Plas Teg posh people, I'd heard, hadn't had a shoot for years. (Plas Teg itself, the Jacobean mansion on the other side of Hope Mountain, was now empty with a

269

Preservation Order on it, and used by an auctioneer for storing furniture.) So the pheasants were free, like the rabbits and the squirrels. I would go down the tunnel and the secret path....

I approached along the farm road. The hawthorn was in bloom in the Cae Cefn boundary hedge – as it used to be! Ahead was the panorama of Hope Mountain. A stranger approaching would be unaware that it is only the upper half of it you see, until you are in the farmyard or in front of the house. For the terrain falls so sharply that a whole valley – sloping fields, wood, marsh and the mountain's lower slopes – is suddenly revealed. I would stop at the farmyard gate and feast my eyes like a newcomer; and, because it was so familiar, absorb again all its intense detail. And then begin my descent of the fields.

I was brought up sharp: for the wood, which in retrospect had always seemed aglow in the sunlight of early spring, was no more. The Coal Board had been, and opencast mining had obliterated the whole of the wood and half the fields. All was devastation: total death – devoid of life and every living thing, a landscape bleak and stark. I turned my gaze towards the house and farm buildings of Pen-y-Wern; they stood like an outpost on the Western Front. And beyond, some way down the slope from Cae Cefn, was the spring which was our well. It was still there, for the heavy machinery's destruction had not yet reached the clump of trees where it bubbled out of the hillside. The grass was still green around it. But the trickle of water, the tiniest of streams, was now a streak of mud;

it oozed into the overturned earth and devastated wood to form a quagmire.

It was a Sunday afternoon. I picked my way down, through mud and slime, past enormous earth-moving machinery and mud-spattered lorries standing silent on the Sabbath; past the remains of burnt-out piles of felled timber and huge, gaping holes from which the coal had been extracted, the holes waiting to be refilled with the mountains of spoil alongside.

There were no birds, except a solitary, squawking, tuneless crow, lost without trees, swooping to limp and briefly peck the barren earth; then fly away, its broad black wings barely able to lift it again into flight.

The railway branch line to Brymbo had closed and the track had been torn up. Weeds grew between the ballast stones. I stooped to put my hand on them. They were strangely warm to the touch. Everything was quiet; but there never were any trains on a Sunday.

The marsh had been half-filled with sludge. A solitary waterhen swam among the few remaining reeds and bulrushes. She did not notice me.

Dad lived to be eighty-three. (Mam had died nine years earlier.) I sorted out his papers: cheque book, insurance policy, letters, passport; photographs: Will Rogers with his lasso, on stage; Arthur on Cae Cefn, holding his ball; and a host of others, all still in their biscuit tin. Among them the group photograph of us – Georgie Jones using a camera of an older generation to achieve a picture of depth and permanence; the three of us natural without posed smiles, with the lilac and the warm light and shade of early spring, the distant fringe of tree tops – the wood as it used to be – with Hope Mountain beyond: a postcard size, its sepia giving the effect of a portrait, much frayed at the corners – it must have travelled around North America quite a bit, in his pocket wallet. Coloured picture postcards: Montreal, Vancouver, Miami... a pack of them; how crude the colours looked now – and yet and yet, somewhere in the mind's eye, they still glowed through the passage of time.

Then something I could not remember having seen before: a menu printed inside a cover of red and gold with a white star. '*MV Britannic*: Farewell Dinner'. I opened it. Inside was a page for autographs, but not one autograph. Printed inside the cover: 'Your last day aboard ship; soon you will hear "We dock very soon, Sir..."' (Ah yes, that was at the landing stage.) It was all in highly embellished lettering. 'The White Star Line hopes your voyage has been delightful, that the expectations you had when you came aboard have been realised. Oh how our service to you could be enhanced if only we could but share your own private thoughts.' (To think Dad had spent the six days of the voyage wondering, wondering how Arthur had died.) The flowery language went on: 'We hope there are pangs of regret that the voyage is nearing its end... and that docking tomorrow will conclude a perfect spell at sea.'

I went through his things before disposing of them; there at the back of the wardrobe was his evening suit. In the inside pocket of the tailcoat, an envelope, neatly folded. It had a George the Fifth penny-ha'penny stamp with the postmark 'Pontybodkin, April 1931'. Over forty years ago. In Arthur's handwriting, addressed to him at Hotel Chelsea, 23rd Street at Seventh Avenue...

Arthur writing that letter all those years ago: that day in April was brought back to me, in all its vivid detail....

✦

'23rd Street...' Arthur was addressing the envelope, muttering as he wrote, his pen scratching horribly. He stopped and looked up, making a dangerous sweep with the pen, and bursting out in a contradictory mood: 'But how can a street be at an avenue?'

'23rd Street at Seventh Avenue,' insisted Mam. 'Just put it.' She was losing patience.

'But how can a street...' Mam exploded: 'Well that's what Dad says. Write it. Go on, write it.'

Once more the pen began the scrawl on the envelope. With bad temper, the address was written.

Mam had persuaded him to write the envelope first just to get him started. Now for the letter itself. More attempts to put it off. Then at last he began, now using red ink. 'Dear Dad,' he uttered the words, barely audible, as he wrote: 'When you come on the *Brit... Britannic...*' He crossed out the word. '...on the boat, stay on top of the oh-shun...' And spelling it out aloud: 'S... H... U... N'. Then a delay due to a blot. 'And don't go down to the bottom.'

The rest was written quietly, with only the scrape of the pen. I took an occasional stealthy look over his shoulder: 'I'm going to be the world's mostest famous singer like you, and go in air... ship. Bring back the big money and cow from stock market. We have surprise for you on the stick more tree by the stile.' Mam quietly told me to go with him as far as the stile, to see him on his way to the post at Pontybodkin.

Another glance over his shoulder: 'May I have a quarter. I lost it...' He paused momentarily: 'Er...' then wrote: 'accidentally...' paused again, 'on purpose. No. Accidentally... er...' Finally, with much crossing out, it became: 'I lost it accidentally by mistake.' Then aloud as he placed the pen back on the inkstand: 'Finished'. His wiggly writing had concluded with 'The End Amen'.

Mam came over and hastily scanned through the letter, not really reading it. She told him to cross a t and dot those i's. He whined, but did so. Then: 'But you haven't asked for a football.'

'Oh!' He quickly picked up the pen again and wrote: 'I want a football 7s. 6d. like Dixie Dean in leather case.'

'You'll have to hurry. Finish it. Put kisses.'

'Kiss, kiss, kiss, kiss...'

'That's enough.' But the pen scratched a few more crosses, each bigger than the last: 'Kiss, kiss, kiss...'

'Put it in the envelope.'

'Kiss, kiss. Full... stop.' He ended with a blob, and immediately the pen was down he began folding the sheet of paper.

'Wait! Blotting paper.'

'Oh.' He placed the blotting paper on the still-wet ink with a few thumps then slowly and painstakingly folded the sheet.

'Put it in. Seal it,' said Mam to hurry him. With the letter sealed: 'Take it straight away. Alun's coming with you as far as the stile.'

'I'll be right off.' He got up, the chair legs scraping the tiled floor, and put on his coat.

'Blow your nose.'

He blew his nose loudly, 'Ta-ta.' He rushed towards the door.

'Rho sws...' (Give a kiss...) said Mam in haste, and he spun round, went back, and gave her a quick peck on the cheek while I waited by the door. And as we hurried across the yard she came to the door and called after him: 'A brysia adre....' (And hurry home....)

We ran and at the same time talked breathlessly: '...and Dad will bring it home with him... we'll have our match with my rubber ball... and then... and then, when Dad comes home, another big Cup Final match! It'll be great... with a real leather-case ball!'

'Yes... better than that rubber ball.'

'...and I'll score a hat-trick.'

'Dad... Dad'll be home.'

'Yes... I'll head the ball... like Dixie Dean.'

'Dad'll... come and watch... on the touchline.'

We were taking the shorter path down through the hayfields. Arthur clutched his letter in his hand, the envelope beginning to look a little crumpled.

'We'll show Dad...' he paused for breath '...initials on the sycamore tree.'

'Yes... we'll have to finish it.' It was difficult to keep up with him.

'...and I'll sing... Rwy'n canu... I Sing as the Songbird is Singing.'

'Dad will come... to the school concert... and we'll have the electric light!'

'Yes... I'll sing it... like Mr Hayes says.' He stopped speaking, panting for breath; one sock now down to his ankle. 'And for the encore...'

'What?'

'"I'm living o'er the mem'ries..."'

'Yes! "...my childhood days..."' I was puffed out '"...now gone."'

We were approaching the wood, running with heavy breath, and collapsed exhausted against the stile. Then, after a moment or two to revive, I said, 'I'll wait for you here.'

'Okay.' Recovered, he jumped over the stile.

'I'll carve the initials. Get them finished.'

'Yeah. Work on it.'

'You'll have to hurry. Must get there before Dad sails on the fourteenth.'

'Won't take long. Downhill all the way.'

'So long.'

'Ta-ra...' He moved off down the tunnel.

'And hurry back.'

'Yippee!' His exclamation of joy and anticipation of a new football and events to come resounded through the wood.

'On your way back,' I called after him, 'buy mint imperials!'

From deep down the tunnel, back came his Red Indian war cry, reverberating up through the trees with a resonance that strangely made his voice more mature and yet ethereal.

'And monkey nuts,' I called, louder – he was now out of sight.

I faintly heard another war cry.

Then at the top of my voice: 'I'll wait for you...'

I listened intently for a moment; but he was gone.

I sat on the stile, my tired legs dangling down. There was a faint rumble of train wheels in the distance, and the train whistle that told us the time. He'll make it. The

Royal Mail, the motorbike with a red mailbox instead of a sidecar which we sometimes saw on the Tyrpeg, would be picking up the letters from Pontybodkin Post Office soon. And if his letter catches the mail boat from Liverpool tomorrow morning... he'll make it.

I climbed off the stile up into the sycamore, brought out my pocketknife and began putting a few more touches to the initials on the trunk of the tree. But there was no fun doing it on my own. I waited. Arthur would be a long time. A bird sang: that cheerful, warbling song; it sang again, a soaring descant above the chorus of birds: the loud, melodious song thrushes, the flute-like blackbirds, the sweet, plaintive robins and other birds round about, who knew spring was here... the young nestlings too would soon learn their song from their elders. The birds' chorus brought alive the fresh young foliage, each tree with its own shade of green, and made it appear more profuse in the light air. Then the descant and chorus ceased, and with a gentle flap of wings the bird rose from the tree into the clear blue sky above, and was gone. There was a sudden stillness. I stayed a moment, hearing the silence. It seemed timeless. Everything was tranquil. Then a sigh of the wind. Arthur would be a long while.

So I walked back slowly, up the longer and steeper path round the hayfields to make time pass. I took an outside left kick at a daisy. An outside right pass with a buttercup... centre forward: no, that was Arthur. He was centre forward. Always that. Or singing. Dad said (but not to him) that he had good breath control... I quickened my pace across the yard.

I opened the door slowly. The cat followed me in. Mam was somewhere at the back of the house feeding the hens for Arthur or perhaps upstairs tidying up for Dad coming home. I wound the gramophone:

> I'm living o'er the mem'ries
> Of my childhood days now gone...

I turned the horn towards the door and opened the door wide so that wherever she was she would hear it and know I was back.

> ...And then came life's awakening...

I sat down in the rocking chair with my atlas, idly scanning the pages: 'New York to Liverpool: 3036 nautical miles' but, ill at ease, my mind wasn't on it.

Instead I went out and sat on the low garden wall to wait. I would sit a while before fetching water from the well. Arthur would be a long time. The cat followed and sat beside me, tucking in her paws and blinking in the evening sun. Then Mam singing, somewhere in the house, singing at the top of her voice:

> 'I want you in the morning
> When the dawn comes stealing in'

She knew I was back.

It was early evening. The sun was warm on the red-brick wall, warming my legs under my knees. There was a gentle light.

> 'I want you in the evening
> When the sun sinks in the west'

Below the lawn and lilac tree at the bottom of the garden, in our nearest hayfield, was the cow with head down, grazing for all she was worth, unconcerned with the world. She knew when the grass was sweetest: in early springtime in the hayfields before they were put down to hay. Their carpet of green was shooting up. She would have to be out soon for the hay to grow.

Mam's voice and the gramophone brought the song to an end on that thrilling top G:

'I want you ev'ry moment...
Just because dear, I love you.'

I nipped in to switch off the gramophone, and came out again. It was a warm evening. I would wait outside.

The air was still; there was a quiet emptiness. But below the fields the wood was coming into leaf. And beyond and above the wood, Hope Mountain, which for so long had appeared an irregular patchwork of fields, unkempt with uncut quick-set hedges. Now it was a strangely and wonderfully well-defined, well-ordered pattern, as if it had always been and always would be. It was green and glowing softly, gloriously transformed in the clear light of the April evening sun.

ACKNOWLEDGEMENTS

Grateful acknowledgement is made to the following for permission to reproduce material, as indicated:

Gerallt Richards, Ammanford, Dyfed: the words, written by the Rev Alfa Richards (1876–1931), of the hymn 'Rwy'n Canu Fel Cana'r Aderyn'.

The Rev David J. Griffith, Milwaukee, Wisconsin: the English version, by the Rev William J. Griffith (1882–1956), of the above-named hymn, titled 'I Sing as the Songbird is Singing'.

The Society of Authors, in their capacity as the Literary Representative of the Estate of Lawrence Binyon: quotations from the fourth stanza of the poet's 'For the Fallen'.

Warner Bros Music, successor-in-interest to the Gamble Hinged Music Co and Remick Music Corp: the words, by Helen Hindson and Margaret Ringgold, of the song 'Dawn of Love'.

Oxford University Press: children's nonsense rhymes, etc, from the following books by I. and P. Opie – *The Lore and Language of School Children* (OUP 1959). *Children's Games in Street and Playground* (OUP 1969). *The Singing Game* (OUP 1985).

Grateful thanks are also due to the following for their help in tracing copyright holders: Alison Davey (Messrs Boosey and Hawkes); Carl Michaelson (Messrs Carl Fischer, Inc, New York); D. Islwyn Davies (Baptist Union of Wales, Swansea); Aelwen Jenkins, Swansea; Arturo L. Roberts (editor, *Ninnau*), Basking Ridge, New Jersey; Joan Owen Mandry, Lisbon, Ohio; Olwen M. Welk, Ripon, Wisconsin; John I. Price, Treherbert, Rhondda, Cynon Taff; Huw Williams, Bangor, Gwynedd.

And finally, thanks above all to the publishers of the volumes of *Pictorial Knowledge*, George Newnes Ltd.